IGNITE

HERITAGE OF FIRE: BOOK ONE

EMMA L. ADAMS

This book was written, produced and edited in the UK, where some spelling, grammar and word usage will vary from US English.

Copyright © 2019 Emma L. Adams
All rights reserved.

Want to find out how Cori and her friends met? You can get a free prequel, *Adrift*, if you sign up to my author newsletter.

1

Five years ago, I died.

Let's just say things have gone steadily downhill since. I scanned the plain red-brick terraced house in front of me for any signs of a trap. Pre-faerie invasion, the area would have been the definition of a safe suburban neighbourhood. The lack of shattered windows, piskies nesting in the roof, or scavenger fae waiting to jump on unwary trespassers, told me this place was one of the few safe havens that remained, isolated bubbles in a city ravaged by magic.

"This place belongs to an old human lady called Mrs Tibbs," I told Becks. "She must have been well off."

Becks, literal cat burglar, meowed in agreement. All the neighbouring houses were in a similar condition, neat and shiny. No anti-faerie wards either. Mrs Tibbs had been lucky up until now, but that hadn't stopped her from unwittingly purchasing a dangerous magical device from a sketchy witch at the market, disguised as an old-fashioned record player.

"What kind of sick bastard tries to steal little old ladies' souls?" I remarked aloud. "You'd think she'd know better than to buy anything from a witch with no licence."

Then again, anyone could pretend to be human. Being a dragon shifter, I should know.

Becks padded up to the windowsill, ears pricked. If persuasion didn't work, she'd be ready to create a diversion so we could steal the record player back before it could backfire on its owner. My sister Ember had taken on the task of hunting down the witch who'd sold it to her, which left it up to me and Becks to get the device away from its innocent target.

I strode through the front garden and knocked on the red-painted front door. The door opened and a short grey-haired woman popped up, a friendly smile on her face. Like a harmless grandmother... who'd accidentally bought the magical equivalent of a live bomb and set it up in her living room.

I smiled at her. "Hey there. Sorry to disturb you. I'm here to talk to you about the record player you purchased earlier today."

The corners of her mouth crinkled. "What's your name, dearie?"

No harm in giving her my real name. "It's Coriander."

"That's a pretty name."

I smiled angelically. "Yes, it is. May I come in?"

"Of course."

Ember hadn't been fooled by my innocent little sister act in years, but I had the settings turned to max and the old lady practically fell over herself to let me in. I'd turned twenty-one six months ago, but as a younger sibling, I'd still be the baby when I was ninety. Might as well take advantage.

I kept on my smile all the way into the living room, gushing over the mahogany furniture and the hundred-year-old china as though I'd suddenly developed a passionate interest in antiques. Maybe I should've opted to bring in the witch instead. Calm persuasiveness wasn't on my skill list. Brawling and running for my life, yes. Playing human, not so much.

"Oh, is this it?" I pretended to spot the record player, which I'd taken note of the instant I'd entered the room. "It's wonderful, but I'm afraid there's a problem with it."

"I don't see a problem with it," she said. "I've always wanted a device that can absorb human souls."

My heart missed a beat. "Excuse me?"

This isn't how it was supposed to go. Low-risk mission, my arse.

The old woman threw back her head and screamed. The noise ripped through my eardrums, shattered the glass in the window, and caused Becks to slip off the windowsill with a yowl. The screaming went on and on, forcing me to my knees, and when I wrenched my head upright, it was to see the old woman's friendly smile and wrinkles were gone, replaced by a younger, harsher face framed with dark curls. Her skin was pale and blemish-free, glowing with the beauty of someone whose nature was designed to lure humans into a trap. Her hair was wild and tangled, her eyes bright blue with the glint of an Unseelie fae.

Banshee.

The echo of her scream rendered me immobile for an instant, lingering in my ears, then she lunged at me with pointed teeth. I rolled to the side, tangling my legs with hers in an attempt to trip her. She sprang onto the sofa with lithe grace, baring her teeth. Did banshees eat people? I'd rather not find out when my head was already lodged in her jaws. The sensible thing to do was to dive out the window and run, but I'd come here for the record player and I was damned if I left without it.

I bounced to my feet, one eye on the prize, the other on

my enemy. She might be fae, but shifters had an advantage over normal humans speed-wise. Hovering on the balls of my feet, I eased a binding spell from my wrist into my palm, and when she jumped, I flung it into her face. Crisscrossing red lines appeared in a halo of sparks, pushing her head over heels and pinning her body to the sofa. She screamed again, this time with less volume. Pity trapping spells didn't come with a built-in muting function.

"Quiet," I hissed over my shoulder, reaching out for the record player.

The banshee broke free of the trap with a wild lunge, her long fingernails scraping my cheek. I shot out an elbow, which she avoided with the same preternatural grace as before. With a swift lunge, I swept her feet out from underneath her, and she fell to the carpeted floor. Maybe this house really had belonged to a nice old human lady at one time, but the monster baring her teeth at me had never been human. And her magic had broken my trapping spell way too fast. I made a mental note to give Will a stern talking-to later and kicked her in the face. Her nose broke beneath the heel of my boot with a satisfying crunch, her scream turning into a whimper.

I made for my prize again. "They say banshees only scream when someone's about to die. Does that apply when you're about to kill the person yourself?"

She spat out blood. "I don't need to scream for you, my dear," she said. "You've already passed beyond the veil."

I stiffened, one hand on the record player. How in hell did she know that? *Well, she* is *a death faerie.* For all I knew, I had a sign visible only to death fae and ghosts hovering over my head, saying, 'I got dragged into Death and all I got was this lousy placard.'

Flippancy aside, I *had* died, in technical terms, but since my soul was firmly attached to my body, Death would have to wait another day to claim me.

The banshee's hands hooked around my ankle, and the record player and I hit the carpet with a thump. I kicked, her talon-like nails breaking the skin of my leg. With a yowl, Becks cleared the window in a flying leap and landed on her head. The banshee stumbled, hands tearing at Becks, but her wildcat shifter's claws hung on tenaciously. I was on my feet again in a second, tucking the record player under my arm.

Time to leave.

I sprinted over the armchair and leapt through the empty window frame into the front garden. Over my shoulder, I called, "Come on, Becks, let's get backup."

I'd never tried capturing a full-blooded banshee even *with* backup, but someone at Darcy's place had some serious explaining to do.

A guttural scream shattered the remainder of the glass in the window frame and the banshee hurtled through, tackling me to the ground. Fingers clawing at my throat, she let out another cry, a cross between a mournful wail and a predator's triumphant screech. Greyness hazed over the corners of my vision, blurring the world, while a roaring in my ears drowned out all other sound. She was scrawny, not strong, but that scream echoed through my very bones, conjuring memories of being dragged from my body into a grey whirlwind, into a place so cold that no fire could touch me.

My hand closed around her wrist, wrenching her away from my face. Droplets of blood streamed from her broken nose, and her scream became thicker, more distorted.

I gritted my teeth and reached for another spell.

Sparks flew and blasted her several feet into the air, mouth agape, hair flying behind her. *Bye, bye, banshee.*

The fae crashed through the garden wall and landed in an inelegant sprawl, out cold. Victory was mine.

"Ow." I climbed to my feet, checking for injuries. Scrapes, bruises, and gouge marks on my leg where the faerie had dug her nails in. Not worth wasting a healing spell on.

Becks jumped out the window, shifting to human form mid-leap. She landed at a crouch, no longer a small tabby cat but a woman in her mid-to-late twenties with light brown skin and hair tinted in the same manner as the markings on her tabby form. Her long trench coat brushed the ground as she walked to my side to look at our prisoner. "We should have done worse than knock her out."

I adjusted the remaining band-shaped spells arranged on my wrists like a colourful display of bracelets. "If we don't take her to Darcy alive, he'll be able to deny sending us on a mission way beyond our pay grade and we'll get no compensation for this crap."

She scowled. "You're right, but I don't like it."

"Didn't you check for glamours?" I shook my sleeves down to hide the spells from sight. "She was barely pretending to be human."

"Dude, that's not my job. I don't have the Sight, either. We should have brought Kit with us."

"He'd have freaked out the instant she started screaming." Kit, our half-faerie friend, wasn't cut out for mercenary work. He got on much better helping Will to run the shelter for vulnerable shifters we helped run in our spare time. When we weren't saving not-so-human little old ladies from soul-stealing record players, that is.

I tied the banshee's hands together with a binding spell, hauling her into an upright position. Who knew, maybe her attack was a blessing in disguise. Full-blooded rogue fae were worth a decent pay raise.

Becks and I began the long walk back to Darcy's place with our captive in tow. I kept the fake record player tucked under my arm, which made hauling the banshee along doubly awkward. I was the stronger of the two of us, but that wasn't saying a lot. Becks was small and wiry like the cat she shifted into, while I assumed that whenever I gained the ability to shift into a dragon, I'd be the runt of the litter. The banshee's feet dragged on the pavement and her hair tickled the side of my face like tangled vines.

The banshee situation didn't bode well for Ember's mission, either. There were no signs of her when Becks and I dragged our prisoner through the automatic doors of the local branch of the Official Order of Mercenaries for this district of London. A wide building of metal and chrome, it was practically state of the art compared to its predecessor. In the last few years, the mages had decided that the city's rampant monster problem wasn't going to clear itself up, and if plucky and desperate humans were determined to make martyrs of themselves, they might as well give them the funding to do so. Becks and I made no secret of the fact that we were supernaturals, but our skills weren't exactly useable on the regular job market, which was why we'd wound up working with people who thought that sticking a knife in someone until they stopped moving was the height of diplomacy.

Luck wasn't with us. Instead of Darcy, the only person in the reception area was Jake. The gargoyle hybrid thought he was hot stuff, but everyone knew he bribed Darcy to get out of the more dangerous missions. When he'd claimed to be part dragon shifter, I'd had nearly burst a lung from laughing. I was more inclined to think half-human—with the attitude of a troll.

He raised a brow when we deposited the banshee on the polished floor of the lobby. A smirk played on his mouth as he took in my bruises and Becks's battered coat. "Run into trouble?"

"Nothing I couldn't handle. Where's Darcy?"

"In the back." He moved closer to the prisoner, crouching beside her. "Huh, she's fit. Didn't know you were into bondage."

"You're a sick human being." Where *was* Darcy? He knew perfectly well that leaving Jake on the door was an invitation for trouble.

"Ooh, shouldn't have pissed off the redhead. Watch it, she might start breathing fire next."

"Did it take you all day to think of that one or did someone hand you a prompt?" My hands fisted at my sides. The bloody cheek. The red hair is a side effect of being a dragon shifter, not the other way around.

"Why're you skulking around here and not out on a mission?" Becks put in. "Did you get a scratch from a wildcat shifter and call in sick again?"

He leaned against the desk as though he owned it. "You haven't got clearance to haul in a banshee."

"That'd be because *someone* didn't tell me that's what I'd be dealing with today." I spoke loudly, hoping Darcy would show his face before I knocked Jake's cocky smirk clean off.

The back door opened, and Darcy's broad gargoyle shifter's frame filled the doorway. He was a balding man in his forties who preferred playing human to gargoyle most of the time, and his brows rose in apparent unfeigned surprise when he set eyes on the banshee.

"Did you order one of these, sir?" said Jake, jumping off the desk and grabbing for the banshee's hair.

I got there first, and my fist connected with his throat. Puny I might be, but I hit hard. He went down fast, gasping for breath.

"Break it up," said Darcy in a bored voice. "What have we here?"

"You specifically said I'd be dealing with a harmless old woman." I waved a hand at the unconscious faerie.

"She wasn't," he said, frowning at the sprawling woman. "You don't have clearance to bring in a banshee."

Jake shot me a triumphant look, clutching his throat.

"What, you wanted us to leave her to use this on innocent humans?" Becks deposited the ruined record player on the desk. "Thanks for the warning."

Darcy scowled. "Third misleading query in a week. Bloody cretins. Rebecca, take that to the back room. As for you, Coriander, I have some paperwork for you to sign."

"As long as it comes with payment." I glanced pointedly at the banshee. "Where's she meant to go, then?"

"I'll put in a call for a faerie response team to handle her. She didn't kill anyone, did she?"

"She tried. Also, that knockout spell has a time limit on it."

"We'll do her for attempted murder," he muttered. "Jake, go and fetch the response team. Try not to walk into any fists on the way out."

"Right." Jake looked at her, then back at me. "She hit me, sir."

"I noticed. Go on." Darcy waved a hand, and I suppressed a grin. Darcy didn't interfere in his employees' battles. With my hair-trigger dragon shifter temper, it was probably the only reason I'd lasted so long working here.

Becks took the record player into the storage area for dangerous items while I stood by the desk, drumming my fingers impatiently while Darcy called the clean-up unit in to take away our wayward faerie. Every time he gave us bullshit, I got the strong urge to just... walk out. *Think calming thoughts, Cori. We need the funds for the shelter.*

Speaking of which. I scanned the paperwork Darcy had given me. "You owe us a raise."

"I do not." He put his phone into the pocket of his suit and gave the paperwork a once-over. He might look the other way when anyone started fights and bend the rules if necessary, but he was as much of a tight-fisted bastard as all the bosses I'd had.

"She was a banshee!" I said. "Not human."

"Same difference."

"No, it bloody well isn't," I said. "Banshees are to humans what dragon shifters are to… uh, cat shifters."

"Predators?" He laughed. "Banshees are hardly high-risk."

The banshee stirred with an inhuman hissing noise, and he darted a look at her, apparently regretting that last statement. "The clean-up people will be here soon."

"Better hope so." I shoved the paperwork at him. "A raise, *please.* It's in line with standard rates."

You'd better believe I had it memorised. A full-blooded banshee was on the same level as a high-ranked fae. Not that she'd had much power, really, since being away from Faerie sapped her strength.

I had no such excuse for being a pitiful specimen for a dragon shifter, but hey, maybe I'd luck out and get my claws any day now. Or maybe I'd have better luck trying to squeeze money out of Darcy.

Becks returned from the back room, minus one record player but with her glasses back on. After breaking three pairs in a week, she'd started stashing them in her pocket on missions. "That banshee's worth more than a few pennies, Darcy. Don't be a dick."

He scowled and angled behind the desk, reaching for something on the lower shelf. "Got your payment right here. Also, someone left a package for you, Cori." He held out an envelope stuffed with ten-pound notes and an oval-shaped package. "It's from someone called You Know Who."

"Is that a joke?"

"I didn't know you were in correspondence with Lord

Voldemort," Becks said, taking the envelope with our payment.

I hit her in the arm with my free hand and took the package with the other. "Now you're accepting suspicious packages from pranksters?"

Why send it here and not my home address? Weird. I turned the package over in my hands and found the opening, tugging it open.

Within the package was a giant egg, half the length of my forearm. It was covered in gleaming red scales that reflected the ceiling lights.

"This isn't for us." I let the packaging fall to the floor. "It's a joke, right?"

The egg was warm, the scales sharp, and a raging desire to break it over Darcy's head tore through me like wildfire through a forest.

Only one person could have sent it to me. I had one enemy in all the world, and he was locked in jail where he belonged.

Lorne. The man—or rather, dragon shifter—who'd killed me.

2

One fact I should start with: dragon shifters are almost extinct.

Note the 'almost'.

A lot of people had tried to wipe us out. A lot of not-quite-people had, too. Ghosts, fae, zombies... you get the idea. The thing is, when you're hunted from birth, you develop survival mechanisms. And maybe because of our need to blend in, we weren't capable of shifting into the form of a dragon until we reached a certain age, from late teens to early twenties.

The dragon egg in front of me was a biological impossibility, nothing more than a sick joke from someone who got a kick out of our pain.

"Take this," I said, shoving the egg at Darcy, "and get rid of it before I test to see if it's harder than your head."

"You can't break it," said Darcy, looking a little cowed. "I tried beating the shit out of it with a hammer, and it didn't cave. That thing's real."

"It's bullshit, is what it is." I slid a knife from my pocket and drove it into the egg's scaled side.

The knife bounced off the egg like it was made of concrete. I pushed the blade into the scale-like surface again, and the knife *bent* in my hand, the handle twisting to the side as though the stainless steel had turned into rubber. I tossed the knife aside and made a beeline for the collection of weapons in the back room.

"Hey!" Darcy barred my way. "There's no need to break all my weapons."

Damn. I'd wrecked one of my best knives on top of everything else. "It's not unbreakable," I said. "Nothing is, given the right pressure."

"Then good luck finding whatever it is, but I'm not keeping that thing in the office. If it hatches, we don't need a baby dragon flying around the premises."

"It's not a dragon egg." But it was no use arguing the point. Most people knew next to nothing about dragon shifters, and I wasn't in the mood to give him a refresher.

Tucking the egg under my arm, I marched out of the doors. Cold air whipped at my auburn curls but didn't do much to calm my temper. Dragon shifters gave 'hot-headed' a whole new meaning.

Becks followed on my heels. "Cori, what're you gonna do with it?"

"Ask Ember to torch it," I said. "There's nothing dragon-fire can't melt."

"I don't know..." Becks hesitated. "Suppose it's real?"

"It's impossible," I said. "As for the note—who in the world is You Know Who? Joke or not, it's a spectacularly shitty one, because I *don't* know who it is. Jake, maybe."

How he'd got his slimy hands on something that looked and felt like a dragon egg was a mystery, but who else would have reason to fuck with me?

"Maybe it's..." She broke off before the name 'Lorne' could escape, but I saw it in her eyes.

If the Orion League's hunters weren't as extinct as people had once believed the dragon shifters to be, I'd pin the blame for the egg on them. As it was, the only one of their allies who'd survived was Lorne, who'd been locked in a secure cell for five years and counting. Not the sort of place where it was easy to engineer a delivery of a fake dragon egg to your mortal enemy. The mages wouldn't be thrilled if I showed up on their doorstep to ask if they'd given a little too much freedom to their highest security prisoner. Or worse, they'd offer me another job.

Most people would jump at the chance to work for the Mage Lords, but I'd almost become the Orion League's pet project and I had no desire to repeat the experience at the mages' hands. They weren't above using people if it suited them, and considering I had yet to pull off even a partial shift, it couldn't be more obvious they only wanted to hire me to ensure nobody else did. A dragon shifter, as they'd learned the hard way, could give the mages a serious run for their money. The mages were known for keeping their enemies closer than their friends. Me, I preferred mine behind bars or buried underground.

Granted, the mages did technically own Darcy's place, too, but before they'd bought it from its human owner and refurbished the place, there was a swamp troll living in the showers and a distinct lack of security wards. It was a trade-off: security or freedom. The heavy weight of the dragon egg tucked under my arm was a reminder of how tenuous that freedom was.

I pulled out my phone with my free hand. "I'm gonna see if Ember dealt with the witch who sold that record player."

Ember's phone rang once, twice. Busy, no doubt thanks to whoever hadn't checked if old Mrs Tibbs was an evil soul-stealing monster before he gave me the job. I mean, you wouldn't think it'd be difficult to tell the difference between a harmless little old lady and a harbinger of death.

"I think it was a setup." Becks huddled deep in her thick trench coat. "The whole mission, I mean."

"Maybe Jake screwed with the schedule." I rubbed the back of my neck with my free hand. It was too late to use a healing spell on my bruises, so I'd be aching for a while.

The knot in my chest loosened as we reached Magic Avenue. Once invisible to human eyes, the narrow, winding road housed exclusively supernaturals. Keira, our main ingredients supplier, waved at us as we walked past. She was a fifty-something black woman with braided hair and a friendly smile. "Having a rough day, love?"

"That's one way of putting it." I adjusted my grip on the egg, which I'd slipped inside my padded jacket to avoid anyone seeing me walking around with it in public. With its scaly shape pressed to my side, I kept thinking I felt it vibrating faintly, but since my own heart was still racing, there was no way to be sure.

"I have some spare ingredients if you need them," Keira said.

"Cheers." I took the bag from her and reached into my pocket for a handful of notes from our payment. If nothing else, we had enough not to worry about paying rent on the shelter for the next month or so.

The shelter was a simple brick terraced house next door to our shop, where Will and Kit sold handmade witch spells to the general public. Six of us lived above the shop, which sounded cosy until you considered that two of our number were dragon shifters and another was an ex-Orion League hunter. Yeah, my sister was dating an ex-assassin, but I didn't hold it against her. Most of the time.

The mages had given us the original funding for the shelter as a thank-you for bringing an end to the Orion

League, but over the last five years, the cash had leaked away due to a never-ending series of emergencies. Becks and I had signed up at Darcy's in an attempt to plug the leaking hole, but I wished there was a more stable way to keep it running than by risking our necks hauling in enraged banshees. Still, a similar shelter had saved both of us from a life on the streets, and the least we could do was return the favour.

Today, the words 'Here be Dragons' filled the shop window, flashing in neon pink like a sign on a night club's door.

"Will's at it again." Becks flipped the sign over. "That means he's bored, which means we can expect another ridiculous moneymaking scheme within the next week."

"We raked in cash on the last one." I'd found it hilarious that he'd stocked the shop with bright red dragon plushies wearing T-shirts saying, "London's Loch Ness Monster". Ember had been less amused. But hey, the public loved them.

"Are you forgetting the time he decided to open a pet shop and used a charm to draw in all the neighbourhood mice?"

"You're a cat. You're not supposed to be scared of mice."

She pulled a face at me. "And you're a dragon shifter. You're supposed to roar and terrify our boss into giving us a fifty per cent raise."

"I got us thirty per cent," I pointed out. "Yes, I know we nearly got screamed to death in the process, but I'd say we did pretty well for ourselves."

If not for the egg tucked under my arm, I'd call this a win. Inside the shop, Kit staffed the front desk, wearing his human glamour. His fine black hair appeared shorter than it usually was, his eyes the pale green of a human rather than vibrant emerald, and there was a noticeable absence of pointed ears. He claimed to prefer to play human in front of potential customers, and to be fair, a lot of them had reason to be wary of the fae, even harmless half-faeries like Kit. Will had said it didn't matter what they thought, but Kit could be damned stubborn when he wanted to be.

"Hey," said Kit. "You're back early."

"Mrs Tibbs turned out to be a soul-sucking banshee."

He wrinkled his nose. "Ugh. Banshees. I haven't seen one of those for a while."

"No shortage of souls to feed on here, is there?" I shrugged off my coat. Beneath it, I wore a stripy top and bright scarf. It was a compromise: I could wear all the bright colours I liked as long as I wore practical ones on stealth missions. Not that stealth was a high priority, thanks to my flaming red hair which did not stop growing no matter how many times I cut it.

Kit's boyfriend, Will, walked into the shop through the back door. "What did you do this time, Cori?"

"Did I say I did anything?" I tried a toned-down version of the adorable baby sister smile I'd used on Mrs Tibbs, but Will merely rolled his eyes at me. "I may have punched Jake."

"He deserved it," added Becks. "How's business?"

"Bloody awful. What's that?" Will's gaze fell on the egg tucked under my arm. "Win a raffle, did you?"

"Nope. It's a practical joke." I deposited the egg on the desk in front of Kit, whose glamour snapped off as he jumped to his feet.

"It's alive!" he exclaimed in alarm.

"No, it isn't," I said. "Someone dumped this off at Darcy's place and addressed it to me."

Kit pressed his hands to the egg's surface, a faint green glow spreading from his palms to the egg. "It's alive," he repeated. "There's a heartbeat. Can't you hear it?"

Faerie hearing was more sensitive than humans', but then again, so was shifters'. And while I'd been in denial the whole time I'd been carrying it, now I pressed my palms to the rough edge of sharp scale, an answering thrum vibrated against my palms.

"Maybe someone put a recording of a heartbeat inside it," I said, undeterred. "Or used a spell."

"I can sense life forms," Kit said. "Trust me, there's something living inside that egg."

Being a Summer faerie, he had the expertise in that area. But *what* was in there?

"Damn," said Becks. "Dragon or not, this is probably an illegal trade item. You'd think the guild would have confiscated it and stuck a 'do not touch' label on it."

"Most guilds would," I said. "Darcy probably figured it'd get him in the shit with the mages if they found it, so he foisted it on us instead."

Darcy, like most mercenary outlet owners, had ended up in his position because it offered the security of an office job along with the street cred of killing monsters for profit, even if he didn't actually do any of the killing himself. Mercenaries, humans or not, didn't have long lifespans. Price you paid for taking the hit so a few more humans could sleep in peace without being eaten. Ember's insistence on taking over all the riskier missions had set me behind the other mercs a good three years so the banshee incident was among the most serious I'd handled. That was overprotective older siblings for you. It was cute when I signed up at seventeen—not so much four years later.

"Have you heard from Ember?" I asked Will.

"No," he said. "I thought she was with you. Has *she* ever seen a dragon egg?"

"Nope, because they don't exist." Now I sounded like a sceptical human, but even the magical world had its limits. "Anyway, I also got this." I threw the envelope of cash down on the counter and Will predictably forgot all about the egg.

"Good timing." He grabbed the envelope. "I need some

ingredients for a repair spell. Those two gargoyles busted a hole in the back wall of their room."

"How'd they manage that?"

"Gargoyle claws and family arguments don't mix." Will opened the envelope to count out the cash. While there was no route into the shelter through the shop, the two houses were connected through the living room in the back. I'd never envied my sister's claws quite as much as when I'd seen her tear a hole right through the wall to make a doorway, so we could get in and out of the shelter without leaving the house if the mages imposed a curfew.

"These might help." I handed him the bag of ingredients from Keira, picked up the egg, and carried it to the door behind the counter leading into the back room. "Maybe we should put this up for sale in the shop. How much is a rare monster egg worth, do you know?"

Kit twisted around to face me. "You're going to sell it?"

Becks's eyes were wide behind her glasses. "You wouldn't, would you?

"I'm not *keeping* it," I said. "You need a permit to even own an egg belonging to an unknown magical creature, let alone sell it. Otherwise the mages will slap us with a hefty fine, at the very least."

"My magical practitioner's licence doesn't cover mystery monsters," Will put in. "Now if it's worth a fortune, on the other hand..."

Kit looked scandalised. "But it's *living*." I hadn't seen him this upset in a long time. Being a Summer faerie, he was highly attuned to nature, and whatever he'd felt from that egg was enough to make the idea of selling it utterly repellent.

In fairness, I wasn't at all keen on the idea either. But neither was I keen on the mages shutting down our shop for illegal monster trade. And if I tried to give the egg away and got caught, it'd wind up with the same outcome. Unfortunately, the sensible thing to do would be to hand it over to the mages, but if it *was* booby-trapped, I didn't need to be jailed for attempted murder.

Heaving a sigh, I pushed open the door to the back room. It was a combination of a kitchen, living room and laboratory, with the kitchen and lab at the back and several armchairs and a sofa in front. Through a door on the right were the stairs to our rooms on the upper floor. Six people in one house was cramped enough without adding a mysterious new housemate who could be a man-eating fae monster for all we knew.

I sat in one of the second-hand armchairs and rested the egg in my lap. Becks switched the light on and padded over to join me. The egg's scales shone like rubies, the same colour my sister turned when she shifted into her dragon form.

"If it *is* the real deal?" Becks kept her voice low. She might not be a dragon shifter, but like me, she'd grown up as an orphan who'd never known her family. Becks and I had first met seven years ago during the chaotic aftermath of the faerie invasion, but she'd been at my side through the worst moments of my life almost as much as Ember had.

"We'll deal with that when we get to it." I rested my palm on the egg's spiked edge. The scales were sharp enough to break the skin, and the hum from inside it echoed my own pulse. *Damn. What have I got my hands on?* "There are other kinds of creatures with red scales. Maybe it's a rare species of fae. If we can get our hands on a book…"

"What, *Monsters for Dummies?*" Becks said sceptically, picking up the egg. "Or *The Guide to Caring for Your Unexpected Fanged Pet?* You think they have that in the British Library? Besides, what if it hatches before we find out?"

"At least we'll know what it is." I walked to the kitchen to pour a glass of water. "No use worrying about what you can't control."

I wasn't fooling either of us, but until Ember got back, we'd put the decision on hold. Not that my sister was the definition of level-headed, either.

Shit on toast. What am I supposed to tell the other dragons?

If I wanted to put that egg somewhere nobody would find it, carrying it through the enchanted mirror connecting our house to the home of our fellow dragon shifters seemed the strongest option, but the other dragons had more than enough problems to deal with. For the last five years, they'd been struggling to rebuild the small village in Scotland they'd called home ever since Lorne had first taken leadership over the survivors of the dragon clan wars. Ember and I had only survived because our parents had sent us to London shortly before they lost their lives in the war. The dragon egg, for all I knew, might be a souvenir from that very same conflict.

For now, our best bet was to keep it under wraps until we found out where it came from and what was inside it. Just as long as it didn't hatch before then.

The door clicked open and my sister Ember strode into the back room. Her auburn hair was streaked with mud, and so was her face. Patches of green slime clung to her dark clothes, which were plastered to her lean and muscular body with what looked like swamp water.

"You're okay!" I put the glass down. "What did you do to your phone, turn it off?"

"A troll *ate* it," she said, stripping off her muddy coat. "I've had a hell of a morning. Would you believe the witch was a fucking swamp troll? I had to swim under Tower Bridge, and let me tell you, there's a good reason even the trolls avoid it. Either someone needs their eyes testing, or they need their face rearranging."

"Or both," I said. "That's what I was trying to tell you over the phone. Little old Mrs Tibbs turned out to be a banshee, so someone fucked up majorly. And on top of that, another someone left us an anonymous present at Darcy's."

Her gaze fell on the egg in Becks's hands. It was sort of hard *not* to notice its bright glowing red scales. "What in hell is that?"

"A problem," I said. "You might want to clean yourself up first."

3

Fifteen minutes later, we closed up the shop early and gathered in the living room. After we'd passed the egg around enough times to ascertain the heartbeat was real, I put it down in the central space between the sofa and the three occupied armchairs. Ember's boyfriend Astor was the only person missing, but there wasn't much an ex-assassin might know about dragon eggs. Except possibly how to destroy it.

"We're not selling it," Kit said firmly.

"We already established that," I said. "Selling it is illegal. So's giving it away. That slippery sod Darcy backed us into a corner."

"More like the person who gave it to him." If it wasn't Lorne, then maybe someone from the Orion League had survived. They'd made no secret of their depraved experiments on dragon shifters they'd captured. I'd almost been one of them.

I clenched my fists as though I could crush the weight of bad memories beneath my knuckles. "The note was from You Know Who. So, uh, does anyone actually know who?"

Silence fell, and all our eyes followed the light glinting off the egg's ruby red scales.

"They're loaded, whoever they are," Will said. He sat on the floor with his back to the sofa, his long legs stretched out on the carpet. "Even if it's a fake, it's made of a rare magical substance. Or a convincing substitute."

"Sure looks that way." I reached out and tapped its surface. "I broke my knife on it. Stainless steel, totally wrecked."

"Shit, really?" Ember knew as well as I did that dragon scales were highly resistant to most weapons. Yet that didn't make the egg ours.

"It's got to be fae," I said. "Almost every mystery monster that shows up at Darcy's turns out to be an escapee from Faerie. They like shiny rare things."

"I've never seen anything like it," Kit said. "It doesn't feel Seelie or Unseelie. I'd be able to sense its magic."

"Perhaps it's one of the monsters they kicked out in the invasion." It wasn't outside the realm of possibility that the darkest regions of Faerie had a giant worm beast with scales that looked exactly like a dragon's, but trade in faerie monsters was fiercely outlawed by the mage council. If it'd come from anywhere, it'd be from the underground realm of behind-the-scenes monster trade—not somewhere I particularly wanted to get tangled with.

"All right," Becks said. "Are you one hundred per cent positive wild dragons are extinct?"

"Someone would have told us if they weren't," I said, with another glance at Ember. There was a good reason we'd evolved to shift at a later age: dragon eggs weren't easy to hide in a world full of curious humans. And the post-fae world carried even more threats to our species. "How's it even possible for that egg to exist?"

"Well," Will said, "when a pair of loved-up dragon shifters

—or a dragon shifter and an assassin, as it were—" He yelped when Ember swatted him over the head with a rolled-up newspaper.

"Cut the crap, Will," she said, picking up the egg. "We can't normally shift until we're at least eighteen years old. You don't get baby dragon shifters running around."

Will recoiled. "Are you saying there's a human baby in there?"

"Yeah, that's not possible either," Ember said. "The process of childbirth forces a shifter back into their human form. That's what Noll told me."

"Didn't know you were still in touch."

Noll was one of the few other dragon shifters who lived near London, and we'd helped her start a new life away from the bad memories of being Lorne's consort. She'd been pregnant at the time, so she'd know all about the fun side of giving birth as a shifter. Not so much about mysterious dragon eggs.

"We talk occasionally." Ember ran a hand over the egg's surface. Her fingers faltered as though she felt what I did— the hum of *something* living. Dragon or not, who knew. "Wild dragons… nobody says they *are* extinct. We just assume it."

"Like everyone used to assume dragon shifters were extinct," Becks put in. "Which, considering there are two of them in this room, is clearly bullshit."

London's supernaturals assumed Ember and I were the only two left, and we let them believe it. Our parents had even gone so far as to wipe our memories so nobody could force the location of the dragon shifters' village from us by force, and while we'd had a witch reverse the memory spell, I'd forgotten most of my early childhood. My memories of London were much stronger. We might have forged a new life here, but our species had roots in the ancient past, a time almost forgotten even in this new post-magic world.

"Exactly." Ember looked up, a hint of a spark growing in her grey eyes. "The League failed to wipe us out. Maybe they didn't wipe out the wild dragons either."

The Orion League had only existed in its modern form for the last century until five years ago, but it hadn't sprung up out of the ground. Humans had a nasty habit of chasing us off with pitchforks and sending sword-wielding knights to slay us.

"Fine," I said. "Say it's real. What the hell do we do with it? The village wouldn't take in an unknown dragon egg if they had any sense, and they do."

Ember's mouth pressed together. "Did anyone aside from Darcy see you take it home?"

"No," I said. "Unless Jake was listening in, but he was supposed to be fetching someone to take the banshee away."

"And the package arrived in the mail?"

"Addressed directly to me."

Ember exhaled slowly. "Right. We'll put it to a vote. I don't know where Astor is, but you know he'll vote to get rid of it. I vote we keep it until we find out what it is. What about you guys?"

"Keep it." Kit moved protectively behind the egg. While he'd undergone a dramatic change from the terrified prisoner we'd rescued from the Orion League's prison cells, he could still be startlingly naive. There was no place here for a baby dragon—or monster.

"What, and then apply for a Highly Dangerous Pets permit?" Becks shook her head. "I vote we keep it hidden until we find out what it is, but if it turns out not to be a dragon, we're throwing it out."

"Agreed," I said. "Will?"

"I'm outvoted," he responded. "How do you plan to find out what it is, raid the mages' archives?"

"No, find the person who sold it," I said. "I get the impression they're not working on the legal side."

"And you're the one with the contacts, Will," added Becks.

"You have got to be kidding me," Will said. "If I wander into a rogue gargoyle hideout and ask if anyone's brought in a dragon egg, they'll use me as a punching bag."

"You don't have to mention a dragon egg," Becks said. "Hell, *I* can spy on them if it bothers you. If they have a secret stash of dragon eggs, I'll find it."

"I somehow doubt there's a stash," I said, but a flicker of doubt stirred. What if the person who'd sent the egg had done so to bait us? If we believed the impossible, that wild dragons survived, the egg wouldn't exist in isolation. It had come from somewhere, after all.

It wasn't a well-kept secret that gargoyles still ran a large portion of London's supernatural underworld, but I didn't blame Will for not wanting to get involved. A clan of rogues called the Fanged had killed his father, and while that particular group had disbanded, the gargoyles were the supernaturals most likely to know where an illegal dragon egg had come from. Poking the gargoyles, however, was like kicking a nest of fire ants and then dancing barefoot in its ruins.

Ember put the egg back down on the carpet. "Someone needs to get out a book on reptile eggs so we can estimate how long we have until it hatches."

"You want to break into a library?" I forced a laugh. "Dragon shifters don't follow the rules of normal reptiles, you know that, right? We're mammals. Half, anyway."

Ember made a frustrated noise that sounded like a snarl. "Well, I don't know. We can't just sit and wait for it to hatch. Are we meant to put it into the fire to keep it warm?"

"It feels pretty warm as it is," Becks commented. "Unless someone wants to volunteer to sit on it."

The door blew open without warning, and all of us looked in that direction.

"Uh, Astor?" Ember walked to the open door and peered into the empty shop. "Nobody's there."

I tensed, wishing I hadn't taken off my coat. At least I'd kept my knives handy. "Did you lock the front door?"

"Yes, I did," Will said. "Don't look at me like that, Ember. That assassin of yours normally climbs through the window anyway."

Becks shifted into cat form and made for the door. I moved into the shop behind her. The front door rattled, then the window. Uh-oh.

"I think," I said, "someone might want to get in."

Becks sprinted to the window, standing on her hind legs to peer through the glass. Then she turned human again, stashing her glasses in her pocket. "Nobody's outside."

There came a distant rumbling sound, and a thin trail of plaster dust rained down from the ceiling. Then, from outside, came a loud crash.

"Falling roof tile," said Ember. "They're on the roof."

Oh, wonderful.

"I'll knock them off," said Becks, pushing the window open. Before any of us could object, she'd shifted to cat form and wriggled out of the gap.

Ember and I both looked at each other. While Becks was the best climber out of our group, only one type of supernatural would land on the roof: gargoyles.

So much for not kicking over the nest of fire ants.

"She's going to get herself killed." I ran through the living room into the hall, then climbed the stairs, Ember close on my heels.

The bedroom I shared with Becks was closest, so I opened the door and made for the window.

Ember caught my arm. "Cori…"

"Please don't start. I did knock out a banshee today, you know that, right?"

Ember shook her head. "It's not that you can't take down a gargoyle, but someone has to protect the families in the shelter."

Damn. She had a point—if the attackers were on our roof, they might well be on the roof next door, too. There were a dozen innocent people in that house.

Swearing under my breath, I backed away from the window. Ember pushed it open and climbed onto the ledge, the wind catching her auburn hair. Then she jumped.

For an instant, she free-fell from the window—and then an explosion of red scales filled my vision as her long, lean dragon form took over. Her tail lashed out, knocking the window closed, and her large leathery wings beat once, the updraft rattling the glass in its pane.

Bye bye, gargoyles. Have fun burning in dragonfire.

Ember's roar reverberated through the house as I pelted back downstairs, through the hall and into the back room. Kit stood with his back to the shelter door, his hands still clutching the egg. "The shelter's okay," he said. "Will went to check up on them."

There was another deafening roar, and the house trembled again. "I can't stay in here."

Dragons were hard-wired to protect one another, and Ember didn't use her dragon form on just any opponent. I ran into the shop and through the front door, closing it behind me. Ember flew above the house, her majestic scaled form six feet or longer, not including the tail. The neighbours had come out of their houses to stare at her, too, as she snapped and swiped at the three gargoyles who'd landed on our roof. Judging by their size and the feathers sprouting between their leathery wings, all three were male.

One of them slashed at her with his talons, and Ember

kicked him in the face. The gargoyle flipped head over heels and slammed into the street a few metres from me. The nearest neighbours retreated into their doorways as the gargoyle stirred, letting out a feeble groan. It was maybe six and a half feet tall and twice as wide with its wings extended, but one leathery wing hung at a crooked angle, damaged from his landing. *Try flying onto the roof now, will you?*

"Hey." I ran to him, knife in hand. The gargoyle clawed his way to his feet, tearing holes in the already-scarred tarmac in the process. "Get out of here. Now."

The gargoyle gave a feeble swipe, and I ducked, my knife sinking into the leathery skin between his claws. He howled, toppling backwards, and house opposite rippled with light as its owner's protective shield spell stopped the beast's wing from knocking out the windows.

"Get. Out." I yanked the knife free and hurled a witch charm into his face. As he fell unconscious, the huge grey gargoyle turned into a stocky male human. I readied my knife for the killing blow, and fire exploded behind my head.

I spun on the spot, seeing the other two gargoyles had flown backwards out of range of Ember's fire. She stood on the roof of our house, gripping the tiles with her clawed feet, her body language clear—*you're not getting inside.*

The stocky man stirred at my side and I threw a binding spell at him, locking his body to the tarmac. Aware of the onlooking crowd, I ducked down beside him and hissed, "Tell me who sent you here. What do you want?"

He let out a faint groan. "Dragon shifter scum."

"That wasn't an answer." My foot slammed into his ribs, and he let out a screeching noise more like a gargoyle than a human. "Tell me who sent you. Why are you here?"

"You have something we want."

The image of the dragon egg entered my mind's eye. *Why would the gargoyles want that? How did they even know we had it?*

"All right." I grabbed his shoulder, yanking him to his feet. "You and I are gonna have a chat somewhere more private, mate."

A deafening crash dragged him from my grip—the sound of a dragon landing on a roof. I whirled around as several roof tiles fell, clattering to the pavement from the impact. The huge red dragon had disappeared, and my sister's red hair was visible against the roof tiles. If Ember had shifted back to human, she must be seriously hurt.

Damn them.

Turning my back on the gargoyle, I ran. The door to the shop flew open and Will exited, shifting into gargoyle form. As a half-gargoyle, he was smaller than the three attackers, but the two who'd been on the roof were no longer there. Will's leathery wings beat as he flew up to the roof where Ember had fallen. I clenched my hands, wishing they were claws, wishing I could jump up and join him.

A moment later, Will dropped from the roof, his clawed talons holding Ember's limp human body. He landed on the ground, hopping on one foot to knock the door open. Ember's hair was tangled, her eyes were closed, and bright red blood stained Will's claws where he held her. He shifted to human form again and said, "She's alive. Get a healing spell."

"Got one." I pulled the wristband-shaped backup spell from my pocket, glad I hadn't wasted it on my minor injuries from the banshee. Will carried Ember into the hall, staggering under her weight. He was stronger in shifted form but had trouble fitting his wings through doorways, and the quicker we got Ember away from the gawking neighbours, the better. The entire street would be talking about Ember's crash-landing for the next six months.

She's okay. She has to be okay.

I activated the healing spell the instant Will laid her down on the living room floor. A flash of light illuminated the deep claw wounds on her chest, which began to seal closed immediately. If she hadn't been in dragon form, the gargoyles' claws would have crushed her ribs and pierced the organs underneath. As it was, the scales had kept off most of the damage, but bile seared the back of my throat at the very thought of my sister breathing her last right here in my arms.

I tensed when Ember made a faint groaning noise. It wasn't uncommon for her to fall unconscious after a rough shift, but a pair of rogue gargoyles shouldn't have been able to do so much damage to a dragon shifter. I'd seen her take on more formidable opponents and remain in one piece.

"What did they do to her?" I whispered.

"I was gonna ask you that." Will was uninjured because he'd been in the shelter, probably reassuring the others and forming an escape plan. "Where's Kit?"

"I don't know. Maybe he went upstairs." I got to my feet, my nerves jangling with adrenaline. "Kit?"

Becks ran into the living room, shifting into human form. "The gargoyle you left outside did a runner. The other two pricks flew off, too."

Kit bounded in from the hallway with a faerie's quick grace. "The roof's in bad shape but the ceiling's not going to come crashing down," he announced. "The wards held up. Is Ember okay?"

"She's unconscious." I took a step towards the door Becks had come through, my heart continuing to pound. "Watch her. I'm going to make sure they're gone."

"I'll go with you," Becks said. "At least they didn't break the wards."

"There is that." I scanned the room, my gaze snagging on the door to the shelter, which was partly open. "Did someone move the egg?"

"Move it?" Becks echoed. "Thought Kit had it."

All eyes went to Kit. "I dropped it when Ember fell on the roof," he said, crossing the room to the shelter door. "Right... here."

There was no sign of the dragon egg.

"Will?" I looked at him.

"I didn't see it when I was last in here." He circled the sofa then paced to the lab, running a hand through his blond hair. "Did one of the attackers get in here?"

"No," I said. "Two of them flew off, and I hit the other with a trapping spell in the street. One of us would have seen him come in."

There was a momentary pause. Kit sat on the sofa arm beside Ember's body, holding out his hands above her chest. Green light spread from him to her until her whole body glowed. Faerie healing power was as strong as a witch healing spell, if not stronger. She'd be back on her feet in no time. But the dragon egg...

I ran into the hallway and made for the trapdoor hidden under a piece of loose carpet at the back. I pulled it open, climbing down the short staircase into the darkness. A faint white light permeated the gloom, and a sigh of relief slipped free. The mirror was still there, glowing dimly. I scanned the room for the sealed door at the back that led underground. We didn't use it anymore—the tunnels weren't the safe haven they used to be—but in theory, someone could get in that way, if they broke through the wards and risked being eaten by a monster in the dark.

I grabbed the handle and rattled the wooden door. Still locked, sealed, with the wards in place. No... they hadn't come in through the tunnels.

"Anything?" Becks's voice came from the staircase behind me.

"Nope." I turned my back on the door. "They didn't come in this way."

Which left one option: the shelter.

Please no. Please not them.

I sprang upstairs, closed the trapdoor and pulled the carpet back over it, and retraced my steps to the living room. Ember and Kit were still on the sofa, while Will continued to circle the room, his hands buried in his blond hair.

"What are you doing?" he asked, when I stopped beside the shelter door. It wasn't locked or warded, because we were the only people who could get in or out.

I pulled the door open. "Someone took the egg."

"They wouldn't." Will's eyes widened at the sight of plaster dust in the shelter's hallway from the tremors when Ember had hit the roof.

The house was a mirror of ours. Two doors off the hallway led into rooms set up to house at least two people, sometimes more. I ran through a mental list of our current guests, then turned to the right. "Didn't the gargoyles in there knock a hole through the wall this morning?"

Muttering a curse under his breath, Will tried the door handle, which swung open easily. The room inside was empty, its only remarkable feature the huge claw-shaped gouges in the wall. Big enough for a human to climb out.

"Did you see the Morrises today? At all?" They were two brothers who'd showed up a couple of days ago, a little older than we usually dealt with—most rogues were either teenagers or families with young kids. Adult shifters generally went it alone, but our policy was that we didn't ask questions. We'd lived on the streets for a while ourselves, after all.

Will swore again, kicking the carpet up to expose the faded marks of a spell circle. "They were dabbling in magic."

"What—they were gargoyle-witches, like you?" I scanned the claw-marks. Gargoyle claws weren't that big, and the shape was wrong.

"I'm not convinced they were gargoyles at all." He walked

to the door and tapped the mark with his hand. "No… there's spell residue here. A witch did this. Not a skilled one, either."

"Did they look like gargoyles to you?" I asked.

"Of course they bloody well did." He scowled. "They might have used an illusion spell."

"Can't you see through them?"

"No. And Kit can only see through glamours, not witch illusions." Will kicked at the nearest chair, which had been knocked over. "They took the egg and ran."

"How'd they even know we had it?" How could word have spread so quickly? Nobody had seen me carrying the egg, I was certain.

"I spoke to the other families just then," he said. "They weren't involved, I'm sure of it."

Small comfort. Not only had we been played, three innocent families were in peril. And my sister….

Will started to speak, then stopped. I knew from the wariness on his face that my eyes were glowing faintly orange, a sign of one seriously pissed-off dragon shifter. But no shift accompanied the rage.

My voice came out in a low growl. "They'll burn for this."

4

Ember didn't wake up in the half-hour it took Will to pull together the repair spells to fix the roof, aided by Kit.

I, in the meantime, took to the street, asking every person who'd been watching the fight if they'd seen where the gargoyles had flown off to. The best way to chase them was by flight, but if Will left, nobody would be able to make any spells to heal Ember or fix the damage. Until Ember woke up, we were grounded. It pissed me off beyond measure.

"Keira." I approached the older witch, one of the few people who'd stayed in the street after the excitement was over. "Did you see which way he went? The guy I used a trapping spell on? He can't have flown."

"I saw one of the others pick him up and fly that way." She pointed to the right, which didn't help, considering the street had only one way out. If the gargoyles had come in through the tunnels, I might have been able to chase them, but gargoyles preferred open skies. They could be halfway across the city by now. I'd never catch them on foot.

Once I'd finished my search, I returned home. In the

kitchen, I found Will up to his elbows in spell ingredients, a cauldron atop the stove next to him. "Got a tracking spell?"

"What d'you want one of these for?" He snapped his fingers and activated a spell circle chalked on the work surface.

I held myself at a safe distance from its flaming edges. "A tracker might help me find the scumbag who ran away."

Will pushed his sweaty hair from his eyes. "Might help us find the Morrises, too, for all the good it does. Pretty sure they used false names anyway."

"Not the same anonymous people who sent the egg." I never should have let it out of my sight, but the gargoyles had been counting on the element of surprise.

How had they knocked out Ember? I walked away from the kitchen, finding Kit anxiously hovering over my sister's sleeping form.

"What's wrong with her, do you know?"

He shook his head. "I fixed all her physical injuries. If she's infected with poison or something... I don't know. She had claw wounds, but I healed them."

I brushed a strand of auburn hair from my sister's face, my throat tightening. "Bastards."

The door to the shop flew open again, and a man with pale brown hair entered with the swift, silent steps of someone who'd once made a living creeping over the rooftops to sneak up on unwary prey. He was the only human I'd met who tripped my fight or flight instinct, maybe a leftover effect of his history as an Orion League assassin who'd hunted dragon shifters like us.

His gaze went right to Ember's body. "What the hell happened to her?"

"Gargoyles," I answered. "Three of them tried to tear the roof off."

He swore under his breath, reaching to touch Ember's

face. Being human, there was nothing he could do for her. Other than punish the people responsible, that is, and I'd prefer to take that job for myself.

Astor's gaze snapped onto Will. "Friends of yours, were they?"

"No," said Will, without turning around from the potion brewing on the stove. "I've no idea who they were, but I think it was Ember or Cori they were after."

"Really." Astor's pale stare affixed me to the spot. "What did you do?"

"I didn't do a thing," I said. "Someone thought it was funny to deliver an anonymous package to me containing a dragon egg."

Astor's jaw locked. "A *dragon* egg?"

"I don't know if that's what it contained," I said. "It was sent from someone going by the name You Know Who, so I thought it was a shitty practical joke."

"It wasn't a joke," said Kit, unnecessarily. "Someone wanted us to take custody of the egg, didn't they?"

"What's the use in that now?" I let out a frustrated noise. "We didn't even manage to keep it an hour before the gargoyles' allies stole it back. For all I know they're the ones who sent it in the first place, but who knows."

"Here's your tracker." Will tossed a band-shaped spell in my direction. I snagged it by my fingertips. "Cori, you can do the honours. Becks, stop the assassin from tearing any heads off."

Astor scowled. "Who are you tracking?"

I crouched on the carpet and pulled out my knife, still stained in the gargoyle's blood. "Our attacker."

Laying the knife down, I shook the band-shaped spell to activate it, and it ignited, forming a circle around the bloody knife. I leaned in, pressing my hands to the glowing green edges. *Show me what they did.*

A black-and-white scene filled my vision, showing me a bird's eye view—or rather, gargoyle's eye view—of the street outside. Two gargoyles flew on either side of me, taking swipes at Ember's scaled dragon form. I winced at the impact as the gargoyle slammed into the top of the house, knocking roof tiles flying. A glow enveloped the gargoyle's claws, visible even through the black-and-white colouring of the tracking spell.

Gargoyle claws didn't glow.

The aggressor's claw sank into Ember's leg, and she roared. Trackers played images and not sound, but I still winced. For a moment, my gaze caught on two men slinking away down an alley. While I couldn't see their faces from this angle, one of them was bald, the other had a full head of black hair, and while neither of them looked anything like the gargoyle shifters, the way they walked indicated they didn't want to be followed.

The spell cut out, and the living room came back into view. I looked up at the others. "Becks, were the gargoyles' claws glowing when you saw them?"

"I didn't see," she said. "I don't think so. Why?"

"Looked that way in the vision," I said. "I think they had something on their claws. Poison, maybe."

Astor swore. "Poison? What type?"

"It's got to be something strong," Will said from the kitchen. "Aren't dragon shifters immune to a lot of toxins?"

"We are." Which meant they'd come prepared. "I also think I saw the Morrises—or whoever they really are."

They sure as hell hadn't looked like young, orphaned gargoyle shifters who'd come here off the streets to beg for shelter. They'd been older, forties at a guess, and had moved in a coordinated manner that suggested they'd pulled the same scam before. Maybe we weren't the only shifters they'd relieved of their valuables, but most raiders wouldn't dare rob a supernaturals-only district. They were more than human, that was for sure.

"Would you recognise them if you saw them again?" asked Astor. "Maybe the others in the shelter saw their real faces." His tone was deceptively calm, his face a mask of indifference. I didn't doubt that he was as angry as me; he just hid it better.

"I think so," I said. "They left by foot, not the air, and sneaked out through the alley between the shelter and the shop on the other side."

"Right." Astor made for the door. Without waiting for an invitation, I followed.

Like a lot of locations hidden pre-invasion, Magic Avenue was crammed between two existing streets and didn't have much in the way of back alleys. The Morrises must have already undone whatever spells they'd been using to hide their appearances before fleeing. The alley contained no signs of their presence and no traces of any spells that I could see. Then again, I wasn't a witch.

"Bastards." My hands curled into fists and I suppressed the urge to punch the wall. While Ember could claw chunks out of brick when she was pissed or crush a car into scrap metal, I'd break my hand, which wouldn't help anyone.

Astor's soft footfalls behind me announced his presence. "Well?"

"Nothing here," I said. "It'll take wings to find them."

"Not if we find a witness."

"That was next on the list. I'll do the talking."

Astor terrified most people without even speaking to them. Murdering people for a living wasn't exactly conducive to developing a friendly rapport. Sometimes I wondered what in the world my sister saw in him, but he'd stuck around for five years, for what it was worth.

I knocked on the door of the shop on the alley's left-hand

side. Ahmed, a young man with light brown skin and dark brown hair—shifter or witch, I wasn't sure—answered, his gaze moving warily between us. "You're not gargoyles, are you?"

"Nope. Did you see any, just then? Heading that way?" I pointed down the road.

"Yeah, I saw one of them," he said. "I think he was injured. Then two more scooped him up and flew off with him."

As I'd suspected. "All right, thanks. Did you see two human-looking strangers walk past, too?"

"Human strangers?" he echoed. "No. Why?"

"They came through the alley," I explained. "Not sure if they were human or not, but one was a bald guy, the other had black hair, and they used illusions…"

His eyes went wide. "Humans and gargoyles? As in, two humans directing a team of gargoyles?"

"I don't know about directing, but they worked together. Why?"

"They walked outside my door?" He leaned on the door frame like he was about to faint. "Please tell me you didn't make enemies of the Faulkner twins. What'd you do to piss them off?"

"Nothing." That was the downright infuriating part. I like to feel a grudge is hard-earned. "The Faulkners… the name rings a bell."

"You know who they are," he said. "Half the gargoyle rogues this side of the Thames work for them. You're not going after them, are you?"

"If they stole from us?" I said. "Yeah, we are."

"Then I'm not getting involved." He made to close the door, and Astor stuck his foot in the way. The young man flinched, and I prepared to intervene if the ex-assassin went too far.

"Your life won't be in any danger if you tell us what we

need to know," Astor said in a low, measured voice. "Tell us everything you know about these Faulkners."

"I don't," Ahmed said quickly. "I mean, I know they're twin brothers, human, and they trade in rare items. They say they often sponsor arena matches, too."

Several things clicked into place. "Of course they do."

Everyone knew of the arena, even if all they knew was the name. A place where shifters put their lives on the line to compete for riches—and dragon eggs, apparently.

If they'd taken the egg to one of the underground fighting rings, it'd be worth a fortune to the right person. Of course, going to the arena wouldn't tell me who'd sent me the egg to begin with, but it was a starting point.

Besides, someone had to pay for hurting Ember.

"Thanks," I said to Ahmed.

Astor caught my arm as he closed the door. "We weren't done questioning him."

"I got what I needed. Let go of me."

He released my arm. "Habit."

That's what passed for an apology from Astor. Don't piss off the ex-assassin. It wasn't me he was mad at, so I let it slide. "Will's contacts will know how to get to the arena, so I guess that's where we're going tonight."

"What exactly is the arena?" he asked.

"Underground fighting ring for supernaturals only," I answered. "Sorry, Astor, but you'll have to sit this one out."

He gave me a look that said *we'll see about that*, then turned his back and walked away.

That went well. Two humans who directed teams of gargoyles competed in the arena fights, did they? If they wanted to wager a dragon egg, they deserved to get burned.

I surveyed my reflection in the bathroom mirror, attempting to tie back my mass of auburn curls for the fifth time. I'd stand out too much with it on full display, but illusions, hats and other tricks would fall apart the instant punches started flying.

After three phone calls to former contacts, Will had produced an address which reportedly led to the arena, so Becks and I opted to go and check it out. Knives were concealed up my sleeves, in my pockets, strapped to my belt. Witch spells on both wrists were colour-coded according to Will's system, which he'd borrowed from the local witch coven's standard guide. Knockout spells like the one I'd used on the banshee, and a new itching spell which Will claimed would turn the toughest gargoyle into a whimpering wreck in five seconds flat.

Astor was *not* thrilled at staying behind. I was glad not to have to wait out the night in the same house as an enraged ex-assassin, but leaving my sister behind tied me in knots. She was usually the one who risked her neck on my behalf, not the other way around, and she'd be pissed as hell when she woke up and found me gone. Still, there was no need to take part in any fighting if the scumbags who'd poisoned her weren't there. I knew how to pick my battles, and the reason I'd survived this long was by avoiding these exact scenarios. On the other hand, dragon shifters were prone to running on impulse, and white-hot rage continued to burn deep inside me, threatening to burn reason and caution to cinders.

I tugged my coat straight to hide my weapons. I'd heard arena fights were strictly hand-to-hand, but I'd be a fool to go in there unarmed. Every week came rumours of more deaths, disappearances off the streets of victors and losers alike. I'd fought for my life for too long to casually throw it away to win a prize. Even a dragon egg… which shouldn't exist, and which I wouldn't know about if someone hadn't foisted it on us. Whoever had decided it was worth endangering our lives for would get a sharp kick to the teeth when I found them.

"Ready?" Becks entered the room behind me. She wore her long trench coat, her hair tied back, and her glasses tucked away in her pocket. They vanished when she shifted but tended to fall off when she turned human again. Her short-sightedness didn't matter so much as a cat. Despite the fierce glint in her amber-coloured eyes, I knew she was as nervous as I was.

"Sure." I stepped back from the mirror. "You know what to do."

"Don't get into any fights I don't have to." Becks's survival instincts were as well-honed as mine, and she knew when to fight and when to run. "I think this is nuts, for the record."

"Me too. But Ember's counting on us."

Becks and I trod silently through the shop and out into the night. Magic Avenue was practically dead at this hour. No street lamps illuminated the darkness, but the residents would be watching through their blinds to see if any other attackers showed up.

Becks's hands were trembling. "I've never been to the arena," she said, her voice low. "But someone started a rumour at the first shelter I lived at that it's where my parents sold me off."

"What?" I looked at her in disbelief. "That is utter bullshit."

"I don't think they did." She fiddled with her sleeve, her head bowed. "I think I was stolen from them. They don't just wager cash on those fights."

My stomach turned over. *They bet living shifters as prizes?* Maybe it didn't matter to them if the egg hatched after all. "Scumbags."

Becks didn't talk much about her past. Ember and I had

found her huddled in the ruins of a collapsed building when we'd fled the chaos of the faerie invasion. The Orion League, free to unleash their violence against the supernatural world, had gunned down Rhea, who owned the shelter Ember and I had grown up in. They'd nearly killed Ember and me, too, until my sister had shifted for the first time and saved our necks. My earliest memory was of my sister's hand firmly gripping mine, guiding me through the confusion and clamour of Euston's Underground station, and while her insistence on maintaining that same role in adulthood was sometimes annoying, not everyone was fortunate enough to have someone who'd literally bargain with the forces of life and death to keep them safe.

I'd never felt so damned vulnerable, heading out into the night without my sister at my back. A human and a cat were walking targets, wandering through London's once-bustling tourist district at night. Becks's sharp eyes scanned the darkness for threats, but the only people around were a group of teens smoking beside the fountain in Trafalgar Square. Humans, flirting with danger. Sure, this area was well-lit, but the bright street lamps only made the shadows seem darker. Empty theatres greeted us on either side as we walked towards Leicester Square, halting at the designated meeting spot: a booth which had once sold theatre tickets. Fitting, I supposed.

I walked up to the counter and peered through the grimy glass. "Anyone in?"

"You're s'posed to ring the bell," growled a voice. A man appeared—shifter, by his growling voice and six-foot-something frame. It was a wonder his wide shoulders even fit into the ticket booth.

"Hey there," I said. "We're looking for info on the arena."

He grunted. "Spectator or participant?"

"Can I decide when I'm there?"

He raised a brow. "Testing the waters, are we?"

"No, looking for some friends of mine," I said. "If they're not there, I won't want to waste my time. Know what I mean?"

I did my best to project an air of *I'm totally the sort of hard-as-nails street shifter who participates in public brawls and definitely isn't wearing socks with the Powerpuff Girls on them under these leather boots.*

He gave another grunt. "What're you, shifters? What type?"

"Cat." I indicated Becks. "As for me, I'm saving the reveal for when I win."

"Special attraction, are you?" He held up a stamp, and I extended my hand, beckoning to Becks with my other one. She didn't move. The guy stamped my hand, and I crouched down next to her. Becks shook her head, her whiskers trembling.

I rose to my feet. "Can she come in as a spectator?"

"Fine." His terseness implied he wanted us gone. "Make trouble, you get thrown out. Steal anything, you get skewered. Deal?"

"Deal. Where do I go?"

"That way." He jerked his thumb towards the dimly lit square. "Someone'll come and get you."

That was easier than I expected. For once, being the harmless younger sister who couldn't shift worked in my favour, because the shifter dude had no idea who I was. Maybe I'd be the first dragon shifter to anonymously infiltrate the arena.

Now all I needed to do was survive it.

5

Becks and I waited in Leicester Square for at least fifteen minutes. It was cold for March, but dragon shifters had a higher body temperature than humans, and Becks had fur. She prowled along the low stone wall while I sat down, tapping my foot impatiently. Just when I'd started to think we'd been duped, a short guy wearing a hoody who gave off distinct rat-shifter vibes approached us.

"Are you spectators or participants?" His voice was low and raspy. Definitely a rat shifter.

"Spectators, unless we get lucky," I said, revealing the stamp on my hand. "She's my Second."

"Witch, are you?"

"That's for me to know." The more contradictory clues I left behind me, the harder it'd be for people to guess what I was. Once my secret was out, the dragon egg would be long gone.

"Have it your way." He eyed the knife sticking from my upper pocket. "Weapons aren't allowed in most bouts. Same goes for spells."

"Not gonna be a problem." *Because I'll get my hands on that egg first.* Stealing might not be allowed, but I'd kept the envelope the egg had been delivered in, complete with my work address. Not that I could count on Darcy to back me up, but with any luck, I wouldn't need to.

The rat shifter led us to a narrow passage between two theatres, both shut down and locked up, and opened a door on our right-hand side. The passage smelt strongly of gargoyle shifter. *This is the place.*

The door led to a narrow staircase which disappeared into darkness. The rat shifter dropped his gaze to Becks as she slunk in ahead of me. "Does your friend know the risks?"

"Yes. She's not participating." Becks's meow from further down told me it was safe to climb in.

A short staircase and a couple of corridors later brought us to the main theatre—or rather, the arena. It'd hardly changed from its former pre-invasion appearance, except every person sitting in the rows of seats was a supernatural.

And the stage was a battleground.

Two shifters ripped into one another under the garish lights. Both were in human form, muscle-bound males who already bore visible scars on their bare torsos. I walked up the aisle, pretending to search for a seat while I scanned the spectators. A group of male rat shifters sat in a tight-knit pack, recognisable by their short stature and whiskered faces. Nearby, a burly group of gargoyles were drinking cheap beer and making loud exaggerated claims about their own prowess in arena matches. I nearly cracked up laughing and blew my cover when one of them said, in serious tones, "I once punched a dragon shifter's teeth out, while in human form."

Not likely, mate.

"You're full of shit," said his neighbour. "I, on the other hand, am tipped to be the next leader of the Fanged."

"And I'm the Queen of the Unseelie Court," I muttered, standing on tip-toe to see past the gargoyles' towering heads.

Where's that dragon egg?

A gargoyle's screech came from the stage, followed by a shout. "Stop the match!"

I darted into the nearest row of seats in case anyone called me out for acting suspicious, but all eyes were on the stage. One of the shifters had transformed from human to gargoyle, his leathery wings spread beneath the stage lights.

A raspy voice echoed from somewhere above my right-hand side. "Rule breach. No shifting allowed."

Two huge, brutish gargoyles closed in on the guy who'd just transformed, and he turned human again, spitting out blood. "Lost my head for a second."

"You'll be lucky not to lose it for real," said the raspy voice. "The match is over."

The guards frog-marched him from the arena to loud booing from the crowd. I turned to my right, looking up to see where the amplified voice had come from and spotted a short man leaning on the balcony on my right. Another rat shifter, I'd guess, and presumably the guy running the show. Not one of the two men I'd seen in the vision, but I bet he knew who the Faulkner brothers were.

I climbed up the stairs to the balcony, tugging my hood down to hide my bright hair. With the brutality of the fighting, it made sense that most of the participants were shifters. The faeries kept to their own fighting rings, since their magical skills gave them an unfair advantage. Meanwhile, the witches typically had pacifist tendencies, necromancers weren't the competitive sort, and mages thought street brawling beneath them.

"Hey," I said to the shifter wielding the microphone, whose whiskery face made him look like an oversized rat even as a human. "How do I sign up?"

"Right here," he said. The two brutish gargoyle shifters standing behind him moved forwards an inch or so, as though to remind me of their presence. Now I looked more closely, similar guards stood at intervals around the arena's edges, clothed in smart suits that didn't hide their bulging muscles.

Maybe this wasn't such a good idea. For all I knew, mentioning the Faulkners' names in conjunction with a mysterious dragon egg would get me a beating, or thrown out into the street.

"Going to sign up?" he asked, with a touch of impatience.

"I'm a spectator for now," I said. "Do people often place bets on the matches?"

"Sure. I don't stop them." He shrugged. "Got a couple of serious ones later… rumour has it, we're in for quite a show."

A dragon egg kind of show? Unless I blew my cover, I'd have to sit through the whole damned thing to see if the egg was here, unless Becks managed to sniff it out. Since I didn't fancy being a gargoyle's punching bag, I'd have to suck it up and draw on all the patience I could muster. Not that patience was in any way a dragon shifter virtue.

"Thanks," I said, picking out a new seat on the balcony. The fights weren't ticketed, and people came and went as they wished. It made it easier for me to hide, but more difficult to pinpoint Becks. There were a fair few cat shifters scattered among the crowd, most rangy and scarred with patchy fur. A cat and a gargoyle might look like an unfair match, but I'd seen Becks bring a full-grown troll crashing down when she darted underneath his feet. Never underestimate cat shifters for speed and tenacity.

I leaned over the balcony, looking down at the restless crowd as the next bout began. It was rare for anyone to die during a match, but the losers or even the winners often showed up dead in an alley the next day, or floating face-down in the river. Nobody batted an eyelid. You were on your own if you made an enemy of someone who frequented the arena.

For that reason, I'd prefer to avoid fighting if I could avoid it. Not because I was scared I'd lose, but because winning might prove as fatal as the alternative.

Becks nudged my leg, and I lowered my head to her. "Find anything?"

She jabbed a paw at the balcony just in front of me. I leaned over again, my gaze scanning the row directly beneath me.

Not five metres away were bald head and a head full of darker hair bowed in conversation at the very back of the row.

It's them. The Faulkners.

Liquid fury bubbled inside me. If they weren't actively taking part in the fighting, I wouldn't be able to take them down, but my non-existent claws itched to inflict pain on them for what they'd done to my sister. They wore dark suits, a marked contrast to the majority of the clientele, with the notable exceptions of the muscle-bound guards. It sent a message: that they were exempt from the usual rules of the arena. Even the way they stood set them apart. A glint made my breath stop in my throat, but it was just the bald guy's wristwatch. Real gold, I didn't doubt. Those two oozed a level of sophistication and class that was obvious even from a distance. And to think we'd let them stay in our shelter alongside innocent escapees from this very arena. Nausea rose, and I briefly entertained the idea of vomiting directly onto their heads.

Becks gave me another nudge, asking for permission to jump on them from above. As much as I'd have liked to see her claws make mincemeat of their faces, I shook my head. Getting kicked out would send us back to square one and alert them to our presence. They didn't appear to have the dragon egg on them, but if they planned to bet wager it on an arena match, it couldn't be far off.

I left my seat and approached the dude with the microphone again.

"Hey, mate," I muttered. "Those two down there. Are they fighting?"

"Betting, I heard."

Figures. "Pit me against whoever they're sponsoring."

"Can't do that." He consulted the sheet of paper in his hand. "Pre-arranged match."

I swore. Whoever won would get the dragon egg. I couldn't let that happen.

"Sorry to disappoint you," he said, with absolutely no sincerity. "They're up after this next bout. I wouldn't do anything rash."

The two gargoyles on either side of him cracked their knuckles. *Damn it all.* "All right. Whoever wins, can I challenge them?"

"If you like, but that's between you and them."

Fine, then. I returned to my spot, finding Becks curled underneath my seat, her eyes wide and anxious. She'd probably bite me if I tried to stroke her in reassurance like a real cat, so I settled for letting her sit on my feet to see through the balcony. She'd overheard my conversation with the rat shifter so there was no need to tell her my plan.

The next fight kicked into gear. I fidgeted, picking at a loose thread in the fabric of the seat, and my gaze snagged on a young man in the front row, inches away from the fight. In any other circumstances, I'd worry he might get hit by a stray punch, but for him, that wouldn't be an issue.

He was kinda *dead*, for one thing.

I kept my eye on the stage, hoping the dead man would fade out without noticing I'd spotted him. Generally, when ghosts knew you could see them, they decided to act out and make a scene in any way possible. Highly distracting at best, destructive at worst. It was safe to say nobody else in the arena possessed an iota of the spirit sight, since the ghost floated directly on top of the row of eager spectators without any of them having the faintest clue that there was a dead person standing on top of them.

Of all the times to start seeing ghosts again. It'd been weeks since the last *incident*, where I'd punched out a guy who kept hitting on me and hadn't realised he was a ghost until I'd landed flat on my face. In my defence, it'd been a foggy day, and ghosts resembled transparent versions of their living counterparts. Most of the time they didn't know they were dead, either. It took a gift exclusive to necromancers known as the spirit sight to be able to see them. No other supernaturals had that power. Or so they said.

You've already passed beyond the veil, my dear, a ghost who'd accosted me at Covent Garden market had said. And now the banshee, too. They weren't wrong. I *had* died. Then my sister had used the Moonbeam, a magical artefact rumoured to have been created by the first dragon shifters, to bring me back to life. And now, as the universe liked to remind me, a door had been opened that could never be closed again.

One of the shifters onstage hurled his opponent to the ground, and even the ghost recoiled from the crash. The gargoyle hit the stage and came to a halt inches from the front row, his arm hanging at a crooked angle.

"He's out cold!" someone shouted.

A chorus of shouts accompanied the victor's march away from the stage. I remained tense, hoping everyone would assume I was on the edge of my seat because I was so invested in the match. My glowing red-orange eyes would be harder to explain, but the restless crowd had no need to look in my direction.

A frisson of anger rippled through my veins as the Faulkners moved up the stairs to the balcony where the rat shifter stood. They bent their heads to talk to him, and the rat shifter gave a nod, raising his microphone.

"Now this is new," said the rat shifter, his voice echoing around the arena. "Seems we have a prearranged match, and neither of the participants has disclosed *what*, exactly, they're betting on their candidate's victory. But I believe they're ready to make the announcement now."

"Correct," said a low, resonant voice, as the bald man took the microphone. His pale face was hawkish, his slight frame unimpressive even in his polished suit. "My brother Bryan and I have a show planned for you today. Let's just say things are about to get... *heated.*"

All eyes went to the stage, and a flare of golden light momentarily blinded me. When the light cleared, a cage hung suspended above the arena. Inside it was the dragon egg. Its scales caught the light, washing the arena floor in blood red.

My nails dug into my palms. What the hell were they thinking? Why risk a prize like that in so public a location? Their opponents must have something they *really* wanted. Something more valuable, even. *Not good.*

"Isn't that a beauty?" said the rat shifter in tones of reverence. "A real, genuine dragon egg. Worth millions, if you can put a price on something absolutely priceless. And take a look at their combatant."

A gargoyle shifter strode onto the stage beneath the suspended cage. He looked like he'd got stuck halfway through a shift and never made it all the way back to human. His skin had a leathery texture with a scale-like pattern in places on his thick arms, and while he didn't have wings, his shoulders looked padded. Unless it was all the muscle. He was easily three times my size, and the promise of violence radiated from every inch of him. Their opponent would have to put someone with serious skills forward if they wanted a chance of winning.

But they won't. It was a show. They planned to wager the egg because they knew their candidate wouldn't lose. Everyone would have seen it, realised its worth, and word would spread around the entire shifter community by tomorrow. Then they'd try to sell it to the highest bidder. It'd be a literal bloodbath.

What the hell am I supposed to do? A dozen brutish shifters guarded both sides of the stage, preventing anyone from walking on. The cage was too high, and too far from the balconies for Becks to be able to jump and reach it, let alone me.

"And now, the challenger," said the rat shifter. "Seems he's brought his own microphone."

"I have," said a thick voice, from somewhere in the shadows behind the golden cage. "Here's my candidate."

Another gargoyle shifter took to the stage, significantly smaller than his opponent. His face was flat and broad, his knuckles the size of my head even with the size difference. *Jesus. They must offer these people a fortune to do their dirty work.*

The rat shifter spoke. "And what exactly are *you* betting? How much?"

"I'm not betting cash," said the thick voice from behind the golden cage. "I'm betting him."

Silence hushed the restless crowd as two of the suited guards appeared from backstage, dragging a struggling man between them. His hands were bound, his face bloody.

They're wagering a person?

Shit. I hadn't seen this one coming. If the Faulkners' candidate won, they'd keep the egg and get to sell it. But if the other sponsors won, what did they plan to do with their prisoner?

"Clear the arena," said the announcer, and the two guards dragged their captive to the edge of the stage. The dragon egg remained in its cage above the combatants. Neither of them spared a glance at the prizes as they squared up to one another.

"Do you accept the terms of the match?" said the raspy voice.

"Absolutely," the bald man said into the microphone.

I stood rigid, my careful plans crumbling. Stealing the egg in public view was out of the question. I might have an arsenal of spells on me, but there was a limit, especially in a room packed with over a hundred rowdy shifters and at least twenty brutish guards. None of them had given me a second's glance yet, but that would change if I got near their precious arena floor.

Becks nudged my leg again. "I know, I know. I'm trying to think…"

She gave me another firm nudge, indicating the prisoner with an outstretched paw. The guards had pulled him back to make room for the battle, but he was still visible between two hulking gargoyle shifters. Despite his predicament, he didn't look like the sort of person who got tied up on purpose. He was as powerfully built as one of the arena fighters. And—wait a second.

His hair was coppery red, and his eyes, when they met mine from the arena floor, were ashy grey with the merest hint of a spark.

Another dragon shifter.

6

I forgot the fight, the crowd, the rising noise as the two shifters ripped into one another. I also forgot the dead guy. *Another dragon shifter.* Never mind the egg... he was one of my people. Definitely not one I'd met before either. I'd remember.

A horrible noise came from the stage. The bigger shifter had a grip on the smaller guy's throat, and from the way his skin tore, there was more than a hint of claw there. It wasn't a fair fight at all. He was as good as dead. Which meant the Faulkners would walk away with more than a dragon egg.

They'd get a genuine dragon shifter as a prize.

Anger fuelled my resolve. *Not happening.* Dragon shifters were so rare, either he was one of Lorne's former helpers or he was a rogue like me. Considering he was tied up with his life on the line on a brutal arena match, I'd go with the rogue option.

I bent down to whisper instructions to Becks. We wouldn't have long. The match would be over soon—hell, it should be already. Inflicting mortal wounds on one's opponent would not win any popularity contests, but with the high stakes of this match, it was easy to lose control. When I looked up, the big shifter had dropped the smaller one. His neck bled freely, but he leapt into action again, delivering a hail of punches. A roar struck up from the crowd as the big shifter bent double under the smaller guy's relentless strikes.

Becks slipped away under the seats, while I straightened, tilting my head to better see the prisoner's predicament. Looked like only his hands were bound, with rope. It wasn't the rope that held him captive, though, but the thuggish guards and the limited space to manoeuvre. The only way out was past the two heavily muscled gargoyles holding his bound arms.

I flexed my hands, adjusting the wristband-shaped spells I'd worn under my coat sleeves. I'd memorised the order. Now to see if my speed was up to scratch.

I moved downstairs with my head bowed as quickly as I dared. The crowd roared, and I pretended to roar along with them, slipping down the back row until I was as close to the exit as possible. Then I slid one of the bands off my wrist, activating it with a faint twist.

Smoke seeped out. Not as subtle as I'd have liked, but the crowd barely stirred, no doubt thinking it was a special effect designed for the match. A smokescreen spell would make it harder for anyone to see our escape. Using the smoke as a cover, I slid among the burly gargoyle shifters—who were still arguing about their various fictional accomplishments—and swiped one of their plastic beer cups. Then, with a quick twist, I poured the contents of said cup over the head of the tall gargoyle shifter in the row in front.

I dove to the ground as the shifter in front whirled, flinging a punch at the unsuspecting guy directly behind him. Snarls and screeches broke out, and I crawled underneath the row of seats, for once grateful for my small stature.

By the time I surfaced, the guards who'd been directly by

the exit had moved in to break up the fight. *Have fun with that.*

Grinning, I spotted Becks's sleek form slipping behind the two shifters guarding their prisoner at the side of the stage. There was a faint flash, lost in the roar of stamping feet as the big shifter fell.

No way. Is he actually going to lose?

The huge shifter roared, hitting out at his opponent. There was zero actual skill involved—it was a brawl, plain and simple. Both of them were bleeding from multiple wounds, especially the smaller shifter. The match wouldn't end until one of them was utterly beaten into submission.

Go on. Make a big show of it. Nobody pay any attention to the cat...

One of the suit-wearing shifter guards turned on the spot, apparently hearing the grunts and shouts from the inelegant brawl near the exit, and I held my breath. Becks had disappeared behind the edge of the curtain. I exhaled slowly, and as he returned his attention to the match, I moved to the second row from the front.

Right behind the ghost.

His head whipped around. "Hey," he whispered. "Can you see me?"

I closed my eyes for a moment and then opened them, looking right through the transparent man at the stage in front of me. I was *so* close.

"You can see me," he repeated. "Help me. I'm stuck in here and I can't get out."

He probably wasn't lying. Ghosts tended to get stuck in the place they'd died, so chances were, he'd breathed his last in this very theatre. In one of these matches. But I didn't have time to help a lost spirit.

"Help," he whispered in my ear. "Hellllp."

I'm not going to die because of a ghost. "I'll help you if you stop whispering at me," I said through clenched teeth.

"Oh, thank god you can hear me!"

Thank my sister. She's the one who brought me back from the dead. With side effects. Every single time I saw the faint shimmer that accompanied a ghost's appearance, I remembered that if not for my sister's desperate plea to the Moonbeam, I'd have stayed on the other side of the veil and never come back.

As it was, I *did* come back, but not the same. The fact that I was the only person in the room who could hear and see this irritating spirit was proof enough.

"I'll do anything to help you if you get me out of here," he said, his transparent hands gesturing. "Anything."

"Can't make any promises," I muttered. "But I could use a diversion right now. Anything you can manage." Most spirits didn't have much in the way of magical talent, but I could use all the help I could get.

One of the shifter guards moved again, scratching his leg. The second guy began to twitch, too. I hid a smile. Itching spells were dismissed as childish pranks, but damn, did they come in handy in situations like this.

A keening noise came from the smaller shifter on the stage. Oh, shit. The bigger guy had grabbed him by the throat again, lifting him off the ground.

"I... give," he croaked.

"We have a winner!" crowed the rat shifter. "Excellent. It looks like that dragon egg will be staying with its owners, folks."

Like hell it will.

"Actually," said the bald man's voice, "it won't. I'm going to an auction tomorrow, and I'll be taking the egg with me. It's likely that such a rare and valuable prize will be snapped up fast, so I'd advise you to make your plans ready for tomorrow morning."

I knew it. The moment he'd announced the bet, I'd known he didn't want to wager it on a simple brawl. Everyone in this room would be telling every single person they knew that there was a dragon egg on offer at the auction. By tomorrow, London's entire supernatural community would be scraping out their savings accounts in order to claim it.

"What's their problem?" muttered someone nearby, watching the increasingly uncomfortable-looking guards. One had started to hop from one leg to the other, scratching frantically. By now, the itching would have spread all over their bodies with the ruthlessness of a magically engineered rash. *Good luck guarding your prisoner now.*

"We've been spelled!" the guard rasped.

At that moment, the stage lights went out. Silently thanking the ghost, I spotted the hulking forms of the shifters and the outline of their prisoner between them. He hadn't even moved, which was a bit odd. If I'd been in his position, you'd better believe I'd have made a run for it the instant the guards' attention slipped.

Becks jumped in front of the prisoner, tugging on his feet with her teeth. Finally, he moved, stepping away from the guards. I jumped up behind him, grabbing his arm. "Come with us."

He backed off the stage in one quick jump. I jumped, too, hoping I didn't land on someone. The place was pitch black, and the darkness made it difficult to see. Becks nudged my leg, and I swore. The dragon shifter was climbing onto the stage again.

"Hey!" I caught his arm, pulling him backwards. He landed with a grunt. "I'm saving your life. That power cut won't last forever."

I tugged him after me down the aisle, which was now so

thick with smoke that the exit was totally obscured. He fought me with every step, and I kept losing my grip. Did he not *want* to get out of here?

"I said I'm saving your life." Maybe he thought I was another one of the scumbags who wanted to capture a dragon shifter and wager him as a prize.

He stopped struggling when we passed through the exit and up the stairs into the alley. I looked around for Becks and saw a pair of amber eyes blinking in the darkness.

Rescue mission accomplished.

The instant we crossed the square and disappeared into the safety of a side street, the dragon shifter pulled himself free from my grip.

"Hey," I said. "Let me untie your hands."

Without speaking, he held out his hands. An unlocking spell wouldn't work on rope, so I pulled one of my knives. The rope was thick and tough, and it took a few moments to make a dent in it.

"Are you going to speak?" I whispered. "Look, if we get somewhere sheltered, nobody'll come after us. They're too busy running around in there looking for the source of the itching spell."

"You fool," he hissed, and I nearly let go of the knife, startled by his sharp tone.

"I'm sorry, what?" I hacked through another thread. "I saved your life. You're welcome."

"I didn't need saving."

I stopped sawing. "You like to wager your life on shifter brawls for fun? All right, next time I'll make sure to stop and ask you if you want to be rescued before saving your sorry neck."

"I wanted that egg," he said. "Logan and Bryan Faulkner rarely bring their prizes out in the open."

"I'm the one they stole it from." I pocketed the knife,

content to leave him to get the rope off himself. "Less than six hours ago."

He yanked his hands away, breaking the remainder of the rope and tossing it aside. "*You?* A likely story. You look like someone's kid sister."

I kicked him in the kneecap. He stumbled, swearing. *Didn't think I could kick that hard, did you?*

"You have some nerve tossing insults at me, dickhead," I said. "How did you plan on getting that egg out of the cage?"

"I didn't," he growled. "Soon as those bastards hauled me away, I planned to break these ropes and swipe it from them. Dragon claws can break through anything."

"I *am* a dragon shifter." Maybe I'd been a fool for thinking he needed saving. But barging in and breathing fire everywhere was more of a typical dragon shifter approach than letting oneself get captured by a bunch of thugs and humiliated in front of an audience.

Becks ran to my side, turning into her human form. "I'd move out of sight. Those gargoyle guards are *pissed.*"

I swore. "Right, we're moving. That means you too, dickhead. Why not swipe the egg before the match so the whole supernatural community didn't find out about it? Is that not a little more logical?"

He glared at me, his ashy eyes turning to embers. "If you're lying—"

"I'm not lying. I'm a dragon shifter, and that egg is mine. I'm going to take proof right to his public spectacle." I turned my back and walked in the direction of Trafalgar Square, and after a moment, he followed.

"You'll do no such thing," he said. "Make a public attempt to grab the egg and everyone will know about it."

"Like that wasn't public?" He might well be right, but my stealth rescue mission would have worked just fine if the person I'd rescued wasn't an ungrateful wanker. I should have gone for the egg instead of playing Good Samaritan. "Whereabouts are you hanging out, then? Who are your people?"

His angry grey eyes met mine. "None of your business."

"You want that dragon egg, you have to go through me. We can play nice or nasty, be my guest."

He must know I was bluffing. He could fully shift into a giant reptile, while I couldn't even produce a claw. Ember could probably take him on in a fight, but I'd never even managed to find out what they'd poisoned her with.

"That so?" He folded his arms across his broad chest. "And just how do you plan to do that?"

"You saw what I did to those two gargoyle guards."

A brow cocked. "Death by itching spell?"

"That stuff's lethal in a high dose." I pulled up my sleeve, revealing a flash of the wristbands I wore. Okay, I had *one* itching spell and it had a ten-minute time limit, but he didn't have to know.

"How'd you knock the lights out, then?"

I teamed up with an annoying ghost. I hadn't been able to stick around and keep up my end of the bargain, but that was the least of tonight's failures. "That's for me to know."

"Your name?" he asked.

Oh, now he wants to know who I am. "Cori. Yours?"

"Zeph. And sorry to disappoint you, but I need that dragon egg."

"For what purpose?"

He was already striding away, as though meeting a fellow dragon shifter wasn't worth the energy. "Guess I'll see you around, Cori."

"Obviously, since we're going to the auction," I said.

"There is no 'we'," he said over his shoulder.

"Did you hear me inviting you?" I pulled my sleeves back

down to hide the spells. "That egg is mine. And I'm sorry I chose to free you instead. Next time I won't bother."

He merely grunted, and he walked away without looking back.

Becks reappeared at my side. "Nice guy, that. Why'd you free him?"

"Why d'you think?" I released a breath. "I didn't think there were any free dragon shifters left." Not outside of the village, anyway. He must be a rogue who'd somehow avoided the Orion League for their entire reign of terror over the supernatural world.

"Come on," Becks muttered. "We shouldn't hang around here after dark."

"What a waste of time." I strode down the gloomy street, anger flickering. "So we don't have the egg. And now it's going up for auction in public—I suppose if the whole city knows about it, at least it'll be easy to find out where it is."

"Damn right," Becks said. "I'll do some snooping and find out where the auction's taking place."

"And I'll get my claws out." Metaphorically speaking. "No rescuing anyone next time."

7

You'd think the adrenaline rush of my night's exploits would have stopped me sleeping, but I passed out cold the instant my head hit the pillow. I woke early, squinting at the grey light seeping through the window of my box-sized room. The three-bedroom house meant I shared with Becks, and her absence told me she hadn't returned from her nocturnal wander.

I reached for my phone on the bedside table and checked the time. Seven in the morning. I'd showered last night before crashing, so my hair had dried in a curly mass. I tugged a brush through it a few times after pulling on jeans and a bright T-shirt, along with a pair of Hello Kitty socks which didn't help the 'cute baby sister' impression, but oh well. I gave up trying to tame my hair and walked downstairs to check up on my sister.

Ember had spent the night on the sofa, the closest spot to Will's spell stores. He stood in the kitchen area, barefoot, his blond hair sticking up from running his hands through it. Open containers of various herbs littered the tables, along with stray leaves and chalked spell circles. I sneezed as the foul smell of whatever was boiling in the pan on the stove dove up my nose and down my throat until my eyes stung.

"Jesus, Will, is the next stage of the itching spell a 'burn your enemy's eyes out' spell instead?" I held my breath and grabbed a cereal bar from the cupboard, scooting out of range.

"I hope not, considering it's for your sister." He gave the contents of the boiling pan a half-hearted stir. "How'd the itching spells do?"

"Brilliant," I said. "Did you even sleep last night?"

"No." He tipped some of an open container of powder into the pan. "I've tried fourteen poison cures on your sister and she still hasn't woken up. I even had to ask Keira for another recipe, which led to some seriously awkward questions. I think she might be telling the other neighbours we're hiding a hellhound in here."

My throat went dry. I should have cornered those Faulkner bastards last night and found out how they'd poisoned her. I'd screwed up in a dozen ways, but failing my sister hit the hardest. Yet I knew as well as anyone that the instant I laid a hand on one of those brothers, a gargoyle shifter would choke me out, sink a claw under my ribcage and leave me bleeding to death in an alley.

I really *hated* when caution was the best option.

"I wish I knew what to do." I took a bite of the cereal bar, more to distract myself than anything else. My stomach was wound in knots, and the foul smell of the boiling antidote didn't help in the slightest.

"I'll find a cure," Will said. "If she was going to die, it'd have happened in the first twelve hours."

I choked on my bite. "Will, if you're trying to reassure me, it's not working."

He moved the pan to the side. "Look, between you and me, most gargoyles aren't too bright, and they had the poison all over their claws. That rules out most of the deadly toxins because they might have accidentally ended up poisoning themselves. You'd be amazed how often that happens."

"It'd serve them right." I took another bite and tossed the wrapper in the bin. "I take it Becks didn't come back last night?"

She'd gone out again not long after we got home, claiming she'd be back when she found out where the auction was being held. Maybe it was a side effect of being a cat shifter, but she never seemed to sleep through the night, preferring to nap throughout the day. It came in handy when we wanted someone to watch the house during the hours of darkness when the monsters came out to play. Kit, on the other hand, would sleep twenty hours a day if we let him.

"Haven't seen her." Will yawned. "Nor Astor."

"He went out, too?" I wouldn't have expected him to lie around at home when Ember's life was at risk. To be honest, I had no idea *what* he did with his time. When it came to ex-assassins who'd once worked for my mortal enemies, I was probably better off not knowing.

"Yep." He added a few more herbs to the pan and gave it a stir. "So you're going to this auction?"

"Ideally, we either need to ambush the Faulkners before they get there or sneak up on the person who buys the egg from them when they're leaving with their prize," I said. "Going *into* the auction is way too risky. If anyone sees us carrying it, they'll come and torch us all even if we hide the egg on the other side of the mirror."

He frowned. "Have you asked them?"

"The other dragon shifters? Hell, no. They have enough to worry about. Besides, I lost the egg before I could even think about how to break the news to them."

"About that," Will said. "Are you sure it's a good idea, stealing it back? I mean, the thing was more trouble than it was worth. For all you know, the British Museum will put in a bid for it."

"And when it hatches?" I shook my head. "Look, I don't know what I planned to do with it. I just know I don't want it with *them*, and not just because they're the ones who poisoned Ember. They might be the only people who can help us fix her, too."

"I get it, believe me, Cori," he said. "I just don't know if we're going about this the right way."

I glanced at Ember, my chest tightening. "If the poison turns out to be a rare one, they'll have the antidote for sure. And I'm not letting them get away without punishment. Dragon egg or not."

"Your choice," he said. "I agree, for the record—the longer we go without answers on the poison, the worse it might end up being for her. Being a dragon shifter helps, but that she's been unconscious this long…"

"Will. Shut up." I squeezed my eyes shut, gritting my teeth. I'd only let the anger give way to fear and grief when all else failed.

But there was someone I hadn't accounted for in my plans: Zeph. I assumed *he* had a plan to get the dragon egg, too, and the practical side of me whispered that I ought to have convinced him to join forces. He might be an ungrateful dick, but he was also a dragon shifter. He could wipe those two gargoyles off the face of the planet in a single breath if he'd wanted to. He seemed determined to do everything alone, unless he had a cat shifter spy on his team, too. But I had my doubts. Everything about him had screamed, *loner.*

Since I had zero clue what Zeph's plan might be, I could only work with what I knew. He'd deliberately got himself kidnapped and tied up last time, but the same strategy wouldn't work in an open auction which masqueraded as being on the right side of the law. That his life had never been in any real danger was a moot point.

He's too unpredictable.

The door inched open and Becks slinked in, turning human. Her hair was dishevelled and her coat drenched in muddy water. "Fell out of a gutter," she said in explanation. "The auction's at Garland Street, at twelve. That gives us about five hours to ambush the Faulkners."

"Did you find out where they're hanging out?" I asked.

"No." She shook herself, more like a dog than a cat, and pulled her glasses out of her pocket, setting them on her nose. "Got a cleansing spell?"

"You could just take a shower," Will said. "Waste of resources, that. It's the sort of lazy shit the mages do."

"I don't have time to clean my coat," she responded, walking to the rows of spells laid out on the table. "And for the record, I *did* find out that Jake at the mercenary guild might be involved."

"Shit, he is?" There was a flash as she activated the cleansing spell, banishing every splash of dirty water from her coat. "I should have known. What's he involved in?"

"Messenger boy," she responded. "Makes sense. The guild's pay's shit at his level, and gargoyle shifters tend to have a pack mentality. Bet he has family involved."

"They do seem close-knit," I said, thinking of the suit-wearing guards at the theatre last night. "In what way is he involved? I mean, he was seconds from seeing the egg himself. I thought he might have overheard us talking to Darcy."

"I don't know about the egg, but he was skulking around one of their places carrying a couple of packages," she said. "I think he's just a grunt, so he might not have much useful info."

"Worth a shot," I said. "I should have hit him harder yesterday."

Either way, I was going to that auction, and if I got to take a swing at Jake beforehand, so much the better.

I walked to the mercenary office, Becks padding at my side. Like yesterday, I covered my bright clothes with a long coat but didn't bother to tame my hair this time. Zeph's comments about me looking like someone's kid sister had rubbed me up the wrong way. Sure, I *was* Ember's kid sister, but that didn't mean she didn't count on me as much as I counted on her.

If Ember was awake now, she'd reprimand me for taking risks and then order me to drop a message at the mages' place tipping them off about the auction. And then lie low.

I can always do both. I didn't trust the mages to have my back, but it was a simple matter to write a message ready to send to the mages before the auction started.

"They won't show," Becks had muttered. "Too scared to get their hands dirty."

"I dunno, auctions are more their thing than arena fights."

If they showed up at the auction and arrested everyone, it would solve most of our problems in one go—the dragon egg being the obvious exception.

I walked through the automatic doors into the mercenaries' place, spotting Darcy behind the desk. The sight of any gargoyle unnerved me after last night, but he wasn't the sort to get tangled in underground fighting rings. He wouldn't have been put in charge of a place that mostly employed humans if he had any unsavoury connections. The mages must have a rough idea who did. They might deliberately hold themselves apart from the rest of us, but there wasn't much they didn't know. Which suggested they might at least consider my tip-off about the auction, but I wasn't about to take any chances. If the Faulkners got wind that someone had told tales on them to the mages, they might cancel or change location. I'd need to wait as close to the starting time as possible to send my warning.

"Cori," said Darcy. "You're not in until nine."

"I'm looking for Jake," I said. "And as a matter of fact, I'm taking the day off. Family business."

"I don't think so."

"My sister was poisoned yesterday," I said. "I'm shopping around for an antidote. Sorry to disappoint you."

He scowled. "You're the third person to show up with a bullshit excuse today. Nice try."

"I'm not lying," I said. "Come to my house if you don't believe me. We were attacked by a bunch of rogue gargoyles. Know anything about that?"

"Me? No. I don't do business with rogues."

"Except Jake." With spectacular timing, Jake chose that moment to walk into the guild. "Oh, he's here. Excellent."

"If you're going to fight, take it outside," said Darcy. "I just cleaned those carpets."

"With pleasure." I marched to Jake and gave him a shove, causing him to trip over through the glass doors.

"The hell?" He caught himself before he hit the pavement. "What'd I do to you, runt?"

I grabbed the scruff of his shirt, yanking him close and sinking a punch into his gut. He doubled over with a curse. "I heard you're a messenger for the Faulkners."

He straightened upright in time for me to headbutt him in the face. Then he was down again, swearing, blood splattering the pavement. "Ow! It's not a crime to have a side job, you crazy dragon."

"Oh, come on, you know your employers think the laws

don't apply to them." I crossed my arms, waiting for him to recover enough to lift his head. From the look of things, I'd broken his nose. Totally worth the headache. "They also poisoned my sister, so I'm not in a friendly mood."

He pressed a hand to his nose to stem the bleeding. "Poison?"

"Please don't make me repeat myself. It's no common poison, so I'm taking a wild guess a witch made it. I'm told you're a delivery boy... made any deliveries from a local witch lately?"

Blood dripped through his fingers. "Maybe I did. Didn't see any poison, though."

"Obviously they wouldn't tell you in case you blabbed to everyone you saw," I said. "An address, *please*. I'm not in a diplomatic mood."

"I noticed." He reached into his pocket with a shaky hand and pressed a tissue to his bleeding nose. "The witch is called Brady Locke and lives in Hawthorn Square."

Another supernatural community, not far from the arena. "Do you ever check the packages to make sure they're not having you deliver anything illegal?"

"I'm not hired to ask questions."

"No, that'd require having two brain cells to rub together." If I found this witch, I could at least figure out to handle the poison. That'd leave me with an hour or two to prepare for the auction. Not ideal, but saving Ember was paramount. Then I'd punish the dickheads who'd tried to kill her.

I left Jake bleeding outside the guild doors and walked back to where Becks waited.

"Slight issue," I said to her. "We're going after a witch. Tell Will we'll bring details of the antidote, okay?"

She gave a nod and took off, her lithe tabby form covering far more ground than I could. She'd have no issue catching me up. Now all I needed was—

A ghost.

I stopped walking before I collided with a stocky man floating above the pavement. He was an average-looking guy, from what I could tell, but there was something oddly familiar about him.

Wait a second. He was the gargoyle I'd fought outside our house. Guess he hadn't made it after all.

"Hey." My voice snapped out, and the man turned on me, his eyes widening. Blue light surrounded him, separating his transparent form from the muted tones of the nearby buildings.

"You." He stared at me. "You're... you're not dead."

"I'm aware of that." I remained still, my heart thumping against my ribcage. "You are. Who killed you?"

"The Faulkners, of course," he growled. "Said it was an incentive not to get taken down by a pretty little dragon shifter girl."

I gave a short laugh. "Yeah, right. Didn't work out so well for you, did it? Are your friends still alive and kicking or did they manage to poison themselves to death?"

"I don't know," he mumbled. "The poison doesn't affect..."

"Gargoyles." My heart sank. "It's dragon-specific, isn't it? Am I right in thinking this poison found its way to you by way of a witch called Brady Locke?"

"How do you know?" He frowned. "How do you *see* me? Nobody else can."

"Spirit sight, obviously," I said. There was no point in beating around the bush. When it came to the dead, you had limited time to ask questions. "And this witch has the antidote?"

"Yeah... yes."

Good. We're on the right track. "And the auction? Were you supposed to go?"

He shook his head. "No, course not. It's way too high-class for the likes of me."

"They'll go in alone, dressed as respectable businessmen," I surmised. "Pretend they came by that egg legally—goes without saying."

"How'd you get that egg to begin with?" he asked. "You can trust me, pretty dragon shifter. I can't talk to nobody else. I'm gone. Going, going, gone."

He was starting to lose it. No surprises there. Most ghosts lost their minds within seconds of passing over the veil, so he must be more strong-willed than he looked to have stuck around this long.

"Someone mailed it to me," I said. "Is it the first dragon egg you've handled?"

"Me? Yeah. Don't know about the Faulkners, though. They told us nothing, told us none. I'm going, going, going, gone..." He was babbling now. "Don't leave me!" He reached out to grab my coat and fell right through me, sprawling in mid-air. I suppressed a snort. Okay, maybe ghosts weren't that scary after all. I didn't think they could even shift. At least, I'd never seen a ghostly gargoyle flying through the sky.

"Tell me more." I took a step back to rid myself of the weird sight of him sprawled transparently on top of my legs.

"Tell you what?" said a voice from beside my shoulder, and I tripped backwards into Astor. He didn't even try to stop me from falling, but I caught the nearest wall with my fingertips before I hit the ground.

"Do you mind not creeping up on me?" I turned and scowled at him. "At least give me some warning first."

"Who were you talking to just then?"

"The ghost of one of those scumbags who attacked Ember," I responded. "I'm on my way to hunt the witch who made the poison they used on her."

His face hardened. "Tell me."

"Witch, called Brady Locke. Lives in Hawthorn Square…" I trailed off, realising the ghost was almost gone, hardly visible against the dull backdrop. "Hey. Tell me where your people are staying."

"New Hostel, Russell Square, but you're wasting your time," he said. "They're dead—we're all as good as dead."

"Says who?"

His mouth moved, his body fading until nothing remained but grey sky and greyer buildings.

I glared at the spot where he'd vanished. "Damn… he said he and the other gargoyles were staying in Russell Square. Bit of a walk from here, but maybe they have the antidote with them."

"Go there," Astor said. "I'll handle the witch."

"Astor, you're not good at leaving people alive to question," I said.

His expression said, *duh*. I mean, with a former assassin, you didn't really get the 'leave people alive' option. What he'd been doing all night, who knew.

"When did you plan to mention you can talk to ghosts?" he queried.

"I told Ember." She'd been concerned enough to tell me to check in at the local necromancer guild, but they knew I was a dragon shifter. They'd think I was taking the piss out of them if I claimed to also have an affinity with the dead. "Fine, let's flip a coin. Want to go to the hostel or to the witch? The hostel might have more of those gargoyles to beat up."

I'd rather have Astor out from under my feet if I went after the witch, but on the other hand, the gargoyles might know their master's supplier of dragon eggs. If the Faulkners had ordered them to help steal it from me, perhaps they knew who'd sent it to begin with.

Astor made the decision for me. He strode right through

the spot where the ghost had been hovering. "I'll try to leave enough of the witch left for you to finish off."

"Astor!" I said, but he crossed the road without looking back.

Great. The ex-assassin had stolen my mission. Then again, the gargoyles might have some of the antidote in their lair, just in case.

Becks ran up to me, shifting to human form. "What did Astor want?"

"He swiped our mission," I told her. "Which works in our favour, because I just found out where those other two gargoyles who attacked Ember are staying. What do you say we go and use them for target practise?"

"Sounds like a plan."

8

The hostel looked like the type of place which had been a rat-infested hellhole for tourists or students on a budget *before* the invasion, let alone after. You know the type. *Pay less than £20 a night and walk away with a suspicious rash and someone else's laundry as a bonus!*

Becks wrinkled her nose. "Those Faulkners don't take care of their people."

"I'm not surprised in the slightest." The hostel's black-painted door hung from its hinges, like the owners weren't even trying not to let wild faerie beasts gnaw on their guests. I didn't smell anything suspicious, though, so I let Becks run ahead while I waited on the doorstep. If the gargoyles tried to escape, I'd block their path.

Becks returned a moment later. "First floor. Want me to go in through the window?"

"Yep. I'll head upstairs."

The reception area contained a run-down desk behind a door on my right, and stairs on the left covered in bright blue carpet that did nothing to improve the atmosphere. I casually walked upstairs like I had the right to be here, and the dozing receptionist didn't even look up. *Honestly.* I wondered if guests often showed up dead in their beds. Wouldn't surprise me.

The first rooms I came to were built like bunkers—a dragon's worst nightmare. The sight of a dozen three-storey bunk beds crammed into the tight space made me shudder. I hurried along the corridor, and a yowl sounded from behind the door on my right. Becks's signal.

I kicked the door in, drawing a knife. Two things hit me: the dragon egg was not in this room, and both shifters had been expecting an attack. The towering forms of two full-grown gargoyle shifters filled the twin room, claws at the ready.

I ducked underneath a swiping claw, my knife sinking into leathery skin. Blood spurted onto the already filthy carpet, and the gargoyle reeled backwards with a cry.

Becks darted around the room, causing the second gargoyle's huge wings to smack into the walls in his attempts to catch her. At first, I thought she was just trying to confuse him—then I saw she held something in her mouth. Before I could see what it was, the first gargoyle took another jab at me. I rolled under his feet, slashing at his exposed ankles with my blade. They weren't that bright, electing to fight us in an enclosed space ill-suited to those massive wings.

"Come on, give me a real fight." I took another swipe, drawing blood. I didn't want to kill them until they gave me some answers on the dragon egg, but no gargoyles could talk in shifted form. "You're not saying you have no weapons in here aside from those clumsy claws?"

The gargoyle's clawed foot slammed down. I rolled over on the filthy carpet, blood splattering my jacket on top of whatever questionable stains were on the floor. I'd need to take a bath in bleach after this. Becks streaked past me, a bottle clamped in her mouth. That's what she'd picked up. Had she found the antidote to the poison?

My knife sank deep into the nearest gargoyle's leg. With a screech, he fell to his knees. "That's for my sister."

A gurgling cry escaped him as I pressed the knife to his throat. *Come on. Shift back.*

There was a faint crash from under our feet, and the room trembled all over. My knife sank deep into his throat, and blood fountained over my hand. Too much blood. "Oh, *shit.*"

He coughed, a gargling noise that gave way to a death rattle. I mouthed, *get out* at Becks, but the second gargoyle reached the window first. Glass shattered, showering the carpet. Becks yowled in alarm and I shouted her name, but she was already toppling over the edge of the windowsill.

A deafening blast rocked the room. I dove for the open window, grabbing the nearest solid object—the fleeing gargoyle. My hands locked around his ankle as he took flight, just as the building collapsed behind us in a shower of brick and dust.

Smoke billowed up in clouds, catching in my throat. I dug my nails into the gargoyle's leathery skin. He rotated in a circle, kicking out in an attempt to dislodge me. My grip slipped. Crap. I was too far from the ground to land safely.

The gargoyle gave one powerful kick, and my grip broke. Panic tore through my mind, the wind roared in my ears, and the world turned into a foggy grey haze. A thousand transparent faces surrounded me, seeming to whisper my name. Death called.

No.

A roar of fire ignited in my veins, and a moment later, I hit the earth, hands-first.

Not hands. Claws.

Ruby red scales covered curved claws, buried deep into

the tarmac. My feet touched the road as I skidded to a halt, shaken, but alive.

Death's grey fog lurked at the edges of my vision, filling my ears with the whispers of a thousand ghosts. My stomach turned over when I looked up at the hostel, covered in a grey film above the rising cloud of smoke.

"Cori!" Becks ran to my side, her face covered in plaster dust. "Thank god—I thought you were dead."

"Not quite yet." I yanked my claws out of the tarmac, my body trembling. "Cats always land on their feet, dragons always land on their claws."

"Lucky you." Becks wiped dust from her face. "I'm sorry, Cori. I dropped the bottle when I fell out. It smashed in the road. I never saw if it was the antidote or not, but it looked like it might be."

Damn them. In a flicker, my claws disappeared. Ruby red claws, like my sister's. I pressed my hand to my mouth. No way was anyone alive in that hostel. A few dozen innocent humans had died. "What the hell was the point in blowing the place up?"

"I don't know." Becks took a half-step towards the cloud of smoke engulfing the building and its neighbours. "But you *shifted.*"

"I still lost him." I scowled at the shape of the gargoyle disappearing into the sky. "I should have known our little friends would have no issues with blowing up a hostel with a bunch of humans inside it."

The explosion had taken place downstairs, which meant either the place was booby-trapped, or someone had brought in the explosive right after Becks and I had walked in. Either we'd been followed, or the gargoyles had been the target.

Becks shook dust off her coat, backing away from the hostel. "We need to get the hell out before we're blamed."

"Wise idea." Now we had to rely on Astor to get the antidote from the witch. And I had a new incentive to track down the Faulkners and bury my new ruby-red claws in their throats.

We hurried towards the nearest main road, where we'd stand a good chance of losing any tail we might have picked up. There was a fair bit of traffic, though nowhere near the volume there'd been before the invasion. Most people couldn't afford the skyrocketing fuel prices, let alone the damages from driving on roads that had been neglected for the last seven years.

A rattling noise sounded from the sky, making the hairs stand up on my arms, and I tensed for a gargoyle attack before I spotted a white helicopter hovering over the rooftops.

"Who the bloody hell is that?" I turned to Becks, whose eyes widened.

"Some rich arsehole who's asking for a mid-air collision with a gargoyle," she said, shaking her head.

I watched the helicopter until it passed beyond sight, then spotted someone very familiar walking towards us. Even though he wore dark jeans and a hoody, with his bright hair hidden, I'd know him anywhere. Zeph—the dragon shifter I'd saved at the arena.

Oh, wonderful. No point in pretending I hadn't seen him. I kept walking, and Becks made a faint noise of disgust when she recognised him, too.

Zeph stopped when we were about a metre apart. So did I. A breeze stirred, lifting his hood to reveal a few auburn curls against his pale forehead.

"You." I'd never thought I'd *not* be glad to see another dragon shifter, but couldn't he have appeared before the hostel had blown up? I mean, he could fly. What was he doing skulking around like a human?

"I was a dick last night," he began.

"Do you want a medal for admitting it?" I said. "I don't know if you saw, but someone just tried to blow me up."

"I think they were aiming for the gargoyles," he said. "That's who you were after, right? I got the address, too."

I'd bet he hadn't got it from a dead man. He must have contacts of his own. "You missed the memo. Looks like the Faulkners want to cover their tracks."

"I don't think it was them," he said.

"Killing off their own people seems to be their thing," I said. "Was that where you were going, the hostel? There's nothing left of it. The humans will pin it on us, no doubt. The way the walls collapsed, it must have been magic that blew it up."

"Figures," he said. "Did one of the gargoyles escape?"

"I tried to tail him, but he shook me off. Literally."

Zeph raised an eyebrow. "You have a death wish. First you barge into an arena match between two of the city's most notorious crime lords to capture a dragon shifter, now this?"

"Speaking of whom, what happened to the guys who caught you and dragged you to the arena?"

"Dead," he said.

He didn't need to tell me who'd been responsible. "Bit of a risk, killing the loser before the auction even started."

"They wouldn't have bid on it," he said. "The people who captured me didn't want the egg, they wanted what's *inside* the egg, and it wouldn't have gone well for them."

My heart missed a beat. For all I'd been through to get it back, I still didn't know what the egg contained. Not a real dragon shifter, like us. Zeph, however, knew. He wasn't bluffing.

I weighed the odds for a moment. Zeph wasn't exactly an ally, but he wasn't on the side of the scumbags who'd stolen the egg from me either. And while I didn't like the thought of him stealing our property, I'd trust him with the egg a damn sight more than those gargoyles.

"What was inside the egg?" I asked. "Someone passed it onto me for safeguarding but neglected to tell me what breed of dragon it is."

He raised his eyes to the sky, where the helicopter had disappeared. "This is not the place to have that conversation."

"Damn right." Becks gave me a nudge. "Less than an hour till the auction. Grab what info you need from him and then go."

"That's the plan." I scanned the road for a likely spot to chat. I still needed to send a warning to the mages, but the explosion at the hostel had rattled me. If we'd been the targets and we brought the mages on their tail, the Faulkners might elevate us to the very top of their hit lists.

Zeph kicked in the door to an empty coffee shop. I followed, my body tensed, but there didn't appear to be any wild fae lurking inside. The merest flash of orange light in his eyes reminded me that he wouldn't care if there was. "You don't know what was in the egg."

"Like I said," I said, leaving the door half open so Becks could watch the street, "I was entrusted with it to safeguard."

"Safeguard?" he echoed. "You're the one who'll need safeguarding when it hatches. Wild dragonlings aren't domesticated."

"Dragonlings?" I'd never heard that term before. "Regardless, I want it out of harm's way. It's a living creature, and those people aren't going to treat it kindly when it hatches."

"Kindly?" He shook his head. "Look, I don't have time to give you a crash course on wild dragonlings, but suffice to say, it needs to be removed from the city as soon as possible. They're like engineered killing machines."

Engineered killing machines? "So not like shifters, then? I thought all wild dragon species were extinct."

"They were," Zeph said. "But you know what the humans are like. Rich humans have been collecting rare species of supernatural creatures for the novelty value since before the invasion. If we're not careful, that egg will end up in someone's private collection. And within a week, everyone in the area will be dead."

Jesus. He's serious. Or he was a *really* good liar. "So the Faulkners are literally playing with fire. Do they know it?"

"I doubt they care," he said flatly. "They see only the potential value in selling it. How can you have got your hands on that egg and not know what it is?"

The patronising note to his voice burned through my shock and surprise. "Because someone sent it to me by first-class post, dickhead. And, for the record, that's not why I went looking for the Faulkners. They poisoned my sister with something toxic to dragons."

"They what?" His grey eyes narrowed. "There's more than one of you?"

Well, well. I knew he couldn't be that disinterested that other dragons lived in London. "Have you been living under a rock for the last five years? Don't tell me you've never heard of Ember."

I knew from his blank expression that he hadn't. That'd explain why I'd never seen him before. He wasn't from London at all.

"I don't know this Ember, but I've never heard of a poison that's toxic to dragons."

"The gargoyles had it," I said. "Why didn't you fly after him, if he's who you were looking for?"

A spark stirred in his eyes. "There's already been a loud explosion in the area. The humans know something's up. Don't you think shifting would draw a little too much attention?"

"You don't want to make a scene," I surmised. "I guess it's

hard for you to stay under the radar if you end up on the front page of the papers like my sister did."

"Papers? I'm taking a wild guess you're *not* under the radar," he said. "In that case, you're best off staying out of the auction altogether."

"Nice try," I said. "Nobody knows who I am. It was a long time ago and I've never made headlines. Besides, that dragon egg is mine."

"The Faulkners know who you are."

"They didn't know I was at the hostel," I said. "Unless Jake tipped them off."

He frowned. "Just how many acquaintances do you have who work with the gargoyles?"

"After I kill him, zero." I took a step backwards. "But we've an auction to infiltrate, so I'd say we find the Faulkners. Deal with the rest of it later."

"I told you I prefer to work alone," Zeph said. "There's no reason to risk your neck."

"Look, you might be a loner, but I'm not. My sister's counting on me." I drew in a breath. "Besides, gambling a living creature's life—engineered killing machine or not—is a dick move."

Walking away now was out of the question.

I met Zeph's gaze, which simmered with an echo of my own fire. "How's this? Tell me your plan, I'll tell you mine. And we'll get our hands on that dragon egg together."

"If you like," he said. "With one condition: the egg leaves the city."

"Done," I said—he didn't have to know about the mirror. "My condition? I get to deal with the person who tried to kill my sister."

"Deal." The grey in his eyes turned to flames. "Here's what I know."

9

Not much more than I did, as it turned out.

Zeph, like me, had no intention of actually setting foot in the auction hall. He agreed that our best bet was to ambush the Faulkners before they arrived, but we'd been circling the neighbourhood for half an hour and still hadn't seen so much as a gargoyle's footprint. Considering the chosen location, I assumed that most people at the auction would be rich humans. Humans who wanted to get their hands on a dragon egg for the novelty value, I guessed. Wankers.

My hands twitched, claws flickering to hands and back again. I'd always wondered how Ember did that, but it seemed to be a reflex. I grinned at the play of light on the ruby red scales extending up my wrists. All the better to punch a gargoyle's lights out with, my dear.

Zeph said, "Can you put those away? You'll draw attention."

Hey, let me have my moment, grump. "All right." I dug my hands in my pockets. I'd celebrate later, after Ember woke up.

Astor had better be having better luck than we were.

"What're they doing, teleporting in?" I checked the time on my phone for the tenth time. "Or did they plan on showing up fashionably late?"

"Maybe they're sending someone else in their place," Zeph suggested. "So they don't have to risk their necks."

"It's an auction with humans, not a wrestling match with a bridge troll. They can't stir everyone up and then not show."

A whirring noise filled the air. The helicopter was back, flying low over the rooftops and making an irritating racket in the process. Why was it moving so slowly? The door looks like it was open, too. Safety hazard, much?

Hang on. "They're in the helicopter."

The Faulkners planned to get to the auction hall from the air. Dragon egg and all, without risking an ambush. Then they'd get out again with minimal damage. Clever bastards.

Zeph tilted his head to look at the helicopter, frowning. "Are you sure?"

"Want to fly up and check?" Becks asked. "You're the only one of the three of us who can get that high."

Zeph's eyes narrowed. "If it *is* them, that helicopter will be protected if they're flaunting it in public. I don't think they're landing, either."

"They're not?" The helicopter kept circling the rooftops but showed no signs of descending. Underneath its incessant whirring came the sound of a muffled thump.

Then the building beneath the helicopter went up in flames.

My instincts snapped on as a plume of orange fire roared to the sky. Becks shifted to cat form and pelted down the road with a yowl of alarm, while I followed her back the way we'd come, feet pounding on the pavement. Zeph overtook me quickly, while Becks was a tabby streak in the distance.

We caught up to her in an alley between two run-down buildings.

Becks turned human, collapsing against the wall in a breathless heap. "Jesus. They were onto us, all right. If we were in the building…"

"We weren't the targets," Zeph interrupted.

"The egg," I said, my voice hollow. "If it wasn't in that building, they just flew off with it. It's gone."

He shook his head. "I don't think they caused the blast. They wanted the money. They wouldn't have gone to the trouble of luring everyone to the auction and then blown it up."

"Then who?" I scanned the smoke-stained sky. It was too far off to see the fire from here, but like the collapsing hotel, it would resemble an accident from an outside view. It'd be pinned on something mundane like a gas leak. *Bastards.*

If we'd been the targets, using fire against a dragon wasn't a smart move. Dragons had a natural immunity to fire—the human-made sort, anyway. Magical fire, I wasn't so sure on. But it was a very good job I hadn't stuck with my initial plan to tip off the mages—if they'd sent anyone to break up the auction, they would have been caught in the blast while the perpetrators flew away and the blame landed on the person who'd made the call—me.

"If I knew, I'd be on their tail," Zeph answered.

"You want to be vaporised?" I said. "I don't know about you, but I'd rather not test whether their magical fire affects dragons by walking into it."

"I concur," Becks said. "What the hell now? The Faulkners are gone. Unless you have their address?"

"Don't you think I'd have used it if I did?" Zeph's eyes burned with simmering flames. "They'll be lying low, if they have any sense."

"In that case, we should tell Will," I said. "Astor, too. See if anyone has any connections we can use to find where they hang out when they're not swooping around the skies or wagering dangerous artefacts on arena matches."

Becks eyed our new companion. "We can't take him back with us."

"I'm not overly keen on the idea either, to be honest," Zeph supplied.

Like hell was I letting him slip away again. "We have resources. Got a witch on your team?"

"No," he said. "But I do have a witch's address."

"Already sent one of our people there," I said. "Speaking of whom, maybe he's brought the antidote back. Or at least some details about the poison."

If he had, then Ember might be awake by now. Despite the urgency of our mission, I needed to talk to her for entirely selfish reasons. I wanted to tell her I'd finally managed a partial shift, even if she wasn't awake to hear it.

"I wouldn't mind learning more about that poison," Zeph said. "All right, I'll come with you. Happy?"

"Not really." I dropped my arms to my sides, thoroughly put out. "Fair warning, my friends have just dealt with a pair of deceiving bastards who wormed their way into our house to steal from us. They're a little on edge."

"So am I," he said. "We might not have been the targets, but I think we just got a glimpse of who we're dealing with."

"Yeah, we did," I said. "I guess we'll have to show them who has the monopoly on all fire-related action in this city."

"Bloody hell," Will said when we walked into the back room of the shop with Zeph in tow. "I thought you were in that place when it blew up."

The shop was closed for the day, and Will was alone in

the back room, sorting out handmade spells on the kitchen table. Ember, meanwhile, lay where we'd left her on the sofa. Zeph glanced at her on the way in, and I could see him putting two and two together.

"You heard?" I said. "Someone blew up the hostel, too. Not sure if we were the targets, but someone's feeling a little trigger-happy today."

"And you brought a friend." Will looked Zeph up and down. "You don't look familiar. Have we met?"

"Name's Zeph," he said. "I'm told there's a witch in here. Gargoyle shifter, are you?"

"Gargoyle-witch," Will corrected. "Yes, I make spells. Sometimes they even work."

"He's messing with you," I said. "They always work. You know what I did in the arena last night? His work."

"Itching spells?" Zeph sounded sceptical.

"Hey, it took a lot of testing on unwitting bystanders before I got that one right." Will picked up a purple band-shaped spell, tossed it into the air and caught it again. "And—oh, hey, Kit."

The door to the shelter opened, and Kit walked in. His human glamour immediately fell off when he set eyes on the newcomer. "Oh. Hi. Who are you?"

I stepped in. "Kit, this is Zeph. He's a dragon shifter."

"And you're a faerie," said Zeph. "This is your team? A gargoyle-witch, a cat shifter, a faerie and two dragons?"

"We also have an assassin," added Will. "Human, but that's his least unappealing quality. What do you want?"

"Want?" Zeph blinked. "Nothing. I'm not here to steal your resources or whatever. I get on fine alone."

Huh. I'd suspected he didn't have a team of allies, since he'd been skulking around on his own last night, but it made his *getting captured on purpose* move even more reckless. Then again, with dragon shifters, impulsiveness was par for the course.

"He's here because we were both on our way to ambush the same guys when someone inconveniently blew up the auction hall," I supplied.

Will frowned. "So, you're saying the Faulkners still have the egg, but they blew up their potential buyers before anyone could bid on it?"

"I'm saying someone else blew up the place in an attempt to destroy the egg and the Faulkner brothers in the process," I said. "That's my guess, anyway."

"You said you sent someone to find the witch they hired?" asked Zeph, his gaze darting over to Ember's inert form on the sofa.

"Yeah. Isn't Astor back yet?"

Will shook his head. "No. I expected him back before you."

So did I. He hadn't run into trouble, had he? The ex-assassin was good at escaping situations that would end fatally for the majority of humans, since he'd been one of the Orion League's elite soldiers before he'd quit. Then again, the witch he pursued had brought a full-grown dragon shifter crashing to earth.

"Well, Zeph here seems to think the Faulkners still have the egg and are lying low until the dust settles," Becks said.

"Then who blew up the hostel?" Will's brow furrowed.

"That one was probably the Faulkners," I said. "More than likely, anyway. The gargoyles who attacked Ember were there."

"One of them flew away, though," Becks added. "He went right for the glass the instant the explosion hit."

"That'd explain why they didn't have the egg hidden in the room." I wished I'd killed the bastard myself. The number of discarded potion bottles on the work surface were a glaring reminder that as long as we didn't have the antidote to the poison, the enemy might use it against Zeph or me at any time as well. "That place was a shithole, though. The Faulkners will be somewhere more high-class. I just wish I'd seen where the guy who escaped flew off to. I nearly had him."

"You nearly *died*," Becks said. "If you hadn't shifted right then…"

"I know."

"Wait, you—" Will cut off as I shot him a warning look. Not that it really mattered if Zeph knew whether I could shift or not at this point. "You nearly died? Damn. Maybe I should be developing explosive-proof shields."

"No spell could have held off that blast," Zeph said. "Maybe a ward, but it was a human establishment. Cowards."

"Why kill humans?" Becks said.

Good question. Their actions showed a callous disregard for human life, and not much regard for supernatural lives, either. Whoever had caused the second explosion, though, seemed to want the egg destroyed and not sold. If anyone got the slightest hint that we'd laid our hands on it, we might well be the next to burn.

I turned to Zeph. "Are the dragons… dragonlings really that dangerous?"

"Is the sky blue?" He snagged a handmade spell with his fingertips and turned it over in his palm. "It's possible that the dragon egg is impervious to fire, in which case, the person who set off the second blast might have intended on fishing it out of the rubble. And if the egg itself was destroyed in the explosion, the dragonling would have survived."

My jaw hit the floor. "You might have told me that before."

"It wouldn't have done any good." He put the spell back

down on the table. "The place was collapsing. Even if we're immune to the fire, we can still get crushed to death."

"The Faulkners weren't in there, either way," I said. "So—you think they still have it?"

"Yes, I do," he said. "But they won't be easy to find, especially now."

"We can track the gargoyle dude who got away," Becks put in. "He bled all over me when I bit him."

"He won't have been important enough for the Faulkners to trust with their location," Zeph said. "I guarantee it. Didn't you say you had an acquaintance who works as a messenger for them?"

"Already asked him," I said. "He doesn't know where they live. He delivers packages for them, though... I guess we can search his flat. I can swipe his address from the guild, no problem."

"I'll handle that," Becks said. "You should be lying low, since you just walked away from two explosions."

"She's right," Zeph said. "Running into one blast is bad enough. Two is downright careless."

"Was that a joke?" I faked a gasp of astonishment. "Forget the morbid subject matter. I thought you didn't have a sense of humour."

He arched a brow. "You met me last night and you feel qualified to judge me?"

"Well," I said, delicately. "Considering you acted like I mugged you rather than saving your life and pretty much called me a disgrace to all dragon shifters—yes, actually. I think that says a lot of things about you."

"I said I was sorry," he said. "You don't know how much trouble it took me to get close to that egg."

I did have a pretty good idea, but I let that one slide. "How'd you know it'd be there to begin with?"

"I'm acquainted with the arena," he said. "I hear rumours.

Besides, it's not the first time one of those eggs has ended up in the city. I know what signs to look for. The ones I can get hold of, I smuggle them out and release the dragonlings into the wild."

"Because you think they're monstrous killing machines who'll run amok slaughtering people." I couldn't keep the scepticism out of my voice.

"What, the baby dragons?" Will's brows shot up. "I mean, I wouldn't call Ember 'harmless', but that sounds like something a human would say."

"I didn't use those words," Zeph said. "But dragonlings are basically like… baby dinosaurs. If a baby T-Rex hatched in your house, you wouldn't set it loose in the city."

"Baby dinosaurs?" Kit blinked. "That's what was in the egg? It didn't feel dangerous."

"Of course it's not—yet," Zeph said. "The point is that they wake up starving and can't tell the difference between humans and prey. Add in the fact that they're supposed to have their parents close by, and it's a recipe for a very pissed off little dragonling. Oh, and they grow fast. Within six months, it'll be fully grown. As big as a dragon shifter."

"I knew we should have given the thing away," said Will. "Kit, we still can't keep it. Don't even think about it."

Kit's face fell. "But—"

"Release it into the wild," I said. "Let the wild fae deal with a new predator running rampant on their territory. How in the world did they end up here? Is someone breeding them in London?"

"That's what I'd like to know," Zeph said. "I have my suspicions, but… getting the egg is my priority."

There must be more he wasn't telling me, but the longer I went without finding out where the Faulkners were hiding, the more likely they were to escape the city with their little pissed-off dragonling in tow.

And leave my sister to die.

"Why not just let it eat them?" Becks said. "The gargoyles, I mean."

"I think they can protect themselves," Zeph said. "They have a poison designed to target dragons. That's proof enough that they planned for this scenario."

I'd been trying to avoid looking at my sister's unconscious body, but my chest tightened like a vice. "Astor's supposed to be dealing with that witch. I don't know what's taking him so long."

"He's probably burying some bodies," said Will. "He'll be fine. You, however, need a shielding spell or three. Won't do much against magical fire, mind."

I don't need a shield. I had claws now… and I intended to use them.

"Damn right," I said. "Time to find out what the Faulkners have Jake delivering for them."

10

Jake's flat was a ten-minute walk from the guild. He lived alone, which was unusual given London's average rental prices but understandable due to his repellent personality. Becks had darted into Darcy's place and out again with his address in a matter of minutes. He'd be out on whatever mission Darcy had sent him on today, so I wasn't worried about him running into us snooping.

The squat block of flats did have security doors, but a single unlocking spell got us inside. Two flights of stairs later and we unlocked the cupboard-sized flat, which contained a bedroom, kitchen and living room crammed into one tiny space.

"This place smells like it's been doused in aftershave." I coughed, grimacing. "Also, has he ever cleaned these carpets?"

"I'm guessing no." Becks closed the door behind us. "Given that nobody stopped us coming in, I'm taking a wild guess he doesn't have any friends here."

'I can't imagine why." I stepped over the dirty clothes on

the floor, and the even dirtier magazines, depicting two winged monsters in anatomically questionable positions. "What the hell is that, gargoyle porn?"

Becks pulled a face. "Are you going to put one of Will's itching spells in his bed?"

"Why do you think I brought it?" I eased the spell off my wrist. "Never pass up an opportunity to screw with your mortal enemy. Though he's not even in my top five enemies after this week."

"Am I?" Zeph enquired.

Unsure whether he was being serious or not, I pretended to think. "Don't worry, I won't put an itching spell in *your* bed."

A smirk lifted the corner of his mouth. "I'd like to see you try. I doubt those things have any effect on a dragon shifter."

"Don't be so sure." Zeph must be warming up to our partnership if he was joining in with our banter. "Those guards from last night will still be feeling the effects." Pity I hadn't targeted the Faulkner brothers while I was at it. Though hitting a mob boss with an itching spell was probably a worse offence than stabbing one of them.

I tossed the discarded covers back onto the narrow bed and found an even more explicit page spread underneath, depicting a dozen winged beasts involved in some kind of orgy. *Oh, so that's how the talons fit into it.* Why wasn't there a mind-wiping spell for occasions like this?

"I'm scarred for life." I dropped the itching spell on the pillow. "All right, let's see what the Faulkners want him to deliver this week."

Jake's flat was such a mess, it took several minutes to find anything with his own address on it, let alone anyone else's. Zeph kept pacing along the same wall, then stopped a bookshelf that overflowed with old DVDs and video games. He reached in between two DVDs and tugged out a large square package.

"How'd you know that was there?" I asked.

"Dragons are good at sniffing out treasure," said Becks. "I guess that's tonight's delivery."

Zeph flashed a claw, slicing open the package. White-blue scales crept up his wrists before his hand turned human again, and he let out a low whistle. "That's rare."

"What is it?" I took the box from him, examined the herbs inside it, then snapped it closed. "Witch props. Same address Astor went to." My senses ignited at the sound of footsteps outside the door, then a key turned in the lock.

I reached the door first, planting myself in front of it.

The door opened, and Jake stopped inches away from me. "What're you doing in here? You're breaking and entering!"

"Like you're not slacking off in the middle of a work day." I rolled my eyes. "The address of your other employer, please. Otherwise *this*—" I held up the box—"Comes home with me."

He paled. "You can't do that. They'll kill you."

"They already tried that today. Didn't quite work out."

He shook his head. "Please don't. I'm hanging on by a thread as it is."

Footsteps behind me told me Zeph was at my shoulder. "Was it you who sent them to blow up the hostel at Russell Square?"

His brows shot up. "They did what? No. I didn't know you were there. Why?"

So the targets had been the other two gargoyles? That meant the person who'd tried to kill them hadn't been after us. We'd just been unlucky.

"Your employers also poisoned my sister," I added. "Do you check what's in the packages before you deliver them?"

"Why the hell would I do that?"

Honestly. "Any more of these hidden in here, then?"

His jaw set. "None of your business."

"Wrong answer." I held up a hand. "If you don't tell us, we'll tear the place up with you still in it."

What little colour was left in his face drained out of it. "Chill, Cori. Jesus. I thought you were the nice one."

"You thought wrong. Packages?"

"Two under the bed."

Right by the gargoyle porn. You might know it. "Becks, go get it. Don't look at page sixteen."

The colour returned to Jake's face in a dramatic sweep of red. "What the fuck are you doing snooping around here anyway? Why not ask my employers, not me?"

"They're proving a little difficult to find," I said. "I'm glad you showed up to make our lives easier."

Becks returned to my side, holding two packages. I took one of them, shifting my other hand to a claw in order to slice the package open like Zeph had. *At least I'll never have to worry about opening packaging again.*

Jake made a small noise like a rat being squashed by a car. "Shit, you're actually a dragon?"

I widened my eyes at the ruby-red claw where my hand had been. "Really? I hadn't noticed."

Inside the package was another box of ingredients, to no surprise. Taking the last package from Becks, I sliced that one open, too. Within, I found a third box of dried leaves and herbs.

"Poison, is it?" Becks asked.

Jake blanched. "I don't know, I'm not a witch."

"No, you're a loser." I threw the packages at him. "Where did you sign up to work for them? Got an address, or do I have to use this?"

At the sight of both clawed hands, he sagged against the door frame as though all the fight had gone out of him.

"Page Street," he muttered. "Happy?"

"Thrilled to bits." I elbowed past him to the door. "Almost as thrilled as I am to be acquainted with your mentally scarring reading material."

Jake made a low, angry noise and moved to follow me, only for Zeph to drive an elbow into his ribs on his way past. Jake tripped over his own feet to get away from him and made to slam the door—not before Becks trod on his foot, hard.

I gave a breezy smile as we walked downstairs. "Pleasant guy, isn't he?"

Becks snorted, pushing open the door out of the building. Zeph gave me an odd look.

"What?" I followed Becks out into the street.

He pulled his hood back up, hiding his auburn hair. "Your interrogation style is a little… unorthodox."

"What, you think I shouldn't have brought up the gargoyle porn? It's going to be haunting my nightmares for the next six months, might as well get some use out of it."

He cracked a grin. "Page Street… I know where that is."

"Glad one of us does," I said. "So you're not totally averse to working with me?"

"Like I said, you got me on a bad day. Or night."

"I think I worked that much out already," I said. "Maybe next time you decide to bet your life on an arena match, you should hold up a placard saying, 'Not Actually A Hostage' so nobody sets you free."

His smile thinned. "That was a shitty plan, to be honest. I was improvising."

"Now you have a team behind you." I fell silent, trying to read his expression. There was no hint of fire in his eyes. "Is now a good time to ask who your people are? I mean, you've met mine. Or are you here alone?"

"In the city? Yes." He didn't elaborate. Maybe I'd pushed too far. Dragon shifters didn't really do small talk.

"Never mind," I said. "I don't normally ask strangers personal questions, except you've met all my friends. Most of my colleagues haven't."

"You work for the mercenaries," he said. "I heard their pay is terrible."

"You aren't wrong," I said. "But we depend on the funding to keep our shelter running."

"Shelter?"

"For shifters who need our help. Like the shelters where most of us grew up." I nodded to Becks, who didn't look thrilled at me telling him so much. But considering London's entire population of rogue gargoyles apparently knew our address, giving Zeph information was way down on my list of concerns.

Zeph's expression cleared, like I'd just answered a question or two he'd been pondering on. "I'm not local, if you hadn't guessed," he said. "I assumed most rogues or orphans were caught by dickheads like the ones in the arena and sold into servitude. I freed a bunch of caged shifters before I killed the guys who took me—there were dozens of them. They'd been there for weeks."

Becks flinched, shifting into cat form so fast that I nearly tripped over her. "Sorry, Becks. Zeph, I hope you made *them* sorry."

Flames flickered in the corners of his eyes. "I did. And to tell you the truth, my people are dead. The Orion League killed them."

My steps faltered, as my mind filled with images of cold metal bars, and the sound of sharp voices that made the dragon inside me scream in helpless rage. My nails bit into my palms and would have broken the skin if my hands hadn't turned to claws, scales creeping up my arms to my elbows.

"Right," I said, my voice sounding distant. "Of course they did."

Lorne and his people might have killed me, but my time as a captive of the Orion League had been like a different kind of death. They'd crushed me into submission, trapped me in a place that still revisited my nightmares almost as often as the grey fog of the spirit realm. Except in there, there'd been no reprieve. Between death and a cage, I'd pick death every time.

Warmth brushed my arm and I jumped a little. Zeph had caught my elbow where the scales ended, just above the spot where they merged with my still-human upper arm. "It gets easier to control the shift if you practise. I'll tell you more when we're somewhere less exposed."

I took in a steadying breath. He'd guessed that I was new to shifting, then. I didn't have the faintest idea what I was supposed to say to that—or what he'd read from my expression.

Did the League kill your family? his eyes asked. But they hadn't. Lorne had. And while the League's prison cells had left scars on me, there was zero chance the Orion League was involved. They were dead.

Lorne, though? He'd worked *with* the League and committed enough atrocities of his own free will that I hadn't ruled out him being involved with this scheme. But I wasn't ready to tear open those wounds in front of a stranger. Fellow dragon shifter or not.

Becks shifted from cat to human again when we found ourselves at a brick building of maybe five storeys, divided into different businesses by floor.

"It doesn't say which floor is for assassins-for-hire or evil mob bosses," I remarked. "We'll have to get inside to find out."

"I can do that," said Becks, shifting to cat form and scaling the drainpipe. I watched her climb, envying her ability to use her shifted form for practical purposes. Zeph was watching her too. I wondered if it bothered him that he couldn't shift in public without creating a spectacle.

A few moments later, Becks hopped off the drainpipe and landed on her paws, shifting to human again. "Fourth floor. Elevators aren't working and we're likely to be stopped on the stairs."

"Can you get inside their office via the window?" I asked, the back of my neck prickling. My dragon instincts weren't as acute as say, a wolf shifter's, but I had the distinct feeling of unseen eyes watching us from somewhere close by. "They're bound to have a copy of their address somewhere inside. Even if it's not a permanent one."

"Sure. Give me one of your unlocking spells."

"Here." I eased the spell off my wrist and handed it to her, and Becks took it in her mouth before scaling the drainpipe again.

Zeph, meanwhile, turned his back to the building. "We're being watched."

"You feel it, too?" I scanned the low-rise rooftops, and sure enough, I spotted the craggy outline of a gargoyle impersonating a statue.

"What're the odds of him being the guy who escaped the blast at the hostel?" I flexed my hands.

"Fairly high," Zeph responded.

"Can you breathe fire at him from here?"

"No," he said. "I'd blast the roof off the building in the process. Then we can say goodbye to keeping a low profile."

"Can he even see us that far off?" I made a rude gesture in the gargoyle's general direction, but he didn't react. "Any ideas?"

"No. You might have noticed I'm prone to winging it."

I snorted. "Good god, that was terrible."

"You're not saying you've never made that one?" He leaned casually against the wall, not taking his eyes off the gargoyle. With his hood down, the weak sunlight caught on his auburn hair. Close up, it had streaks of lighter blond and brown in it, too.

"My jokes are more sophisticated than that," I said.

"Aside from the gargoyle porn."

I groaned. "I wouldn't have brought it up if he hadn't been advertising it for the world to see. Why d'you have to remind me?"

He flashed me a grin. "You look more like a dragon shifter when you're blushing."

What the hell was I meant to say to that? "The mane of bright red hair didn't give you a clue?"

"You were wearing a hood when I first met you," he pointed out.

"Uh, yeah, that'd be because of the stealth issue." I stuck my tongue out at the gargoyle, who still hadn't moved. "Sure you don't wanna fly up there and snarl at him a little?"

"If he has any sense, he's scared shitless of us already. He escaped the explosion at the hostel, you said?"

"He jumped through the window," I said. "I tried to hitch a ride and he kicked me off. If not for my claws, I'd be decorating the tarmac."

"Ah, that's when it happened."

"Yeah." To my own surprise, I found I didn't mind him knowing it was my first time shifting. It wasn't like he had a whole tribe of dragons waiting to laugh and poke fun at me for being a late developer.

Knowing he was alone explained how easily he'd come around to cooperating with us. Pride and defiance were dragon shifter traits, shortly behind a sense of intense protectiveness towards those we cared about, but we weren't natural loners. We were drawn to find each other.

I opened my mouth to ask him where he'd been living, but Becks jumped off the drainpipe beside us. "Got an address. They're staying at a hotel. I think it's a temporary arrangement, but if we hurry, we might catch them before they do a runner."

"Good timing," Zeph said, pointing up at the rooftops. "I think that gargoyle just went to warn his boss."

Sure enough, the winged shape was already disappearing into the cloudy sky. "Damn. Wish we could overtake him in mid-air."

Following on foot was slow and frustrating, even as we walked at a fast pace. I didn't have cash for a taxi, and besides, the fewer people who knew we were living and breathing, the better. I did spot a few cars on the road, but they were mostly the mages' chauffeurs. As the top of the heap, they'd retained all their privileges from the world before the invasion.

I hadn't told Zeph the mages had provided the funds we'd used to set up the shelter—a one-off sum, a reward for saving the city. There was little point, since the money was almost gone. The others had tried to keep our struggles under wraps, but I'd run into enough worried middle-of-the-night discussions between Ember and Will to know the day was approaching when we'd have to decide whether we could afford to keep the shelter running at all. Assuming the gargoyles didn't knock the place down before we ever got to that point.

Zeph came to such an abrupt halt, I nearly crashed into him.

"Jesus." He stared down the long driveway on our right at a massive building with a glass exterior, reflecting the light of the sun in dazzling planes. A shimmering semi-transparent shield lay thickly over the windows—a sign that someone with serious magical connections owned the place.

"Wait, is *that* the hotel?" I blinked to clear the glare of the sun from my eyes. "Bloody hell. How many wards are on that thing?"

"Enough." Zeph's eyes had started to simmer again. Mine probably had, too. *Only the best for the murderous scumbags who want to gain a fortune by selling off dragon eggs.*

My fists clenched. "Becks, can you climb up the wall or is it too steep?"

"I can try." She shifted to cat form, running across the drive to the hulking steel-and-glass construction. I followed, pulling my hood up and wishing I'd asked Will for an illusion spell. I doubted the hotel staff would look at our shabby clothes and let us walk in without a fuss.

Becks got midway up the wall before the wards flashed and she fell. I caught her in my arms, and she wriggled free, turning human again.

"Worth a shot," I said. "Guess we're going in the front way. I have a shadow spell, but it won't do much good in a place that bright."

"Thought not." Zeph scowled. "I think it's safe to say they know we're coming."

"Better hope their helicopter's not around." I didn't see the gargoyle either, but I doubted he'd be able to get inside from the air if all the windows were warded.

"They're on the third floor, if it helps," said Becks. "That's what I guessed from the room number, anyway."

Zeph pulled up his hood, Becks transformed into a cat again, and we walked up the wide stone steps and through the automatic doors into the vast reception area. My shoes squeaked on the polished marble, and bright fluorescent lights shone from all angles. It was like looking into the future—or rather, the past, the world before the faerie invasion. The distance between us and the type of people who could afford to stay in this place might as well have spanned galaxies. Rich travellers, businessmen… and shifter-killing mobsters.

With barely a sound, Becks zipped through the lobby in a blur of tabby fury. Trusting her to keep hidden, I kept my head down and walked on.

"Excuse me," called the blond woman at the reception desk on our right. "Are you lost?"

"No," I said, squarely pegging her as human. "Do you have any rooms?"

This place was about a thousand light years away from my price range, but anything that got her eyes away from whatever Becks was doing, the better.

"I can see if we have any vacancies," she said, giving my jacket a critical look. "It's formal dress in the evenings, by the way… and don't you have any suitcases with you?"

I prepared to unleash a spell, but Zeph strode up to the desk first. Instantly, she stopped talking, her mouth hanging open.

"Hey there," he said. His voice dropped in pitch, and while I couldn't see his eyes, both staff members behind the desk froze, as though his words had paralysed them. *What the hell did he do?*

There'd be time to ask questions later. "Terribly sorry about this." I yanked down my sleeve and activated two knockout spells. I caught the blond woman by the arm before she face-planted. The second tumbled backwards and landed in an awkward sprawl.

"Subtle," I muttered. "How'd you do that? Never mind, tell me later."

We made right for the elevator, where Becks waited. The lift was made of glass and metal, too, and put me in mind of a cage. I didn't like the cramped space, but three staircases would take too long to climb.

I winced at the screeching noise as the lift ascended,

impatience burning within me. The Faulkners would already know we were coming, and there was no exit except the way we'd come in, unless Zeph broke his cover—and the wards—and pulled off a full shift. Even on the inside, the faint hum of magical wards reverberated in the air like electricity. The hotel's owners must have bought them straight from the Mage Lords.

The lift doors opened, and we ran out into the third-floor corridor, following the room number signs. 322, 321—

Zeph reached the door first, kicking it inwards. There was a screech of alarm, then a gargoyle flew at us, claws outstretched.

11

"Get the window!" I yelled to Becks, and jumped at the gargoyle, my claws sliding out. With my left hand, I deflected his strike, sending him staggering back.

No more dancing around with knives—I could match his claws with a set of my own. Ruby red slashes tore open his exposed talons, and he whined in pain.

Behind him, I spotted two people by the window. One bald, one dark-haired, both wearing expressions of fury. And, I'd like to imagine, fear, too.

Waiting for your helicopter to pick you up, are you?

I renewed my attack on the gargoyle, my claws gouging deep holes in his leathery skin until I scraped at bone beneath. A gurgling cry escaped, and he took a weak swipe, only for Zeph to catch his claw and twist, hard. White-blue scales gleamed up to Zeph's elbows, and the gargoyle's clawed hand went limp. My fellow dragon shifter grabbed our adversary by the wing, yanking him to the floor.

"Hey, he was mine," I said breathlessly, giving the gargoyle a vicious kick when he was down. He screamed in agony when I snagged the edge of his wing, tearing into the membrane. *Let's see you fly away this time, dickhead.*

"Do the honours," Zeph said, pinning him down.

"This is for my sister," I said, and ripped out the gargoyle's throat.

My claws slid free, slippery with blood, and there came a yowl from Becks. I jumped to my feet, running towards the Faulkner twins.

"You're not going anywhere with that dragon egg, you cowardly snakes." I skidded to a halt as the bald Faulkner brother—Logan—wheeled around, clutching Becks's struggling cat form by the throat.

"It's too late," he said, in his low, resonant voice. "Sorry to bring an end to your good intentions, but the egg is no longer in our possession."

"The hell it isn't." Fire burned deep inside me, not satiated by the gargoyle's death. My claws itched to bury themselves in both of their throats, a deep instinct from the predator within me. "I know you skipped the auction—"

"The auction?" The dark-haired brother, Bryan, gave a soft laugh. "You expected us to parade the egg in front of humans?"

"Considering the stunt you pulled at the arena? I figured you had a flair for the dramatic."

"Perhaps," he said, "but my brother and I also have a flair for self-preservation. The moment we heard the auction hall might be targeted for an attack, we called off the auction and found an independent buyer. Fetched a nice sum, too."

Damn. Those cowardly bastards. I should have known they'd have had a backup plan.

"Who targeted it?" I asked. "Who blew up the place?"

Who's trying to destroy the dragon egg? It couldn't be the same people who coveted it... so either someone had a vested interest in not letting any wild dragonlings loose in London, or they wanted it for themselves. Either way, though—it was gone. I'd failed.

Logan gave Becks a violent shake, and she shifted to human form, crashing on top of him. Sparks flashed and I shouted a warning, but Becks shifted back into her cat form and pelted across the carpet, dodging whatever spell Logan had used.

"Witch spells?" I kept one eye on each of them, conscious of Zeph's presence behind me. "Part witch, are you? Or did you have someone else sneak into your room at the shelter to help you disguise yourselves as orphaned shifters? I'd have thought that sort of trickery beneath you."

The bald man's lip curled. "I have a little skill with magic. Skill enough to bring down a wild animal like you, at any rate."

A low growl slipped from Zeph's throat, and his anger lit a fire in my own veins. I flung a trapping spell into Logan's face, and net-like red threads of light pinned him to the wall. His brother dodged, his hand in his pocket. There was a clicking sound—a sound that froze the blood in my veins.

Please tell me that isn't what it sounded like.

"I hoped you'd know when to run, Coriander," he said. "I only need one dragon shifter, and I'd prefer a fully mature specimen. You didn't have to interfere."

My instincts screamed to life and I shouted a wordless warning to Zeph, throwing myself to the floor. In the same instant, Bryan whipped a gun from his pocket and fired. A feathery dart whipped over my head, followed by another. *Not a bullet. You're okay. Move, Cori.*

I rolled over, metallic-tasting fear coating the back of my throat. Behind me, Zeph roared, loud enough for both of us. The Faulkners, however, didn't look cowed, not even the one stuck in the trapping spell. His partner fired twice more, and I flattened my body on the carpet.

Zeph lunged at him, claws out, but a blast knocked him flat onto his back. The air rippled in front of the two men, forming a shimmering transparent shield. An advanced shield spell.

I raised an eyebrow. "You're going on the defensive? Guess you're not so competent at magic, huh."

Logan smiled with no warmth. "You're wasting your time. You'll never find the egg, and you can't destroy us."

"You overestimate yourselves," growled Zeph, back on his feet. "Have you any idea of the damage one of those creatures can do?"

"I would love to hear all about it," said Logan, freed from the trapping spell, "but I think we've outstayed our welcome."

The window glass shattered, fanning out with such precision, it could only have been broken with a spell. I ducked the spray of glass and looked up to see a white helicopter outside, whirring loudly.

It *was* their helicopter we'd seen hovering above the auction hall, at a suitable distance from the explosion.

"No, you don't," I growled, shaking glass off my hands.

Darts flew past my head as Bryan covered the window with his back, and his brother climbed out into the helicopter. I dodged each attack and grabbed Bryan by the throat, pinning him to the wall. My claws dug deep into the flesh of his shoulder. He let out a quiet snarl of pain, but before I could move, his hand inched up, and something cold and metal pressed against my chest.

"I wouldn't." Bryan's tone was flat. I didn't dare move to look down at his weapon. Fear and rage warred, and my claws flickered in and out of existence. *Don't disappear on me now.*

"Would you look at that?" I fought to keep the fear out of my voice. "A stalemate. Tell me what you stand to gain in all this, and I might not toss you out the window."

"You're in no position to negotiate, little worm," he said. "Not unless you want to end up the same as your sister. I must admit I don't know the *precise* dosage of the poison which will kill a dragon. I'm rather short on specimens to test them on. But I'm more than willing to find out."

"You scum." My voice rumbled deep in my chest.

My claw moved, but the cold metal against my chest dug in, chilling my blood. "Move, Coriander. Be grateful that I've spared your life… and let your friend's fate be a lesson to you."

Zeph.

I spun around, and Bryan leapt towards the window. I lunged at him with a scream of fury, but he gave another leap through the helicopter's open door, catching his brother's arm for balance.

"I wouldn't bother trying to track us down again," he said. "You'll have much bigger problems to worry about soon enough."

Over his shoulder, his brother took aim at me again. A dart clipped my jacket sleeve, and Zeph caught me, pulling me back into the room. The helicopter rose, and the Faulkners' cold smiles were the last thing I saw before they disappeared into the sky.

I yanked myself free of Zeph's grip. "Bastards."

"It's no use killing them," Zeph said, his voice oddly slurred. "If we do, we might bring half the mob on our tail. Scaring them is more than enough."

"But they sold the egg." My footsteps crunched in broken glass. The blast had even shattered the magical wards on the window. "They made a fortune out of it and now they're leaving the rest of us to clean up the mess."

"I'm aware of that." Zeph's voice was quieter than before, and he'd sunk to the glass-strewn floor, a feathery dart sticking out of his shoulder.

"Shit," I said. "Zeph, you okay? What's in those darts?"

"I'm taking a wild guess it's the same poison they used on your sister."

Damn. "Come on, we have to get out of here. Becks, you okay?"

She meowed from beside the door in answer. I gave the room a cursory scan, but if the Faulkners had always planned to do a runner, they wouldn't have left anything important behind.

Zeph climbed to his feet and stumbled towards the door. I took his elbow to stop him from tripping over. The sounds of a commotion echoed into the corridor from a nearby staircase. Ah, shit. The receptionists would have recovered by now and had probably called security.

We ran into the elevator, where Zeph sagged against the wall, his face pale.

"I'm okay," he said, though he was sweating. "I think it's designed to affect dragons, not humans, so as long as I don't shift, I should be able to make it back home in one piece."

"I bloody hope so. We don't have a car." And the Faulkners had a freaking helicopter. If anything, they had better wings than I did.

The elevator screeched to a halt, and Zeph staggered. I caught his arm, my heart thumping. *Not the time, Zeph. We have to get somewhere safe—*

Oh, shit.

Suited security guards filled the reception area. Human or not, it didn't matter. Zeph couldn't shift and there were three of us and six of them. Not to mention the two dazed-looking receptionists.

"Ah." I took a step forwards, Zeph leaning heavily on me. "You might have noticed you've lost a couple of guests, and I bet they didn't pay before leaving."

There was also the gargoyle, whose dead body I'd left

back in the Faulkners' room, but that was the least of it. My hands were covered in blood to the elbows and Zeph's condition was impossible to hide.

Hide.

I grabbed a smokescreen spell from my wrist, hurling it into the air. Thick grey smoke poured through the reception area, and Becks shifted into cat form, darting in and out of the guards' legs. Cursing, the guards lunged to grab her, but Becks at top speed was like a house cat had got into the catnip and then found a skateboard. If we'd been at normal speed, getting Zeph out would be no problem, but he was rapidly turning into dead weight.

"Come on." I dragged him behind a pillar to avoid tripping over Becks. "We can make it—"

The automatic doors slid open and someone else ran in. The guards turned on the newcomer, but the combination of the smokescreen spell and the element of surprise gave him the edge. Three guards were down before I saw who it was— Astor. I never thought I'd be glad to see a former Orion League assassin.

I dragged Zeph forwards a few more feet. "Backup is here. He must have followed our trail."

And brought the antidote. *I hope.*

At my words, Zeph seemed to revive a little. We made our way past the receptionists cowering behind the counter and through the doors. Navigating the stone steps outside was trickier. By the time Zeph had reached the bottom, his auburn curls were plastered to his forehead with sweat.

Astor landed softly behind us. "What's wrong with him?"

"They hit him with the same poison they used on Ember."

Astor swore. "They won't be down for long. I didn't kill them, since this is a human-owned place."

Right. Ember claimed Astor followed his own moral code,

but I'd never been able to make much sense out of it. "How'd you know where to find us? The witch?"

"Yes, and I borrowed a car." He indicated a sleek black vehicle parked outside.

"Nice," Becks said, appearing at my side in human form. "I assume by 'borrowed', you meant 'nicked it from the hotel car park'?"

Astor opened the door instead of answering, and I helped Zeph into the back seat. That left Astor and Becks to sit in the front. Neither seemed thrilled with that arrangement, but when Zeph fell on top of me, I had to admit they had the better deal. I pushed Zeph back into his own seat with a firm but gentle hand.

"Thanks, Astor," I said, as he started the engine. "I was starting to think you'd been eaten by a troll."

He glared at me through the front mirror. "Nobody said the Faulkners' witch friend had a pet goblin or three."

"Well, that'd be because I didn't know. Did you get the antidote?"

"I got the recipe," he answered.

"Good." Zeph sagged against the window. "What did you do to the witch?"

"Killed him, of course."

Astor drove off at a speed that made my teeth rattle. When we hit a pothole and flew a foot into the air, Zeph groaned, looking even paler than before. "Can you not do that? I don't like cars."

"Well, please try not to throw up on me." I winced as we hit the road with a noise that suggested the car's original owner would not get it back in pristine condition.

"I won't," he said, his eyes sliding closed. "We'll need to get that egg back in the next forty-eight hours if we want to avoid a massacre."

"Massacre?" Astor's sharp voice came from the front. "Nobody mentioned a massacre."

"Zeph's the only one of us who's encountered those dragonlings before," I explained. "They're like wild animals, he says."

"Deadly." Zeph's voice was barely a murmur, and his white-knuckled grip on the door had grown limp. When Astor swerved the car, he fell on top of my legs again. *Ow.*

"Can you drive any quicker, Astor?" I pushed Zeph to the side, panic brewing. He was fading fast, and poisons weren't my area of expertise. *I thought they wanted him alive.* Or maybe they'd been aiming for me and hit him instead.

"This is as fast as it goes." We rattled over another pothole. "I take it your scheme to catch the thieves didn't go as planned?"

"They had a helicopter," Becks said. "Not only that, they sold the egg to some rich bastard friend of theirs. No idea who."

Astor slowed the car. "I'm going to have to abandon this vehicle before we get home so its owners can't follow us."

"Crap." I dug in my pocket for my phone, dried blood cracking on my hands. The gargoyle's blood. I wiped my fingers on my jeans, then called Will's number. "Hey! We're on the way back now. Zeph's injured. Astor stole a car."

"Want me to pick you up?"

"Zeph can't walk, so that'd be ideal. Thank you."

I ended the call. If we all went home, the antidote might take hours to brew and longer to work. The Faulkners might be on their way out of the city by then. If they weren't already.

"Cori?" Becks said from the front. "Let me guess—you're going to follow them."

"Not them. The egg." I wiped more blood from my hands.

"How many rich bastards who covet rare supernatural creatures can there be?"

"More than you think," Astor said.

"What, you personally know them?" Becks said. "All right, I'm with you."

Since when was she on Team Let's Find the Dubious Dragon Egg? "You sure?"

"Sure I don't want a massacre? Hell yes," Becks said.

"There is that." Not that I knew where London's rich collectors of dangerous magical items hung out in their spare time, except for the arena. "If the egg hatches and eats the person who bought it, it would serve them right."

But the idea of letting the Faulkners get away with poisoning my sister and shooting at us did not appeal in the slightest. Thanks to me, their gargoyle allies were dead, so we couldn't question them...

Or could we?

"Astor, can you drop me off at Russell Square?" I asked.

"Why d'you want to go there?" He turned a sharp corner, causing Zeph's semi-conscious body to fall into my lap again.

"A hunch."

Most people didn't become ghosts after death, but it was common after a particularly violent end. Perhaps the Faulkners hadn't told their allies anything worthwhile, but I didn't believe for a minute they were just going to leave the city without finishing what they started. They'd claimed they needed a dragon shifter, and I doubted they'd just let us run.

No. They'd be back. I was sure of it.

Astor took a swift turn, and I fell back in my seat with my legs in the air and Zeph's head beneath my thighs. I gave him a gentle shove to the side before sitting back down properly. "You know, I normally like to get to know a guy a little better before getting this intimate with him. Maybe we should grab a movie later, or..."

Zeph did not find my comment amusing. Neither did Astor. Though in the former's case, it was because he was out cold.

Astor drew the car to a halt at the roadside. "Out," he said. "I won't be able to pick you up."

"I'll survive it." I hopped out the car, after making sure Zeph was in a comfortable position in the back.

Becks bounded out to join me, her glasses back on. "Going to clue me in on whatever wild scheme you're cooking up next?"

"I'm not *that* bad," I protested. "At least I didn't let myself get tied up as bait in an arena match."

She snorted. "That Zeph? He's a piece of work. I can see why you two get along."

"I'll take that as a compliment."

We walked the short distance to the hostel—or what was left of it. While I'd stopped shaking with adrenaline, a familiar chill swept through me, and grey fog permeated my vision.

Every time I went near a place thick with death, the veil closed in. Transparent bodies floated in all directions, unaware of the waking world. Pushing down my apprehension, I scanned the dead, searching for someone familiar. Shifters were forced into human form when they died, but I knew his face.

There he is.

The gargoyle shifter stood, or floated, in the middle of the mass of wandering spirits. I zeroed in on him, waving a hand. "Hey there. Hey, you."

The mass of ghosts closed in on me, wailing faintly. I kept walking, one eye on my target. Just my luck to target the one ghost who *didn't* want to speak to me.

"Who are you talking to?" Becks said from behind me. "You're seeing dead people again, aren't you?"

"On and off." I did my best to ignore the other ghosts, walking right into the gargoyle shifter's line of sight. "Hey. I know you can see me."

The gargoyle roared and lunged at me, only to pass right through my body and fall flat on his face. He floated face-down in mid-air, and I stifled a laugh. After my latest brush with death, ghosts seemed far less scary than the living. Better still, his violent attempt to jump on me had scared the other spirits away.

"You bitch," he said. "You killed me."

"You'd have done the same to me." I folded my arms, burying my hands in my armpits to chase off Death's chill. "You can't hurt me, and when you pass through the gates of Death, you'll never see me again."

Not until I died, anyway. I had every intention of living a long and full life, thanks.

He scowled. "What do you want?"

"You knew your boss planned to sell the egg, right? Who to?"

He released a breath, which he technically didn't need to do, being dead. I'd seen ghosts cling onto all sorts of habits they'd had when they were alive. "Sell it? It still has their name on it."

"Wait, what?" I frowned. "We cornered them at their hotel room, and they said they already sold it before the auction."

"Of course they did," he said, his lip curling. "They'll want to throw everyone off the trace. It'll be in their stronghold, at their house in Kensington."

"What?" That was right next to mage territory—which said something about the connections they kept that I didn't care for at all. "Are you sure?"

"I'm dead," he yelled. "I'm not sure of anything, am I? You killed me."

"You'll get over it." I turned my back on the ghost, my

head spinning. The Faulkners had *kept* the egg. Why? To stick it to the person who'd tried to blow up the auction hall, or had that been their doing, too? Presumably, they didn't expect it to hatch anytime soon. Whatever the case, nobody would guess it was still within the city, much less next door to mage territory. Crafty bastards.

Becks waved at me. "Cori, are you still with us?"

"I am," I said. "And I think I know where the egg is. Problem is, it's in Kensington. Anyone who can afford to buy property there will be able to afford top-level security, too."

The Mage Lords were the most protected individuals in the city, since they kept supernatural society running as well as helping prevent the non-supernatural side from collapsing. If the Faulkners had friends within the mages' ranks, I could say goodbye to finding an easy way out.

I'd see what Ember said when she woke up. Now we had the antidote, she and Zeph would recover from the poison.

The Faulkners might have outsmarted us and wriggled through our fingers, but this wouldn't end until their deaths. I'd make sure of it.

12

"Cori?"

I blinked awake, my face pressed to something rough and scratchy. I'd fallen asleep on the living room floor. I sat up, rubbing my cheek where it'd brushed against the rough carpet. Zeph sat in the armchair we'd left him in in while we waited for the antidote to take effect. Neither he nor Ember had woken up last night, and from Ember's inert state on the sofa, there'd been no change.

"Where am I?" Zeph blinked at me, his grey eyes sleepy.

"You're at my house," I said. "Well, technically, it's Will's house."

"Didn't recognise it in the dark." He leaned forward, frowning at Ember's sleeping form. "Has she woken up yet?"

"I don't think so." My chest tightened. She'd had a worse dose of the poison than Zeph had, and Will had said she might take another day to wake up. I'd offered to watch her overnight and must have dozed off.

Zeph ran a hand over the place where the dart had torn a hole in his grey hoody. "Damn close call there."

"Yeah…" I tore my gaze from Ember. "Glad the antidote worked. How're you feeling?"

"Hungry." He eyed the box of cold pizza leftover from yesterday evening. "Can I warm that up?"

"What, by breathing fire on it?"

"Nah, I don't do that in the house. Safety hazard."

A smile tugged at my mouth. "I guess it is."

I climbed to my feet, stretching. My neck ached from lying on the floor, but I was glad I'd showered last night to wash the taint of the gargoyles' blood. After checking Zeph knew how to use the microwave, I went to my room to change, stopping to have a quick wash in the bathroom. Sleeping on the floor had left a pink mark on my cheek and my eyes didn't *look* any brighter after my shift, but with any luck, the claws were the first sign of something more.

Vaguely refreshed, I returned to the main room to find Zeph leaning back against the kitchen counter as though he lived here. Dragons tended to relax around our own kind in a way that we rarely achieved with other people. I'd forgotten how few dragon shifters around my own age I'd met. Lorne had forced most dragons who were capable of fighting to serve him or die. They could have used someone like Zeph in the village, actually—young, strong and capable. Emphasis on the 'strong' part. It was unfair. I hadn't inherited any of those genes at all. His muscular arms were thicker than my neck.

He raised an eyebrow, seeing me staring. "Something up?"

I shrugged. "Weird coincidence, isn't it? Of all the people to run into, it had to be the only other dragon shifters in the city."

"I've been living near London for a couple of years and I've never crossed paths with any of you," he said. "Met plenty of other supernaturals, and humans, but never anyone like me."

I tapped a foot, not sure what to say. I'd often missed the company of my own kind, but with Ember, I was never really alone.

"Zeph's your real name, then?" I asked. "Let me guess, it's short for Zephyr."

"You've got it," he said. "A bit on the nose, but both of my parents were dragon shifters, so there was no danger of me turning out to be a rat or a wolf shifter instead. I imagine that would have been a disappointment for them."

"Ha. My sister's called Ember, so I can't talk. I think my parents must have run out of imagination by the time they got to me. 'Coriander' is more suited to a witch than a dragon."

He shrugged. "I had a friend called Blaize. Poor kid had to use an alias to pass as human."

"He'd be able to make a hell of an entrance in an arena fight, though."

"Yeah... he was more of a pacifist. Not often heard of from a dragon, but there you have it." His use of the past tense said it all, and his words carried an undercurrent of long-buried pain. I might have lost my community, too, but my memories were too distant to haunt me with the image of what might have been. I didn't even remember my parents' faces.

The microwave dinged and he took out the plate. "Want some of this?"

"Not at this hour in the morning, I don't." I glanced at Ember. "She'll be pissed that this is the first impression you got of her. She likes to play the tough big sister role."

"I'm not one to talk about bad first impressions." He bit into a slice of pizza. "I guess you probably understand, but when I have a plan, I get pissed when it goes off the rails."

"I get that." I knew about dragon shifter temperaments. Ember was worse than I was, so I was used to mediating arguments... or putting on the cute little sister act to get her to stop blowing up at people. "I'm glad you didn't turn out to be a dick."

"You forgive me for it, then?" He finished the slice and picked up another.

"Even if I didn't, I'd rather be on your side than the guys we're fighting."

"Better than you hating me. I'll take it." He set the plate down and poured a glass of water. Watching him move around as a human made me almost forget the scaled beast he could turn into, but the shifter was there in the way he moved. Assured, confident but not to the point of arrogance. The dim kitchen light caught on the strands of blond in his auburn hair and the faint stubble on his face. He was certainly striking-looking, but dragon shifters generally were. I saw something of Ember's fierceness in his ashy grey eyes... which met mine as he caught me looking. Busted.

He tilted his head. "You're staring at me again."

"Trying to work out if we're related."

"We aren't," he said. "Unless you're from a village in Yorkshire."

"Nah, Scotland."

"You don't have the accent."

"I moved to London when I was five," I said. "There are so few of us, I wondered."

"Hmm." The merest flicker of amber danced in his eyes. "You sure that's the only reason you wanted to know?"

I should have seen that one coming. Shifters didn't mince words when it came to expressing interest in one another. While the majority of shifters stayed with one partner for life, casual hook-ups were common, especially among the younger shifters. I'd never been with another dragon shifter, for obvious reasons, but I'd occasionally wondered if the result would be as... *intense* as one dragon shifter and another supernatural.

You're not my type wasn't accurate, so I settled for saying, "Yes, it is. For now."

Now you're flirting with him? Dangerous idea, and even more dangerous was the glint in his eyes as he bit into the pizza slice. Like I was the one he wanted to sink his teeth into. *Okay, now you're reading too much into it.*

"All right, then." He walked past me, holding the plate in one hand, the other brushing my sleeve—just delicately enough to pass off as an accident.

I grabbed my water glass. *Cool it, Cori.* Now wasn't the time to play games, especially as I was sure he hadn't told me everything about himself yet. Yorkshire? If he'd still been there when the invasion happened, he'd have had a hell of a long and dangerous journey to get to London.

He'd come here for a reason.

"Cori? You going to stand there staring into space all morning?"

"Nope." I drained the glass and switched off the kitchen light, following him back into the living room area. "Glad you're okay. You passed out on me in the car."

"Ah, sorry. Moving vehicles... not my thing." He gave a faint shudder, leaning back in the armchair. "Comes with being able to fly, I guess."

"You flew to London?"

"Yeah." He rested the plate on the arm of the chair. "The comment about going out for a movie..."

I groaned. "You heard."

A grin slid onto his mouth. "I like how you handle stress by cracking jokes. Most dragons I've met take themselves way too seriously."

"When you've seen Death, you can either dig your own

grave or laugh in his face. I've never been a fan of being buried."

"Seen death," he said. "You can see dead people, can't you?"

I blinked. "How'd you know?"

"I heard you talking to the others," he said. "I was half conscious at the time, but I thought... that's how you turned the lights off at the theatre, isn't it?"

"Yep," I said. "I like to think of it as a party trick. Anyway, we know who has the egg now. All we need to do is break into a rich guy's house today. If you're up for it."

"Wouldn't miss it." He grinned, showing a dimple. "And afterwards, we can catch a movie."

I didn't miss the suggestive hint in his voice. Oh, boy. If Ember woke up right now, she'd probably try to strangle him.

"Good, one of you is awake," said Will, walking through the door before I could formulate a response. "The assassin had better stop bitching at me about getting the antidote wrong. I told him it might take twenty-four hours to work, but I might as well have yelled at the clouds to stop raining."

"Patience isn't Astor's strong point," I said. "But—are you sure it should be taking this long to work on Ember?"

"Don't you start," Will said, with a sigh. "Chill out. Your sister is going to be fine. A normal person would be dead several times over by now. She got through the first twenty-four hours without the antidote. She'll be okay, Cori."

"All right." I walked to my sister's side. At least she didn't look uncomfortable, or in pain. "Are you coming with us, Will?"

"I should stay here with Kit in case the worst happens, and we have to close the shelter. Besides, Becks is better at stealth than I am."

"I'm about as stealthy as a rampaging troll." I glanced at

Zeph. "Him, too. Are you positive you're not going to keel over on me again, Zeph? I don't know what the long-term effects of that poison are."

"There aren't any," said a voice from the dark corner of the room, and everyone jumped as Astor walked into view from the shadows. I was pretty sure he knew exactly how much it unnerved people when he did that.

"At this rate we'll all drop dead of fright before we even get started." I gave Astor an eye-roll. "Not necessary, Astor. Are you sure?"

"I'm more concerned with the short-term effects."

"Oh, for god's sake," said Will. "Ember will be fine. She had it worse because she was in her shifted form when she impaled herself on the gargoyle's claws. Bound to leave a mark."

Kit entered the room. "Is Ember awake?"

"No," Astor said, through clenched teeth. His agitation did not help my own state of mind one bit. "What exactly did you plan to do if it doesn't work?"

"You stole the bloody antidote recipe, Astor," Will said. "If you'd wanted another one, you shouldn't have killed the witch. Now for god's sake, go with Cori to steal the dragon egg back and quit getting under my feet."

Astor's gaze cut to me. "Steal it back? I thought you were getting rid of the thing."

"That's the plan," I said. "But we kinda need to actually *have* it first."

"We need to get it out of the city," Zeph said, eyeing Astor. The two hadn't been properly introduced yet, thanks to Zeph's half-conscious state on the drive back yesterday. "Fast. The dragonling will be close to hatching by now."

"Is it going to hatch?" Kit asked. "Is that why it felt so alive?"

"If it is, it makes no sense that the Faulkners stashed it at their house," I said. "Unless they wanted the dragonling, not the egg."

Did they plan to sell it after it hatches? Maybe. I wouldn't put anything past them.

"I'm not convinced they want either," Zeph said. "Not now they've got London's supernaturals all stirred up over the egg. Maybe they're counting on a network of fakes showing up and the profits flowing straight to them. I wouldn't have thought they'd go to so much trouble, though."

"Exactly," I said. "If it was just the egg they wanted, they could have just taken it straight to their hideout right after they stole it from me. They didn't need to make a public display. I'm not sure it's the money they wanted."

"No," said Zeph. "There's something else they wanted. I think it's safe to assume that whatever it is, it's worth risking life and limb for."

"Or someone else's life and limb," I said, thinking of those gargoyles. "You know this fancy estate of theirs... it's right next to mage territory. They have friends in *really* high places."

There was an awkward silence in which nobody acknowledged that none of us had ever suggested reporting the issue to the Mage Lords, but everyone was thinking it. Except possibly Zeph, not being local. The mages might have helped us in the past, but they stayed far away from the shifters' underworld. Given the potential connections the Faulkners had, it was pretty safe to say we were on our own in this one.

"Then you'll have to use your ingenuity to get inside," Will said, as Becks walked in. "All right, how many of you will be going?"

"I am," said Becks. "Cori, too, right?"

"Yeah, I am. Zeph, too. Astor, will you be coming with

us?" Either way, with Ember, Will and Kit staying behind, it seemed both too small and too large a group for a robbery.

"I'll go ahead," Astor said. "Someone needs to have a look around the property to see what kind of security they have, and they'll already be looking out for two dragons and a cat. I'll meet you later."

"With another stolen car?"

He didn't dignify that with a response, and briefly paused to look at Ember before walking through the open door to the shop.

Zeph watched him leave. "Why do you have a human living here?"

"I wonder that at least twice a day," Will said.

"He's dating Ember," Becks supplied.

Zeph looked at Ember's sleeping body. "A human and a dragon shifter?"

"If that's the oddest thing you've heard today, then you're in for a hell of a ride," said Will.

13

The Faulkners' place wasn't as big or extravagant as I'd expected, a plain terraced house identical to its neighbours. What set it apart from any other neighbourhood were the shimmering wards covering its whitewashed exterior, and the pair of grim-faced gargoyles crammed into dark suits standing on either side of the front gate.

Zeph and I wore shadow spells, the most basic form of illusion charm. They wouldn't have worked in the bright, glass-walled hotel, but the sun hid behind a bank of clouds and the narrow houses cast long shadows, affording us no shortage of places to hide in.

"They'll be watching for showy diversions," I whispered to Zeph as we walked, heads down, hoods up. "That means we can't do anything too drastic to get inside. They're too smart to fall for a ploy. Pretending to give ourselves up won't work." Besides, I wasn't convinced they wouldn't just kill us if we pulled a stunt like Zeph had in the arena.

"I thought so," he said. "But if one of us got caught on

purpose, we'd get an inside view. We're going by guesswork here."

He was right, but it was too risky. "We're also dealing with humans. They'll be compensating for their lack of supernatural talent in every way possible. They have those darts specially made for dragon shifters. God knows what else the place is booby-trapped with."

All my instincts screamed at me to turn back. Human they might be, but I'd been hunted and captured by humans before. What they lacked in strength and speed, they made up for in persistence and inventiveness. Our handmade spells looked like nothing compared to their wards. Since at least one of the Faulkners was part witch, they had the upper hand in that department, too.

Assuming they were even here.

I truly hated stealth missions. Even with a shadow spell masking me from sight, I was still *there*, clumsy and angry and not at all good at soundlessly running on rooftops like Becks and Astor. Why was blasting the doors off never the best option?

"Hey," I whispered to Zeph. "You know what you did to freeze the receptionists at the hotel? Would it work on the guards?"

"It requires direct eye contact. I'd have to show them my real face. I realise they've already seen it, but they'll have more guards on backup. I can't hit all of them at once."

A cat-shaped shadow streaked past, indicating Becks's return. A moment later, she turned human, a dark outline of a person hidden behind a shadow charm. "Astor claims he knows when the guards change at the gates. He's going to set off a signal when they do."

"Is he going to tell us what his plan is?" I stood on tiptoe to see if I could spot him, but the assassin hid better than I did even without using a spell. "I don't have to ask, do I."

No matter. I had one of my own... and it looked a lot like a rat shifter.

I neared the house, watching from behind a parked van for Astor's signal. I counted to thirty, then there came the sound of a car backfiring. On cue, I broke into a run. The gargoyles, eyes squinted against the setting sun, didn't so much as look at me as I aimed carefully, throwing a spell at their feet. A giant rat appeared where the spell's sparks faded, and only then did they look down.

"Hey," said one of them. "Hey—get away. Shoo."

He waved a hand at the rat, which skittered around in a convincing imitation of the real thing. Illusions didn't last long, so we needed to be quick.

"Chase it off," said his partner, aiming a kick. He missed wildly, but the illusion was set to move fast enough to cover up that the rat didn't actually exist. If he tried to pick it up, he'd know it wasn't real, but it moved too quickly for a big clumsy gargoyle shifter to get his hands on. "What, you're not scared of rodents, are you?"

Two new guards approached the gate. Like the others, they had the big, mean look of the suit-wearing gargoyles we'd seen at the arena. Maybe they were the same ones. A lot of shifters needed two jobs to make ends meet, after all. Guard rich folks by day, supervise illegal arena matches by night.

"What're you so wound up about?" one of the newcomers queried. "Scared of a little mouse?"

Two gargoyles both lunged for the rat, missed, and it ran through the gates into the front garden.

"It's one of those damned shifters!" said the gargoyle on the left, shoving his way through the gate into the garden.

"They said watch out for a cat shifter, not a rat shifter," yelled his partner. "Can't you tell the difference?"

Stifling a laugh, I kept an eye on Becks. *Not a rat shifter, but you're about to be sorry you abandoned your post.* Becks would activate the rest of the spells inside the grounds. That'd keep them busy for a while.

"Hey, there are two of them!" said a voice, then Zeph moved for the gap in the gates. Neither of us could match the mad dash of a hyperactive cat, but Becks was already in there, dropping spells left and right. Shouts and cursing filled the air. Footsteps behind us announced the arrival of a new guard, but Zeph spun on the spot, throwing a knockout spell into his face. He crumpled, and I did the same to the second. Then we ran for the gates, and up the path to the house's front doors.

Now for the tricky bit. One look at the house's glittering exterior told me the place was warded the same as the hotel was, on the off-chance that someone slipped through the gate. Shimmering glyphs danced up and down the brick walls, spells intended to keep out intruders.

The front door opened, and another scowling gargoyle peered out. "What is going on out here?"

"Don't open the door!" yelled the guard. "There are rat shifters loose in the grounds."

"They're not shifters," returned his partner.

The shifter at the door scowled at both of them. "Get them all out."

I took aim, unseen, and the last spell hit the guard full in the face, causing an illusory rat to spring into existence on his shoulder. He half-shifted to gargoyle form in alarm, hopping on the spot.

"There's a rat on me! A rat!"

Becks darted under his feet and gave a firm shove, sending him toppling off the doorstep. Zeph vaulted his flailing legs and climbed to the front door, and I followed close on his heels.

Another guard stood on our left, at the foot of a thickly

carpeted staircase. His gaze flicked to our shadowy forms, and Zeph yanked him off the stairs, an arm around his neck.

The time for subtlety—if you could call a plague of fake rats subtle—was at an end.

Zeph lowered the guard's unconscious body to the ground. "How long do those illusions last?" he whispered.

"Ten minutes." Not enough to thoroughly search every room, but it stood to reason that the dragon egg would be kept in the place with the best wards. The hum of magic in the walls made it difficult to pinpoint the source, but that's why I'd brought a spell sensor. I pulled the stick-shaped device from my pocket, glad that my friends had stolen it from the mages a while ago.

A faint humming noise came from its end, leading us upstairs to a short corridor. Zeph knocked out two more guards on the way. Normally we'd rely on our enhanced shifter senses to track the egg, but the stench of gargoyle masked everything aside from each other.

"Is that thing even working?" Zeph asked, after our third dead end. All the rooms were empty, creating the impression that nobody lived here. Maybe it was all a show, even the guards.

"Yes, but the place is too heavily warded to detect anything subtle," I muttered back.

The device chose that moment to give a loud beep. I followed the sound to a room at the corridor's end and turned the door handle. Locked. I grabbed an unlocking spell, but Zeph had already shoved the door hard with his shoulder.

"Ow," he muttered.

"I could have unlocked that, you know." I had to admit, it was kind of refreshing to be in the company of someone who had even less patience than I did.

My grin slipped away at the sight of the dragon egg in a

sealed transparent case in the centre of the room. Wards flickered around its edges, creating a rippling effect on its ruby scales. Other than that, the room was suspiciously empty. I took a wary step over the threshold, and Zeph caught my arm.

A dozen darts shot at us from all direction. I jerked back, activating a shield spell. The darts bounced off, and I released a sigh of relief when they clattered harmlessly to the floor. They were magical darts, not immune to shielding spells. I waited, counted to five, then inched into the room.

Sharp spikes appeared from the ceiling, stabbing downwards. Zeph and I both leapt through the door at once. Metal bars pierced the floor beneath the door frame, trapping us in the room. *Damn, that was close.*

A thin wailing noise struck up, and a red light flashed overhead. We'd tripped an alarm. I grabbed a silencing spell and threw it at the blinking light, which went out. *Nice try.* But the guards had probably heard the alarm start in the seconds before we'd cut it off. We didn't have much time.

I pulled an explosive spell from my wrist and threw it at the egg. The spell hit the ward with a muffled blast but didn't make a dent. *Thought not.*

Zeph's claws appeared, visible even through his shadow spell. He reached for the egg and jerked back, cursing.

With a snarl, I ran forwards, past the cage, straight at the barrier. My claws flickered to life, hitting the ward, and a sudden pain like an electric shock exploded up my arms. *Ow.*

"What the hell was that?"

"I don't know." Zeph pressed his claws to the barrier. I did likewise, and a second shot of pain ricocheted up my spine.

Cold metallic fear lined the back of my throat. I knew that pain. I'd hoped never to experience it again.

Zeph growled, low and threatening, and made another lunge for the shield. His white-blue claws pressed against the invisible barrier, and he gave a low grunt of pain. "It's got at least three layers on. I thought my claws could get through one."

"I bet only dragonfire can."

"All right. Back up."

"Wait." Oh, no. "Zeph, don't. They already know we're in—"

Claws shot from his hands. His body lengthened, turning scaled, tail lashing the wall. Wings sprouted from his back, opalescent scales gleaming brightly enough to dazzle the eyes. His horned head lowered, and a torrent of blinding white fire engulfed the room.

14

I threw myself flat, the fire whooshing over my head. Screaming alarms filled the air, and the dragon egg clattered to the floor.

Yes.

A scraping noise came from the door, indicating the bars had withdrawn back into the door frame. Then two suited gargoyles ran in behind Zeph. Oh, crap.

Neither of the newcomers looked at me. I crouched down, holding my breath. I was still under the shadow spell, but Zeph's had broken when he'd shifted into dragon form. He turned his head, impeded by the cramped space, and one of the gargoyles pressed a dart gun to his scaled body.

"Don't try anything funny," said the guard. "Those scales of yours can't block the poison. What are you, a stray?"

Fury simmered in Zeph's eyes, but when our gazes connected, he gave the slightest head-shake, telling me not to intervene.

Oh. He wanted me to steal the egg while their attention was on him. *Uh, not sure it's gonna work out that way, Zeph.* I wasn't close enough to reach the egg without alerting the guards, and the shadow spell only made *me* invisible, not anything I touched.

"Damn, he actually destroyed the barrier," said the second guard. "What'll we do with him?"

"Cage him," said the guy on the left. "Get that egg away from him first."

Dammit, Zeph. What were you thinking, breathing fire like that?

I caught his eye and he jerked his head, a minute movement that the guard picked up on. "None of that." He pressed the gun harder into Zeph's back.

A jolt of understanding hit me. He hadn't just been trying to destroy the shields protecting the egg: he'd been trying to get them to move it elsewhere. And when they did, I'd have an opening to snatch it from their hands.

Right Guard grabbed the egg with a belligerent grunt and marched to the door. The murmur of voices from outside told me he wasn't alone. If the guards all had those dart guns, there'd be no way to fight my way out without being turned into a human pincushion. I'd need to pick my moment carefully.

Trusting Left Guard was occupied with Zeph, I shadowed Right Guard out of the room, and aimed a spell at his back.

"What're you doing?" another guard asked him from the corridor. "You're not supposed to move that egg without permission."

"Fucker in there melted the shield spell," Right Guard answered.

"Bryan said not to move it."

"Bryan didn't say anything about what to do when a dragon breathes fire inside the fucking house. Get in there and help restrain him, you dumb fuck."

Guess they're as friendly to each other as they are to us.

It took one corridor for the itching spell to kick in. Right

Guard's pace slowed, then quickened as he tried to scratch his leg while walking on it at the same time. *Ha.*

"Someone take this thing off my hands," he growled. "They got me with one of those itching spells."

The nearest guard laughed, which, to be fair, was what I'd have done if I'd been him. As it was, I wanted to bulldoze the lot of them to the ground and get Zeph out—but he'd be pissed with me if I let the egg out of my sight.

As Right Guard reached the stairs, there came a roar of pain from behind me. *Zeph.*

Bye bye, caution. I kicked Right Guard in the back of the leg, sending him toppling downstairs. His grip broke on the egg and I jumped over him, kicking him in the face in the process. I grabbed the egg before it rolled away, and pain burned my palms, sudden and sharp.

Ow. What the hell? I tucked the egg under my arm, my palms blistering. They must have put some kind of shield on the egg itself. *Not cool.*

Wait. I could see my hands. Which meant...

"Hey, it's her!" yelled Right Guard, whose nose was bleeding.

I legged it. Hampered by the egg, I veered around a corner and collided with another guard. Bugger.

"Ah," I said, backing up. "It's been spectacular to see you all again, but you see, this egg is *mine*. So if you don't mind, I'm taking it back."

I hurled an explosive spell with my free hand. A mild cracking noise came from above, and the spell dissipated before it reached its target. They'd warded the *ceiling*?

A dart flew past my head, then another. I released my claws, sinking them into the nearest guard's leg. Another grabbed for the egg and I kicked him in the shins first, weaving around him.

There came a rumbling growl from above, and the guards

scattered as a gargoyle shifter came tumbling downstairs. He fell in a heap at my feet, and I gave him a swift kick in the crotch before he got up. Zeph appeared at the top of the stairs, slamming into another gargoyle and sending him crashing down to join his buddy. His nose was bleeding, there were scratches on his face, but he'd got out of the room without being impaled.

"Wanna come and lend a hand?" My claws sank into another guard from behind, and he went limp.

"Give that here, you little worm." A pair of rough hands snatched at the egg, seemingly unhurt by its protective spell.

I gripped the egg in both hands, caught in a tug-of-war. The new guard had the same appearance as the half-shifted dude from the arena. His hands were covered in rough leathery skin and while they weren't clawed, he was much stronger than I was. And why did the shielding spell hurt me and not him?

"Give it back." I tugged on the egg. "Why do you all look the same? Did someone with no imagination raid a Build A Villain Factory?"

The guard yanked the egg from my grip, and Zeph shouted a warning from above.

I jumped out of the way as two guards toppled downstairs, followed by Zeph himself. His white-blue claws were stained crimson and his eyes simmered with fire.

"Hand over the egg," he rumbled.

The remaining guard, seeing he was outnumbered, held the egg out. "Give it up. There's a dozen more guards outside the house, and I doubt you'll make it halfway home before the effects of the egg's shield paralyse you. It's up to you to decide whether it's worth the risk."

"What'd you put on it?" Not to say no to an opportunity, I reached for the egg again.

Zeph tackled me from behind, driving both of us to the

floor. Sharp metal bullets pinged off the walls. Someone was firing at us from the open door—and those weren't darts.

I know those bullets.

My body trembled beneath Zeph's, and for a brief moment, my legs went limp. Supernatural-killing bullets weren't supposed to exist anymore.

Zeph made a lunge for the egg, snapping me out of my shock. The guard caught his arm, twisting hard. Zeph roared in pain, and the two went down, grappling with one another. I needed to take out the person with the gun, otherwise one of us would die. But the egg—

A bullet clipped my sleeve and a frisson of alarm sparked inside me. Unlike the darts, there was no getting up from a shot from an anti-supernatural bullet.

Then a tremendous blast came from outside. Shouts of rage erupted, the bullets stopped, and the egg rolled to the floor where the guard had dropped it.

Gotcha.

I grabbed the egg and tucked it under my arm, running onto the doorstep. Two guards lay unconscious at the foot of the steps, but the guy in the house had been right—there were at least four cars parked outside, and more gargoyles behind the front gate. I cracked my knuckles, wondering how many darts I could take before I dropped stone dead.

"Get out," a voice hissed in my ear. Astor stood at a half-crouch in the shadows, and from his positioning, he'd been the one to knock out the guards who'd been shooting at me from the doorstep. "Now."

I shook my head, one foot on the doorstep. "I can't leave Zeph in there. Can you get the egg back to the house? The shield on it is designed to hurt dragon shifters, but you should be fine."

Astor grabbed the egg from me. "Don't get yourself killed in there. Your sister would have my head."

Two more guards burst through the gates, both armed. As their guns fired, I jumped off the doorstep, wishing they'd picked a place with a bigger garden. There was nowhere to hide in the front yard. Astor might have the egg, but he could die from one of those bullets, too.

They *shouldn't* exist anymore. I'd thought they'd died along with the Orion League.

Cold metal brushed against my neck, and I twisted around to see that bars had appeared in the doorway, blocking my path inside.

"Zeph!" I shouted.

I grabbed the bars, and an electric shock jolted through my nerves. My vision turned grey-blue, and I felt my knees hit the ground.

I screamed, kicking at the guard who held me. He was human. He shouldn't be able to hurt me like that, but the slightest touch of his thick gloves sent an electric shock through my entire body and left blisters on my hands.

Cold metal pressed to my spine. A click resounded in my ears, haunting me deep in my soul.

"Stop fighting, you little worm."

I screamed my sister's name.

Blackness claimed me.

Grey fog welcomed me into its depths. Faces flickered by, some familiar, some not, all floating towards a distant shape on the horizon... all floating through Death.

"No," I whispered. "I'm not ready... I can't die without seeing my sister again."

White light flared, blindingly bright. I heard Ember's voice. *"Wake up. Wake up, Cori."*

The light grew, overcoming everything, calling to the dragon within me.

Calling me back into the land of the living.

The light dimmed. Now it looked green, rather than white. My vision flickered, and a pair of hands appeared before me, bathed in green light. Not my sister.

I jerked upright, and Kit jumped, his hands still glowing with healing magic. "You're awake!"

"Good god, Cori," said Becks, who stood beside him. "I thought you were dying. What did they do to you? Your hands were a wreck."

"My hands?" My whole body felt like it'd been run over by a truck, but my hands were numb. I twitched my fingers, relieved when some sensation came back. "The egg burned me when I touched it. So did the bars on the door. I was trying to get to Zeph—"

Fear crashed over me again, and my heart kick-started. My captivity at the hands of the Orion League might have left no physical scars on me, but I'd never forget it. I'd never forget the way those guns had sounded, either. I heard the same clicking noise in my nightmares.

"The egg didn't hurt me when I picked it up," Becks said. "What did they do, make it dragon-proofed?"

"Something like that." I pushed into an upright position. "Did you get the egg home?"

Becks pointed to the spare armchair. The egg lay on its side, nestled in the cushions, and Kit moved to stand behind it.

"Thanks for getting me out of there," I said to Becks, since Astor didn't appear to be around.

"Sorry, Cori," Becks said, her mouth pinched. "Zeph was stuck behind those spikes they put in the doorway. They took him."

"Shit." I swung my legs over the sofa's side, my body shaking. "I can't leave him with them."

"A dozen more of their henchmen showed up when we were trying to get you out of there," Becks said. "Speaking of—why were there so many of them so weird-looking? You know what I mean. They looked like they got halfway through a shift and then stuck."

"Ugh, those guys," said Will's voice from the lab. "They do that on purpose, you know—take drugs to slow the shift down, then change forms really fast until they get stuck like that, in half-form. Supposedly, it's worth the downsides of no longer passing as human."

"Weirdos." I watched Kit pick up the egg and cradle it in his arms. "They didn't seem that keen to hang onto the egg, to be honest. They might have fought harder for it."

"The bright side is, we got it," said Becks. "The not-so-bright side is that whatever's inside it might try to eat us when it hatches."

"And on the extremely shitty side, we lost our ally." My head pounded when I thought of Zeph. I shouldn't have left him behind. The bars hadn't given me much of a choice, but those guards were armed with more than dart guns.

"They're not going to kill him, Cori," said Becks. "He's too valuable to them. Plus they have him as bait to lure you back to the house so you'll give up the egg."

"What makes you think they want the egg back?" I rubbed my forehead. "Maybe they wanted him all along. They need a fully mature dragon, apparently."

"Then why'd they try to kill you?" Becks said, frowning.

"*One* dragon," I emphasised. "Also, a *mature* one. Meaning one who can fully shift."

Her eyes sharpened with understanding. "Did he know that when he let himself get caught?"

"Haven't a clue." I glanced over to the sofa, where my

sister still lay unconscious. On top of our utter clusterfuck of a mission, Ember hadn't woken up yet either. Now I looked more closely around the room, I spotted Astor standing silently in a dark corner.

I swallowed hard. "They shot us with bullets. *Those* bullets."

Everyone tensed, except Astor, who avoided our eyes. We might have collectively forgiven him his history of working for the Orion League, but there was no erasing the past.

"I take it they missed?" Will said, breaking the silence. "I mean, you're not a ghost, so I'm guessing they did."

"Will, it isn't funny," Becks said. "Those bullets... damn. Are *they* Orion League soldiers? The Faulkners?"

"They can't be," I said. "They employ shifters, for one. All their guards are gargoyles. They're just as willing to kill humans as supernaturals. Look what they did to the hostel."

"Whoever makes those bullets is getting their funding from somewhere," Astor said, and this time, everyone did look at him. "You can ask, you know. No, I didn't know any of their weapons survived. I suspected they did, because the League didn't exist as long as it did without having a few contingency plans in motion. And of course, there will always be people who think they had the right idea."

"What, that shifters are vermin and should be exterminated?" Becks said tightly.

"They had a real hate-on for dragon shifters," I said. "So do the Faulkners, which is bizarre, considering they wouldn't know Zeph existed if he hadn't let himself get taken into the arena as bait."

"I think the lesson we can all learn from this is that dragons are about as subtle as a nuclear bomb," Will said.

"Damn right." Ember groaned. "What in the world is going on?"

I gasped, jumping to my feet. "Ember. Are you okay?"

"Ugh." She lifted her head. "I feel like I got hit by a truck."

"Join the club." I threw myself on her, prompting a pained grunt. "Don't do that to me again."

Astor's light footsteps sounded behind me, and I released Ember from my hug. She sat up, her auburn hair tumbling over her shoulders. "Hey, Astor. What did I miss?"

"Long story," I said. "Very long. You might want to grab a snack."

"God, I'm starving," Ember said, sitting upright. "Yeah, go on. Tell me what I missed this time. Aside from the egg hatching."

"You *what?*"

All eyes turned to the armchair, and Kit, who stood frozen beside it. Pieces of scale-like egg lay scattered on the carpet.

Then a small winged reptile shot at me, baring pointed teeth.

15

I yelped as the dragonling's teeth dug deep into the palm of my hand. "Ow!"

Ember wrapped both hands around the dragonling's scaled body. "Hang on, Cori, I've got you!"

She gave a firm tug and the dragon's teeth ripped free, taking a chunk of flesh with them. An impressive amount of blood fountained from the wound, and I leaned against the armchair, my head swimming.

Becks caught my arm to steady me. "Ember, you got it?"

"Just about." Ember held the little winged creature still enough for us to get a good look at it. Its tiny wings fanned out from its body, which was maybe the length of my forearm, and its grey-black eyes were huge and saucer-like. Pinkish red scales covered it from head to toe, and a tiny pair of horns crowned its head.

It would have been absolutely adorable if it didn't still have a chunk of my hand sticking out of its mouth.

"I think we answered the question of whether it eats other dragons." I held out my hand, which bled freely from several jagged holes. "Got a healing spell?"

Kit moved over to me, his hands glowing with green light. Healing magic enveloped my hand, closing the wounds. "Thanks, Kit. Either we need a cage or a muzzle. Or both."

"No," Kit protested. "That'll make it worse."

I looked at Ember, who held the wriggling dragonling in both hands. "Maybe he got freaked out because you smell like…" She trailed off, but I knew what she meant to say. I smelled like the Orion League. The stink of their dragon-proofed shield was all over my hands.

"Did you say 'he'?" I asked.

"Oh, he's definitely male," Ember said.

I wished my senses were as finely attuned. All I could smell was blood, and beneath that, the faint burning scent of a dragon.

The dragonling snapped his little teeth at Ember's face, forcing her to hold him at arm's length. "Relax. I might look human, but I'm a dragon, like you."

Astor moved towards her. "Careful with those teeth, Ember."

"At least they won't steal the egg back now," Will said. "Should we put an ad up asking if anyone's looking for a new reptilian housemate?"

"Yeah, we're not telling anyone," I said. "We can't let him roam free around the house. Imagine if he got his teeth into one of the neighbours?"

"If we cage him, he'll get pissed with us," Ember said, settling the dragonling in the crook of her arm. "There. I just startled him, right?"

The dragon's bloody teeth tore at her sleeve, and he kicked off, wings beating.

"Oh, and he knows how to fly," I said. "How did the egg hatch so bloody quickly?"

"He was ready," Kit said. "I thought so, when I first felt the egg."

Ember jumped to catch the dragon's tail and missed. "Jesus. How long was I out for?"

"A day and a half." I made a grab for the dragonling. His teeth snapped at my outstretched fingers, and I yanked my hand away before he did me another injury. "You were dying. Astor barely got the antidote to you on time."

"You did?" She turned to Astor. "How did you know where to find it?"

"Your sister," Astor answered. "She found the address of the witch supplying the Faulkners with spells, so I went after him while your sister risked her neck hunting gargoyle mobsters."

"Astor!" I grabbed the dragonling's tail. "Way to tell tales on me."

"She did *what?*" Ember said.

I tugged the little dragonling gently by the tail, trying to guide him into my hands. He squirmed and made another attempt to chew my fingers. "Hey, I'm safe. Calm down."

"Orion League?" Ember said, her eyes widening. "Not them."

"It isn't, but they're using the same weapons." I struggled to get a grip on the squirming dragonling. "The Faulkners. They're involved in 'convincing' shifters to fight in the arena for rare artefacts."

"They stole the egg?" She moved to help me with the dragonling and got a set of teeth buried in her upper arm for her trouble. "Ow!"

I lifted the struggling dragonling out of reach before he bit any deeper. "We've been chasing them around for two days. Got the egg, but they captured Zeph."

"Zeph?"

"Another dragon shifter."

The dragon broke free and took flight again, pulling a chunk of my hair out in the process. Will threw a spell at him, but the trapping spell hit the floor instead, thin red lines appearing on the carpet.

"Don't trap him!" yelled Kit.

"If we don't, he'll figure out how to get outside." Becks shifted into a cat, letting out a challenging yowl.

The dragonling dove at her, and Becks ran at the trapping spell, veering to the side at the last second. The dragon didn't stop in time. He landed in the prison of red lines in a tangle of limbs.

Becks turned human again. "Thought he'd fall for that one. Now, we have to release him into the wild."

"What, through the mirror?" Ember turned to me. "Did you decide on a plan?"

"We've spent too long trying to get the egg back to have time to discuss it," I admitted. "Also, if we go through the mirror, we don't want him attacking anyone in the village."

"It's the only way," Astor said. "The dragon will be safe, and so will everyone else."

"Except Zeph," I reminded him. "I'm not dumping anything on the other dragon shifters without warning them first."

"I'll speak to them," Ember said. "What time is it?"

"Five in the evening," said Will. "Ember, I'm glad you can stand, but you shouldn't be doing anything too strenuous. You're lucky to be alive."

"For once, I agree with your friend," Astor said.

Lucky to be alive. Like me, she'd danced on the edge of death. Had she gone close enough to see the ghosts in the fog and hear them whisper her name?

"I'm fine now," Ember insisted. "Takes more than a few gargoyles to keep me down. They stole the egg when they attacked me, right? When did this other dragon shifter show up?"

"He was after the egg, too," I explained. "To get it away

from the Faulkners. He warned us those dragonlings are lethal. He compared them to baby dinosaurs."

"A… baby dinosaur?" Ember looked at the little creature lying in the trapping spell. The dragonling bared his teeth at her.

"Yes, and I believe him," Becks said. "We need to get it out of the city. Then we deal with the gargoyle mobsters who know our address and want us dead."

"They want us dead but the dragonling alive?" Ember frowned. "Why?"

"They claimed to need a dragon shifter," I said. "And now they have Zeph. He pulled off a full shift and breathed fire in the middle of their hideout and it still didn't burn down."

Ember went white. "No. That's not possible. Even the League's headquarters went down when I burned it."

"They built that place like a cage—for us," I said, my skin crawling. "Worse, it's right next to mage territory."

Astor made a sceptical noise. "It's possible the Mage Lords looked the other way. They don't value shifters highly."

"No, they don't," said Becks. "I think it's safe to say *they* won't take our little fanged beast off our hands. More like arrest us for holding an illegal magical creature on our property."

I grimaced. "I'm starting to think we should have let it eat the Faulkners. Zeph, though, he said a dragonling would cause a massacre if left to its own devices in London. In six months, they can grow big enough to swallow a person whole. And they're not domesticated."

"I don't see why not." Kit walked towards the trapping spell. "He's never met a person before. We can tame him."

"He's not a dragon shifter, Kit," Will said. "This isn't gonna work. Ember and Cori can set him free in the wild and that'll be the end of it."

I doubt it'll be that simple. There remained the lingering question of how the egg had wound up in the city to begin with, not to mention the anonymous note.

I walked to Kit's side, crouching down to look at the little dragonling. Including the tail, he'd be as long as my forearm, and indistinguishable from a dragon shifter if he grew to our size. But even my blurred childhood memories showed me nothing about other types of dragons. How could I never have heard of their existence before?

I picked up a fragment of the egg where it'd fallen onto the carpet and shifted my right hand to a claw to compare it to the scales on my arm. The dragonling itself was pale pinkish red, but the egg was the same colour as my own scales and the texture was the same.

Ember gasped. "Cori—your hands shifted?"

"Yeah." I turned my newly formed claw over, smiling. "Not a full shift yet… is that likely?" *Please say yes.* At this rate, we'd have to fly the dragonling out of London ourselves.

"Maybe." Ember approached me, her hands shifting to claws. They were the same colour as mine. When I shifted, I'd look like a smaller version of her. Apparently, the younger sibling thing would continue even when I was in the form of a giant fire-breathing beast. "Was it… was it a life or death situation? That's how my first shift was."

The image of the pavement rushing towards me filled my head. "Yeah, it was. Good job my survival instincts kicked in."

Ember picked up a piece of the egg, then tossed it aside. "I don't like that you had to risk your life for the egg. You shouldn't have—"

"I wasn't alone," I said. "Zeph… he wasn't that friendly when we first met, but that's because I accidentally sabotaged his plan to get rid of the egg on his own terms."

"So he knew?" she asked. "Where's he from, do you know?"

"Not London." I ran my thumb over the egg fragment in

my claw, turning it back to a human hand again. "His people were killed by them. The League."

Ember stiffened. "That explains why he was alone."

"Yeah. I trust his expertise on the dragonling issue, but—"

"It's loose!" Becks yelped.

The dragonling tilted his head upright, apparently realising the trapping spell had worn out. Oh, hell.

"Get another one," I mouthed, shuffling behind the little dragon. "Easy... don't startle. It's just me."

The dragon jumped into the air like a bullet from a cannon and zipped through the room, crashing headlong into the wall. I winced at the impact, but the small creature shook it off and flipped over in mid-air, his thin leathery wings pumping frantically.

"Come here." Ember crouched down, hands outstretched. "Come to us. We won't hurt you."

The dragonling dove to the floor, landing on his clawed feet. The claws were too small to do any significant damage, but if he grew any bigger, we'd have to worry about those as well as the teeth. He inched along the carpet, long tail swaying, wings bunching against his back.

"I think he's learning to walk," I said. "Like a human toddler."

"A slightly more bitey human toddler," Will said. "Watch it..."

The dragonling took a snap at Ember, who moved her fingers backwards, shifting them to claws. Twitching his head, he sniffed at her scaly hand. Ember held still, and so did I.

Then the dragonling ran right into Kit's arms.

The half-faerie froze in disbelief as the dragonling climbed *onto* his arm. Will took a step forwards, but the dragonling didn't move.

Kit looked utterly delighted. "I think he heard me talking to him from the egg."

"Kit," said Will. "Please put the miniature murder dragon down before it gnaws off your arm."

"He's not going to eat me," Kit insisted. The dragonling batted at his arm with his little scaled hands, making an odd crooning noise. "He was just startled. There are a lot of us and you're all too loud."

Ember rose to her feet. "Are you saying he wants to meet one of us at a time?"

"Maybe," Kit said. "He's just learning to experience the world. Be nice."

"I was trying," I protested, looking at my newly healed hand. "How do we get him to trust us when people want to kidnap him?"

Kit lifted his arm to let the dragonling climb over his shoulders. "I don't know. But he likes me."

Will moved forwards, his expression conflicted. "All right, we'll do this slowly. But please don't let him into the shelter. I don't want him attacking any of the others."

"Do they know?" asked Ember.

"The Faulkners were hiding in the shelter when they took the egg." The dragonling tensed at the ex-assassin's voice, to no surprise. Astor terrified most people he met, and animals generally didn't like him a bit. "On that note—have you closed the place?"

"I've had to close both the shop and the shelter, yes," Will said. "It's not a permanent solution. Our funding isn't infinite, and for all we know, an acquaintance might decide we're worth the bounty that'll inevitably end up on our heads when someone finds out we have the egg."

"Are you sure that hasn't already happened?" Astor said.

"Knowing our luck, it has," said Becks. "We'll get rid of it, right, Cori?"

"We're taking him through the mirror," I said. "Ember, you know we can't keep him here. I don't think they could have known the egg was *that* close to hatching, but still."

"Maybe they did," said Ember. "Maybe they needed a murderous baby dragon for their own purposes."

I thought of the dragon-proofed darts, my throat tightening. They hadn't existed when we'd fought the Orion League before. Who was still manufacturing ways to hurt us, and why? And how had the dragon eggs ended up in the city to begin with?

Kit folded his arms protectively over the dragonling. "You can't let them get hold of him again!"

"We won't," I said. "But we *will* consult with the other dragon shifters. This affects them, too, and they deserve to know."

"Right." Ember gave a short nod. "But—does Zeph know them?"

"No. He doesn't." I heaved a sigh. "I can't leave him to the Faulkners' mercy. I just wish I knew how to deal with their dragon-proofed defences."

"Maybe the other dragons have encountered them before," Ember said. "It can't all be new. They'd need someone—a dragon—to test them on."

Silence fell, and I knew both of us were thinking of the older dragon who'd been the Orion League's captive at the same time as I had. Unlike me, he'd never made it out.

They survived. I can't believe they survived.

The League had experimented on us, treated us as expendable lab rats in a bid to exterminate our species. And, like ghosts, they'd never truly left.

16

Half an hour and a bite to eat later, Ember and I left the others trying to figure out what to feed the dragonling that wasn't one of our fingers and walked down to the basement.

The mirror leaned against the back wall, shimmering with a silvery white sheen. I hadn't told Zeph about it, not that I'd had many chances. The mirror was our secret, and the other dragon shifters' lives depended on us keeping it hidden from the rest of the world.

"Are you sure you want to come?" Ember walked up to the mirror. "You've had a tough day already."

"You nearly died as well," I pointed out. "You can't babysit me every moment, and the shift was bound to happen eventually. The amount of trouble we attract, it was inevitable."

"I'm not at all comfortable that the package was addressed to you to begin with," Ember said, concern wrinkling her brow.

"Then I should have taken it to the post office with its envelope labelled 'return to sender'." I rolled my eyes at my older sister. "No matter what, it's done."

I splayed my hands against the mirror and touched it with my fingertips, causing ripples to spread across its surface. Only a dragon shifter could activate the portal, but once they did, anyone could use it. For that reason, we told nobody about the mirror outside of our small group of trusted allies. The mirror's light grew brighter, and as Ember and I walked into the white haze, it turned to grey fog.

I shivered, drawing my coat tighter over my T-shirt and wishing I'd picked something warmer. I'd forgotten how cold Scotland was at this time of year. I'd also forgotten how much the fog looked like the realm of Death. Not really what I wanted to see after almost revisiting my trip over to the other side.

The fog cleared, revealing the walls of a small basement. Water dripped from the low ceiling courtesy of a leak that had never been fixed. Ember led the way up the small staircase and opened the trapdoor into the hall. Cold air blew in, and even my naturally warm body temperature couldn't keep out the chill. Ember knocked on a wooden door on our right. The quietness suggested Azalea's two children weren't at home.

Ember pushed the door inwards. Azalea stood beside the large wooden desk of her office, looking out of the window into the night. "Oh. Ember. I didn't hear you come in."

She must have been lost in thought, because the two of us were not masters of stealth.

"Hey, Azalea," said Ember. The room was small and draughty, filled with old wooden bookcases and shelves. "Sorry to bother you so late."

Azalea swept her long auburn curls over her shoulder. They seemed to contain more grey strands each time we'd visited over the last five years. Azalea had known the two of us as children, but my memories of the earliest years of my life were blurred by time and the lingering effects of the memory spell. I'd hoped that maintaining contact with her would re-establish our connection with our fellow dragon shifters, but Lorne's rule had crushed the villagers' fighting spirit. Despite that, more left the village each day. Others died, of diseases or in fights with wild fae. Yet despite my continuing offer to help them move to London, Azalea seemed determined that she and her family would remain in the village for the rest of their lives.

"It's good to see you, Cori," she said to me. "What can I do for you two tonight?"

"We need advice, if it's okay," Ember said.

I closed the door behind me and took a seat beside my sister in one of the rickety old chairs. Azalea, meanwhile, moved to the sideboard and began taking mugs out of a cupboard.

"I'm not sure I can be much help," she said, an apology in her tone. "You'll have to forgive me. I've had a lot to handle this week."

"If it's too much trouble, we can leave," I said. "Just one thing—have you ever heard of wild dragons making a comeback? I mean, actual dragons. Not shifters."

"Wild dragons?" She turned around with the kettle in one hand. "No... if they ever existed, they've never been seen in my lifetime."

Her words were sincere. She had no reason to lie to us. "Would anyone in the village remember them?"

Her expression clouded. "No. Most of the elders left us a long time ago."

She poured boiling water into mugs with shaking hands, and Ember hastened to help her.

"We... er, came across a dragon egg recently," I said. "And it hatched."

Azalea froze, a mug in each hand. "You obtained a wild dragon egg? How?"

"Someone sent it to me in the post." I shivered as a gust of wind swept through the room from a crack somewhere in the walls.

"An anonymous sender," Ember added, carrying two mugs over to me. I took one of them when she offered, though I wasn't particularly keen on tea. "We don't know who might have sent it."

Azalea took the remaining chair and sat down. "Are you sure it was a dragon?"

"He looks like a miniature version of a dragon shifter," I said. "I met another dragon shifter who knew they existed, too. A rogue, from Yorkshire."

"Really?" Azalea blew on her tea to cool it, her hands trembling a little. "A rogue from outside the village? I didn't think any..."

"Still existed?" I finished. "He's called Zeph, and he's about my age. Is that... common? I mean, might there be others still out there?"

"Very few," she said. "You'll have to ask him for his specific circumstances. But there's never been anyone called Zeph living here, to my knowledge. If you bring him here, we might be able to ask around."

Weird. Or maybe not. According to Astor, the Orion League had been exterminating rogue dragons for longer than a decade. Some would have left Scotland before the war started sixteen years ago. And the League hadn't just hunted dragons here. They'd tried to wipe us out everywhere we existed.

"Slight problem," I said. "He got kidnapped. We got on the bad side of a group of mobsters. They have... they have equipment designed specifically to target dragon shifters."

I didn't mention the League, but I knew her thoughts had immediately gone there from the tense set of her shoulders, and the brief look of a cornered animal in her ashy grey eyes.

"I'm sorry we brought it up," Ember said, "but I have to know... have you ever encountered poison that only affects dragons before? They used it on me. I nearly died. It was a witch's creation."

Azalea was silent for a long moment. Her grip on her mug tightened until scales briefly appeared on her hands, and her eyes darted around the room as though to avoid looking at us in the eyes. "The League captured witches, as well as shifters. They took them from the supernatural community here in Scotland. I... I heard reports from some of the people who were lucky enough to escape."

"Escaped?" My blood chilled. *That could have been me.* Almost had been, too. The reason it wasn't sat on my right-hand side, fidgeting. Ember had saved my life in so many ways.

"It was a long time ago." Her voice was a whisper. "Before the League permanently relocated to London. They made their first base here in Scotland, hidden in the middle of the Highlands. Few people remember those days, but it was before the dragon clan war."

Before our parents had died. "Would Agnes know?"

"Perhaps."

Ember frowned sideways at me. Agnes was an old witch who lived in a nearby village—and also happened to be the person who'd put the memory-wipe spell on both of us. Maybe she also knew about wild dragons, but if the other shifters didn't, perhaps not.

"So the League hunted you before the war," Ember said, turning back to Azalea. "Why not relocate elsewhere?"

"We tried. Lorne hunted us anyway." Her hands clenched at her sides. "The League's intention was for us to destroy one another, and for all intents and purposes, they were successful."

It wasn't worth arguing with her, but Azalea's expression

of resignation made my chest tighten. The League might not have won the war, but they'd lived on, while we were broken and scattered.

But not beaten.

I'll get Zeph back. And I'll set all their dragon-proofed shields ablaze.

"Right." Ember stood, putting her mug down. "Thanks for your help. We should get going."

I knew what she'd concluded. We had no right to bring our drama through the mirror and disrupt everyone's lives. Baby dragonlings included. Let's face it, I hadn't wanted the egg to show up on my doorstep either. But here we were.

"Yeah, thank you." I put down my mug, too. "We appreciate you making us welcome here."

I caught the shimmer of fire in Ember's eyes before she left the room, and hurried after her, sensing her temper rising. Something had ticked her off. Azalea's defeated tone, perhaps. I understood it too well. Lorne, and the Orion League, had wiped out over ninety per cent of Scotland's dragon shifters—and more, if what they'd done to Zeph's village was commonplace. If the hunters had survived in London, we had to destroy them.

Ember reached the mirror first, marching through its surface. A moment later, warmth flooded me, the warmth of a magically heated house.

"Hang on." I caught Ember's arm before she stormed out of the basement. "Don't run off."

Ember turned to me, her grey eyes simmering. "They've given up."

"I know, but *you* know why."

She blew out a breath. "We can't let the League rise again, Cori. I promised. If they do, we have to fight, because there's no alternative. If we don't, they win."

And with that, she raced up the stairs into the hall. I

climbed after her, wondering if Ember's two-day coma had driven her over the edge. If we weren't careful, there'd be an angry dragon spewing flames all over London... which wouldn't help get Zeph back.

"Ember!" I said. "At least tell me your plan."

She turned around, the flames in her eyes shining in the dark hallway. "My plan starts with burning the Faulkners' house to the ground."

"It's dragon-proofed. Also, Zeph might not even be there anymore." If they expected an attack, they might have found another safe house.

She let out an impatient snarl. "This has the League's ugly fingerprints all over it. Just look what they did to the villagers. They've given up."

"I never said *I* gave up," I said. "So please don't leave me behind."

The fire in her eyes dimmed a little. "They nearly killed you, Cori. They know your face, more than they know mine."

"Ember, our faces look almost the same. Anyone can tell we're related. Besides, you were on the cover of all the local newspapers five years ago. If anything, you're more recognisable as a dragon than a human."

"Are you sure this Zeph is trustworthy, then?" she asked. "If we put our necks on the line for his sake and he doublecrosses us, then we're fucked."

"He won't betray us," I said. "He's a dragon shifter."

"So was Lorne."

The name lingered between us, like a third person. A ghost.

"You mean, so *is* Lorne," I said. Much as I wished it were otherwise.

"We should have killed him," Ember said, echoing my thoughts.

"Not our call." The Mage Lords forbade murder except in

the case of war and self-defence, and neither of us had expected Lorne to get up after Ember had skewered him. He'd woken up in a cell, and while I didn't see what he had to gain from setting dragonling eggs loose in the city, he was bound to be nursing one hell of a grudge against us.

She exhaled in a sigh. "If you say Zeph is trustworthy, then I believe you. But it can't be a simple coincidence that he and the dragon egg—*and* the League's successors— showed up at the same time."

"Yeah, his involvement isn't accidental," I acknowledged. "He's no villain, but I'm not sure he told the whole truth about how he found out the egg existed. I'll say that much."

How was it possible that Scotland's dragon shifters hadn't heard of any surviving wild dragons? They'd lived there long before the faerie invasion, for decades if not centuries. I had one theory, but until we spoke to Zeph again, that's all it was: a theory.

I led the way back into the main room, where Will stood laying out spells on the kitchen table, as far from the dragonling as possible. Becks curled up on one side of the sofa, while Astor sat on the other side, polishing a knife. He stood up the instant Ember and I entered.

"No trouble?"

"Nope." My gaze went to the armchair, where Kit lay fast asleep with a restless-looking dragonling crawling all over his face in an apparent attempt to wake him up. "Not much luck, either, though. Would you believe they've never even heard of the dragonlings?"

"Other than that, they're utterly defeated," Ember crossed the room to the sofa and perched on the arm beside Astor. "How's the little terror getting along, then?"

"He *ate* the birdcage I found in the attic," Will said, holding out his arm as though to show us a non-existent scar. "Took a few pieces out of me as well. And I'm out of healing spells, so I'm refreshing our stocks. I think that little bastard could chew through brick if the mood took him. Not sure you'll be able to safely get him through the mirror, to be honest."

"Unless you knock him out first." Becks yawned and stretched, awakening from her cat nap. "Are you sure the other dragons are just pretending so they don't end up with a wild animal on their hands?"

"No, they're not lying," Ember said. "But someone in London is."

"Your friend." Astor cut his gaze to me.

"He's not out to get us," I said. "He got himself locked in a dragon-proofed house filled with Orion League bullets for our sakes."

"To get hold of that egg," Astor added. "Ember, I know you're worried about the other dragon shifters, but I think that dragon will like the taste of freedom more than their fingers. It doesn't matter if it hunts the faerie monsters living in the Highlands."

"Armies of fae monsters will flee in fear," said Will, scowling at the little dragonling. It was a testament to how heavily faeries slept that Kit didn't wake up even with claws digging into his forehead.

"Zeph first," I said. "I think I know what they're planning to do with him. He was a big hit in the arena the first time around."

"You think they'll show themselves in public?" Becks said.

"Even if not, they won't waste their prize. And I'll be there to take him off their hands." I flexed my claws. "We're going back to the arena."

17

Ember was not a big fan of my plan, to no surprise.

"They know your face," she said.

"The Faulkners do. The others at the arena don't. We were hidden when we smuggled Zeph out the first time."

"And they'll expect you to do it again."

"I know," I said. "But they have Zeph, and I don't know how long he has before they'll decide they don't need him anymore. And what if they decide they want you instead? They specifically said *one* mature dragon shifter."

"Then I'll fight them."

"Ember, you won't be able to shift inside the arena." I'd rather she didn't put herself at risk so soon after her narrow escape from death by poisoning, but Will had already brewed up more of the antidote. This time, we were prepared.

She swore. "You're right, but I don't have to like my baby sister risking her neck. Will you at least use an illusion spell?"

"It'll break the instant my claws come out." But she had a point. There were plenty of cat shifters in the arena. Not so many women with bright red hair and hands that turned into scaled claws whenever I got mad. Claws or not, I was under no delusions that I wouldn't be fighting my way out of there this time. "I'm sure Zeph will be there. If he's not dead, they'll be getting some leverage out of him one way or another."

I was through letting them terrorise other shifters.

We'd give them the same warm welcome we gave the Orion League.

Our group set off under cover of darkness. Becks and I went first, while Ember and Astor would follow later.

Becks scouted ahead for obstacles and waited for me down the road from the ticket booth.

"I heard the Faulkners mentioned, but not Zeph," she said. "They're right on the balcony, apparently."

"Guess they're not that concerned about being targeted by a bomb." Which supported the theory that they'd been responsible for both attacks. "Maybe they have Zeph locked up backstage with those dickhead guards."

This time they'd get worse than an itching spell or two.

"Speaking of guards," Becks said. "You know those dragon-proofed suits they were wearing at the house? They wore the same ones at the arena."

"Shit. Forgot about those." If they wore those, then Zeph would be unable to fight them off without risking injury. "Bastards. I wish we could clue the Mage Lords in."

"They won't do anything," Becks said, her hands clenched at her sides. "They must know about the arena, but as long as it doesn't cross into their territory, they don't care."

"Then we'll make them care," I said. "Since the Faulkners showed up in person, it's safe to say they don't expect to be challenged." Their resources were on a level with the Orion

League's—and even the mages hadn't been able to bring down the League without help.

Once again, Becks shifted into cat form and walked at my feet, her amber eyes alert for threats. I yanked my hood up and approached the gargoyle shifter at the booth.

"You again?" he said. "Going to tell me what you are this time?"

"Maybe you'll be lucky and hear about it later." I meant it, too. I didn't expect tonight to go without a hitch, the least of which would be the exposure of my dragon shifter status.

"Have it your way," he said. "Got a taste of the action and wanted more, did you? Fair warning, there's a limit on ticket numbers tonight and the matches start at nine, on the dot. And the doors will stay closed until twelve, so no leaving until then."

Damn. They must have wanted to ensure there wouldn't be a repeat of last time. At least he didn't seem to suspect I'd been involved with Zeph's escape the other night.

This time, the rat shifter was already waiting for us when we reached Leicester Square.

"You again," he said. "And the cat, too. I hope it wasn't you I saw sneaking around the arena half an hour ago."

"There's a lot of cat shifters in there," I said.

He grunted. "There'll be no sneaking in and out tonight. Our sponsors warded the place."

Warded. Bugger. What kind of ward? It couldn't be the magic-proofed sort that the mages used on the outside of their buildings. Those were way too expensive to waste on the arena, even for the Faulkners, and wouldn't do much to prevent anyone from using spells on one another *inside* the theatre.

Witch magic was Will's area, not mine, so I shelved the matter in the back of my head and made my way towards the abandoned theatre. Warded or not, if I backed out now, Zeph might die.

Becks slunk ahead of me downstairs, her lithe cat form disappearing among the rows of seats. The theatre seemed more crowded than last time, with twice the volume of shifter guards as before. Did they have a factory pumping these guys out, or did they just employ London's entire gargoyle population?

I scanned the packed crowd for an available seat and found myself nose to nose with a ghost. "You said you'd help me!"

I stiffened. It was the same guy as last time, and he appeared clearer than before, less transparent. Ghosts were supposed to lose their strength with every day they lingered, unless they'd been necromancers when they were still alive. *What's he still doing here?*

"Sorry, now isn't a good time." I lowered my head and scanned the rows for a free seat, hoping nobody had seen me speaking to thin air.

"You *promised*," he said, his face crumpling. "Please. I've been stuck in here ever since their dragon killed me."

I drew to a halt. Turned to him. *"Who killed you?"*

A dragon? Not Zeph. He hadn't been here before the other night, right? But if not... then that meant he wasn't the first dragon shifter they'd captured.

"Their dragon," the ghost said. "They set him loose on me because they didn't like how I beat their candidate."

"By dragon," I said, my voice low, "do you mean a person? A shifter?"

His brows rose. "A shifter? You're not..." He faded out, disappearing from sight.

I swore and stepped towards the spot where he'd vanished. Becks blocked my path. "Don't tell me you're seeing dead people again."

"Uh-huh." They'd had more than one dragon? "Have you seen Zeph?"

"No, I haven't. Please stop talking to people who aren't here. Those guards aren't playing nice today."

I followed her gaze and saw two guards dragging a struggling fox shifter out of the doors. When one of them glanced my way, I ducked my head. Hoping my hood hadn't slipped, I climbed to the balcony and found a spare seat. The Faulkners weren't in the shadowy alcove they'd been lurking in before—instead, they were right next to the rat shifter at the very front.

The two men both wore confident smiles that made my skin crawl. After the robbery and the attempt on their lives—to say nothing of the pile of bodies Zeph and I had left behind—one might assume they'd think twice before showing their faces in public. I was more certain than ever that their lives had never been in any real danger. Not that anyone else in the room would know that.

The rest of the crowd showed no signs of apprehension. The air was thick with tension, and a number of fights and arguments were in progress. As I passed the back row, I spotted two gargoyles who I'd thought were fighting until I saw they were entwined in a position that wouldn't have looked out of place in one of Jake's erotic magazines. *Ew. At least take it outside.*

Becks moved among the crowd in cat form, sniffing for danger, while I took the closest seat to the Faulkners that I dared, and eavesdropped on the shifters around me until I heard the word *Faulkner* from further down the row.

"Did you hear they survived the bombing?" whispered a burly fox shifter. "Lucky bastards. Some say they walked out of there without a scratch on them."

"Like hell they did. They were never there," growled a second voice that put me in mind of a wolf shifter.

"They're here *now*. Reckon they brought another dragon egg?"

"I heard Vaughn brought one to bet on the third match."

"He's lying."

"Probably, but someone will be thick enough to fall for it."

Damn. It looked like at least one of my suspicions was right—the Faulkners' stunt had provoked a few imitators. I'd bet *their* dragon eggs weren't the real deal, but it wasn't hard to find gullible people to trick. Like little old ladies with record players.

The arena seemed colder than before, and considering my warmer body temperature, that was saying something. I shivered, fidgeting in my seat. By now, the theatre was packed, guards standing in the aisles at intervals, particularly near the Faulkners. Confident though they might be, they'd still brought protection.

I sat up sharply when the rat shifter's microphone clicked on, sending a wave of static through the arena.

"We have some very special matches tonight," he said in his raspy voice. "Seems the *events* the other night sparked rather a frenzy behind the scenes, and there a number of rare artefacts on offer. I never knew there were so many dragon eggs in London."

Cheers and shouts filled the arena. My theory that the Faulkner had staged the dragon egg scenario to whip everyone into a frenzy was dead on target, then. And if they kept hopping between hotels, pretending to leave town and hiding their possessions at empty houses, they'd be able to sell off both real and fake eggs with zero risk to their own lives.

"The esteemed Mr Bryan Faulkner has claimed the first match," the rat shifter went on. "After the popularity of the last one."

Damn. Well, at least I wouldn't have to wait all night.

Blue-white light flickered in the corner of my eye and the ghost reappeared in the aisle. I twitched my numb hands, trying to ignore him. As a hush fell over the crowd, he floated closer.

And he wasn't alone. Other ghosts drifted through the theatre, transparent people surrounded by a haze of grey. Why had my spirit sight chosen *now* to switch on? The entire arena was bathed in grey fog, like someone had set off a smokescreen spell. Transparent overlapping forms covered the whole arena, so many that it seemed impossible that nobody else could see them.

Wait. The arena must be right on top of a spirit hotspot, a key point where two of the spirit lines that divided the living world from the land of the dead overlapped. But it hadn't been obvious at all the last time I'd been here. Something had changed, something that chilled the air and brought me out in shivers. The shifters on either side of me were shivering, too. The theatre wasn't just haunted, it was the stage for a full-on séance visible to me alone. While the crowd appeared restless and uncomfortable, none of them appeared to be aware of the exclusive ghost-only party taking place on top of them.

A key point was where I'd died, ripped out of my body and dragged into the afterlife.

How many people had died in here? And why were they hovering so close to the waking world?

Cold sweat gathered on the back of my neck, my hands numbed, and it took me a full minute to notice the Faulkners were no longer on the balcony. Bryan Faulkner walked *onto* the stage, revealing himself for the entire arena to see.

I looked past the ghosts, pushed the grey fog aside. My hands gripped the edge of my seat, threatening to turn into claws. *Don't blow your cover, Cori.*

Murmurs rippled through the crowd. I tensed, waiting for

him to catch my eye. But he didn't. His gaze passed right over the balcony, skipping past the spot where I sat. I might not be under a spotlight, but I wasn't invisible. *What're you playing at?*

Tension burned in the air. My hand begged to close around his neck, and I felt my claws dig into the seat, gouging holes into the soft padding. I tried to steady my breathing, but calming a dragon shifter down was like waving a piece of cardboard over a fire.

"Greetings," said Bryan, into his microphone. "Some of you will have met me before, but I thought I'd introduce myself properly before tonight's matches."

Damn him. Just in case anyone had any doubts who was really running the show here. If anyone had been living under a rock for the last two days and had somehow missed the dragon egg showdown.

"I'll be sponsoring the first match," he went on. "I have a new candidate *dying* to prove his worth against a worthy adversary."

My heart kick-started. *They didn't. Did they?*

This time when Zeph walked onto the stage, he wasn't bound or bloody. If anything, he looked in better shape than the last time I'd seen him. He wore dark jeans and a plain t-shirt, not in the least bit torn or damaged. His auburn hair gleamed, catching the light. His gaze appeared to be fixed at some point in the distance and he didn't look at me.

Zeph would never agree to fight for them even if he was cornered. He'd die first. *What did they do to him?*

"And my opponent…" Bryan gestured, and his bald, squat partner walked onto the stage from the opposite side.

"I thought we'd make it interesting," said Logan Faulkner, his voice echoing through his own microphone. "Brother against brother. Champion against champion. My candidate…"

A huge shifter walked onstage. He made even the guards look like small children. Either he had some troll or giant blood somewhere, or he'd used a growth spell, because he barely fit under the low ceiling. Seven feet tall, at least, and heavily muscled. Zeph was no piskie, but he appeared diminished next to his opponent. The guy's hands looked strong enough to crush someone's skull.

"And as for what we'll be fighting for?" Bryan gave a wide smile. "I thought I'd make things interesting and wager this very rare device."

"The winner gets to keep it," added Logan. "No hard feelings, brother, but my candidate will win."

With a flourish, Bryan held up the record player I'd confiscated from Mrs Tibbs.

Damn them. I should have guessed they'd been behind that fiasco, too. Everything was a game to them. Someone at Darcy's place had sold us out, for sure, but who even cared at this point?

The record player was a dangerous magical device that could suck out a person's soul with one hit of a button, according to the report Darcy had given me. It seemed surreal that only a few short days had passed since I'd hauled in the banshee.

In the aisles, guards blocked every possible way out. There were easily two hundred shifters trapped in this room... and twice as many ghosts.

"Look at that," said the rat shifter's raspy voice into his microphone. "I think the rest of our candidates will find it hard to beat *this* for a starter. A dragon shifter against a gargoyle-troll hybrid?"

The guy really was part troll? No wonder he was so huge. Zeph might be a dragon, but the rules stated no shifting, and disobeying them might cost his life. Trolls had notoriously tough skin, not to mention skulls as thick as rocks. *It's not a fair fight. Not at all.*

Wearing identical grins, the two Faulkners moved to opposite sides of the stage, leaving the path open for their candidates to face off against one another. Zeph still hadn't looked my way. Either he didn't expect to see me in the audience, or they'd done more than heal his injuries.

A cold, hard hand clenched around my heart. I might have slept through the majority of my imprisonment at the Orion League's hands, but my sister had filled me in on the nightmares she and the others had faced while trying to break me out. Shifters bred to kill and controlled against their will. If the League could knock a shifter into an endless sleep, they could certainly turn one into a willing puppet.

Dammit, Zeph, snap out of it.

The crowd roared, feet pounding on the floors and shaking the whole theatre as the match prepared to start.

I couldn't stay out of reach while Zeph fought for his life. I got to my feet and slipped down the stairs, ducking into the back row before one of the guards spotted me. The noise was worse on the lower level, and the stomping feet and roaring sent my extra-sensitive shifter senses haywire. They were working themselves into such a frenzy, half of them would accidentally shift by the night's end and would forget *why* they were so worked up. There'd be a bloodbath.

The sound of the bell was lost in the crowd's roar, and the two shifters collided like high-speed trains.

18

The force of the shifters' collision shook the floor, jolting the entire arena. I clenched my teeth tight to keep from biting my tongue, my hands ready at my sides. If I brought out my claws, nobody would notice. All eyes were on the stage.

The troll-shifter swung a meaty fist and overbalanced as Zeph stepped aside, retaliating with a strike to the jaw. The troll roared, swaying, his misshapen face even more crooked with a broken jaw. I gave Zeph a silent cheer, then winced when the troll shifter rammed a fist into his opponent's solar plexus. Zeph staggered backwards, winded, and the troll swung his other fist. Zeph dodged, catching the troll's arm and pulling him off balance.

Zeph moved faster, but in sheer brute force, the other shifter had him outclassed. Half his blows didn't seem to cause his opponent any pain, while each strike bloodied Zeph a little more. Before long, his nose was streaming with blood, his knuckles were scraped raw, and multiple cuts lacerated his muscular arms.

Little by little, the troll was wearing him down.

The match wouldn't end until someone gave in, and a dragon shifter's stubbornness easily matched a troll's inability to judge when to quit. Odds were, someone was going to die regardless of the rules.

I had to do something. I glanced to the side, but the guards were the only people not looking at the stage, their sharp eyes daring anyone to try to leave. I slipped around the shifter next to me and climbed over the seat in front, ducking to avoid being elbowed by a gargoyle. I edged around two cheering fox shifters and climbed to the next row.

Becks clambered over the seat behind me and shifted to human at my side. "So much for stealth," she said into my ear. "I could transform into a giant pink mushroom and most of them wouldn't notice."

"The guards would." They also appeared to be immune to the frenzy sweeping the room, which suggested a level of self-control far beyond most shifters. Shifter rage was contagious. Some called it the full moon effect. One person got mad, everyone else in the vicinity did, and the next thing you knew, a full-on brawl had erupted. Punches flew in the row in front of me, and multiple fights had already broken out among the crowd, the crunch of breaking bones lost in the overall clamour. This time, the guards made no move to break up the fighting. Nothing would divert their attention from the bloodbath unfolding onstage.

"Just let me know when to spell them." Becks ducked the flailing limbs from the row in front of us.

I leaned over to whisper, "Even if he wins, he might get trampled to death on the way out."

"Want me to give him a hand up there?" she whispered back. "Give me the word and I'll dispense the itching spell."

"Honestly?" I winced as the troll shifter landed another

punch to Zeph's chin. "I don't think even that would keep him down. He's going for the kill."

Not that Zeph wasn't giving as good as he got... but where in hell had the Faulkners disappeared to? I'd bet they were hiding backstage so they wouldn't get caught off guard by a stray blow. Cowardly bastards.

"I can look for that record player of theirs," Becks whispered. "I can't believe they took it back from the guild."

"I'm going to tear off Jake's ears and shove them down his throat next time I see him," I growled. "Can you check and see if they're hiding backstage?"

"Will do." She disappeared, shrinking into her cat form, and I hoped she'd move fast enough to avoid being trampled. Every other step, someone elbowed me or trod on my feet. By now, Zeph was visibly struggling. His face was bleeding, he moved at a slight crouch that suggested multiple broken ribs, and the crowd had entirely lost interest in the match in favour of pummelling the shit out of one another. If anything, an itching spell might drive the troll-shifter into an even bigger tantrum.

A punch hit the side of my head. Stars exploded across my vision, followed by a grey haze. Even the ghosts were riled up, a mass of agitated spirits shouting as loudly as the living people.

The Faulkners' record player feeds on souls, on spirits. Had their magical weapon screwed up the spirit realm, too?

I blinked away the greyness, finding my hood had fallen down. I yanked it up, scooting out of the way of the brawl in the seat next to me. A gargoyle fought a young woman who kept shifting from cat to human so fast that she was little more than a blur.

Oh, no. Becks had been caught in the frenzy, clawing and biting at the other shifter. The gargoyle guards weren't even trying to keep things calm.

They're just there to stop anyone from getting out—not to stop anyone from being beaten or trampled to death. I could see tomorrow's headlines, putting the deaths down to a simple outbreak of shifter rage.

"Becks!" I tried to grab her, but her wild-tempered cat form was difficult to grab on a good day, let alone in a mass brawl. She screeched and clawed wildly, her amber eyes unfocused. Why was the frenzy affecting her and not me? My head was completely clear, aside from the pain in the back of my skull where I'd been hit. The others behaved more like animals than humans, as though the full moon had taken up residence here in this room and reduced everyone to impulse alone.

Dragon shifters were one of the few shifter types unaffected by the full moon… but so were gargoyles, and there were plenty of them brawling with one another. I inhaled the scent of sweat and blood and fury, but if the spell was in the air, surely it ought to have affected the guards as well.

What did the Faulkners do?

I caught Becks by the scruff of her neck, and her opponent punched me in the arm. I punched him back with my free hand, getting some claw in for good measure, and swept his legs out from underneath him. The crowd moved in, and he disappeared under a roar of stomping feet.

Becks transformed into human form and spat out blood, her gaze unfocused.

"Becks, snap out of it," I hissed, holding her arms to stop her from lunging at the nearest target.

A pained shout came from the stage. Zeph had the other shifter on the ground, unleashing a torrent of punches on him. The troll-shifter roared, his huge arms grabbing for Zeph. Catching him around the waist, the troll-shifter flung him onto the arena floor. This time, it was Zeph who didn't get up.

Becks broke from my grip with a squirm, and I lunged for her, crashing right through the ghost. "Hello!" he said, half-lying on top of me.

"Ow!" I lurched to my feet, feeling wetness on my face. Blood. Worse, Becks must have shifted, because she'd disappeared again. "Go away."

"I'm trapped!" wailed the ghost. "We're all trapped!"

I groaned. "I don't have time for—"

Greyness flooded the room again, thicker than before, filled with the shapes of the restless dead. Even on a spirit line, it was unusual for so many ghosts to appear at once in a single place. Unless there was something holding them here.

"What's trapping you?" I whispered to the ghost, arms over my head to keep from being trampled. "I can't help you if I get knocked unconscious."

"We're trapped in this room!" said the ghost. "All of us. Why aren't you affected by the spell?"

A spell. I'd never heard of a spell that sent shifters into a frenzy before, but it was the only possible explanation. And the guards must have done something to make themselves immune.

But if dragons were unaffected, why was Zeph continuing to fight? They must have done something else to him—and if they hadn't known I'd be immune to the spell, perhaps they were counting on the crowd trampling me flat.

"I promise I'll help you," I said to the ghost. "If you tell me how to undo the spell they're using."

"I don't know," he whispered. "There's a barrier around the arena, I think. Like a ward."

The ward wasn't for protection. It was a cage.

"I'll do my best."

Fixing my eyes on the stage, I climbed over more seats, dodging brawling shifters and the limp bodies of the ones they'd knocked out or worse. I didn't stop, nor did I care if I was spotted. The rat shifter was probably under the spell, too. The match wouldn't stop until someone died, and the arena doors would only open when the Faulkner brothers had had their fill of bloodshed.

I reached the second row from the front, pulling a spell off my wrist. Then I crouched down and took aim.

The explosive spell sent its target—a fox shifter—flying into the air, right at the stage. He crashed into the troll-shifter, knocking him away from Zeph. Hoping the guards took it for an accident, I set off another explosive at the stage's side, knocking a gargoyle shifter off course. The impact carried him into the path of the troll shifter's punch.

Within seconds, the fighting had spread onto the stage, and while the guards moved to intervene, there were too many out-of-control shifters for them to handle. The troll-shifter disappeared, flailing, under a heap of brawling bodies.

Showtime was over.

I jumped onto the stage behind Zeph and caught his arm. "Hey! Zeph, stop. Wait—"

Zeph shook me off as though swatting a fly and made for his opponent again. I caught his arms, pulling him back.

"Snap out of it!"

Zeph stopped. So did the crowd. My breath caught as the spotlight brightened overhead. My hood had fallen down, my bright hair on display. Blood dampened my cheek, and my body ached from a dozen bruises. The quietness was eerie, absolute, and the riot had utterly stopped.

"Well done," said Logan, striding onto the bloodied stage. "As you can see, our matches have *quite* the effect on the crowd. It really can't be beaten. I suppose I must surrender the prize to my brother."

He held up the record player. The eerie silence, and the lingering cold, made the small hairs on my arms stand up, while even the ghosts cringed back, away from the unassuming-looking contraption he held in his hands.

It sucks out souls... and we're on top of a spirit hotspot. Didn't take a genius to work out that combination meant nothing good.

Bryan walked onto the stage from the opposite side, practically bouncing on the balls of his feet in anticipation. A wave of hatred crashed over me, threatening to pull out my claws.

"My prize," he said, reaching out a hand. "If you don't mind."

"My pleasure." Logan approached his brother, handing him the record player. It seemed to shimmer under the stage lights, surrounded by a grey-blue glow. The same colour as the ghosts.

Bryan turned to me. "I have to admit, I haven't tested this on a dragon shifter yet. I hoped to get a little more use out of your friend first, but he's proving problematic to handle. I'm sure you know all about a dragon shifter's fiery temperament, Coriander, right?"

My hands, still gripping Zeph's arms, went numb. The gleam of the spirit device shone brightly under the stage lights.

"Go on," Bryan said. "Release him, or I will see if this device can hold a dragon shifter's soul.

The crowd didn't move an inch. Thanks to the spell, they probably weren't even aware of what was happening.

"Remarkable spell, isn't it?" Logan said. "Total control. I should add, Cori, that I never intended to kill *all* of you tonight. I still need at least one dragon shifter for my assistance. I hoped it might be your sister."

Ember.

"I wouldn't turn to your allies for help," Bryan added. "The doors are sealed. I suppose you wouldn't know what a spirit barrier is... it's a necromancer technique. Nothing enters or leaves this room. Better, the spirits trapped inside these walls are fuel for our hypnosis spell. There's not much else they can do, is there?"

"What gives you the right to toy with people, alive or dead?" I was stalling for time, but there was no way in hell I could keep his attention occupied until Zeph came to his senses. I'd die first.

"You still call these mindless beasts 'people'?" He exchanged amused glances with his brother. "Look at them. They have no independent thoughts. They are nothing more than instinct-driven animals. Besides, you might say I own half the shifters in this room."

"More than half," said Bryan.

"Oh, you own the other half. That's what makes it fun," said Logan.

Nobody else in the crowd reacted. The guards must be watching our exchange, but none of them made a move to stop us. How much had the Faulkner brothers given them to sell out their fellow shifters?

"Of course," said Bryan. "Sometimes we play against one another. It's just a little spirited competition. Harmless."

"What the hell is wrong with you?" A snarl slipped between my teeth. "I know this is all staged. All of it. The bombs, the egg going 'missing'—you let us steal it back, too, didn't you?"

Logan turned to me. "You're welcome to do whatever you like with the dragonling. The last one we kept got a little out of control and had to be put down, but perhaps another dragon shifter might be able to tame it."

"This isn't a game we're talking about, it's people's lives," I said. "Those bombs killed innocent people."

"Their deaths served a purpose." Bryan held up the record

player. "It feeds on spirit energy. Like a battery. And if it gets overloaded…"

A spark rippled through the room, making me shiver. Grey fog seeped into the corners of my vision, tinged with blue light. Could he see it? I doubted it. He didn't have a clue what he was messing with.

The crowd remained, still, transfixed. Becks was in there somewhere. She didn't deserve to die either.

"Leave your friend," Logan said, beckoning to me. "Don't bother using one of those spells of yours. They'll never touch our shields. As for shifting…" He drew a finger across his throat.

The grey fog was getting worse. *Spirit barrier.* He was right—I was no necromancer. I knew they'd stirred up the spirit realm by creating a barrier around this room and trapping the ghosts inside it, but not how to remove it and set everyone free. Dead or living.

But the Faulkners had no idea I'd been over to the other side myself. I *must* be able to use that to my advantage.

I focused on the spirit realm, scanning its grey haze for signs of a barrier. The transparent mass of ghosts must end somewhere. They floated everywhere, yet avoided the area surrounding the record player. Normally physical objects weren't visible in Death, but the record player was surrounded by a glowing mass of white-blue light.

Souls. It already contained the souls of the people who'd died when the bombs went off. That's why their helicopter had been at the auction hall. They were harvesting souls. And now they planned to do the same here.

I jerked my head to the side… and then I saw it. A circle surrounded the edges of the room, its lines glowing faintly.

That must be the barrier.

Could I break it? If I did, the ghosts would escape, and the shifters would be able to get out. The Faulkners' spell must be contained within this room, too.

"I'm waiting, Coriander," said Logan.

I shuffled forwards, pushing Zeph along with me. He went willingly, not showing the slightest sign of the pain he must be in. *Fuck them, for what they did to him. I guess the reason they're not afraid of losing their souls is because they don't have them.*

A glowing light drew my attention. Typically, necromancer barriers required candles to function. Twelve candles. If the spirit barrier was anything like a summoning circle, then there must be candles within the room itself for it to work. So that glow…

"We don't have all night," said Bryan.

There. My gaze pinpointed a candle fixed to the wall on my right, too high for the brawling shifters to reach.

I drew in a breath. Then I let go of Zeph, grabbed an explosive spell, and threw it right at the candle.

Light burst across my vision, blinding me for an instant. As my sight came back, the mass of spirits *moved*. Faces flashed before me, one after the other, too quickly to take note of, floating through the walls and out into the city. A thousand ghosts fleeing in search of freedom.

Not just the ghosts. The shifters were moving, too, on unsteady feet, bruised and bewildered but free of the spell. They poured over the seats, overwhelming the unprepared guards in their rush for the exit.

"You little worm!" screamed Logan. "Close the doors—close the fucking doors!"

The thunder of footsteps filled the room, along with the chill wind of the ghosts' departure. *Too late.* The entire theatre trembled as the shifters moved, in a frenzy for an entirely different reason this time. Logan swore, backing up.

Bryan thrust the record player in my face. "I can still take your soul, you worm."

Becks jumped on his head, causing him to shout in pain as her claws dug into his face. His fancy shield didn't protect him against cat claws, and a scream escaped when she drew bloody furrows into his cheeks.

"Hey!" yelled a voice from the front row. "What the fuck did you do to us?"

The spell must have been fuelled by the spirit barrier, the energy of so many ghosts trapped in one place. Without it, the shifters' control over their actions had returned—and they were *pissed.*

"Let's go," Logan yelled at his brother. "Bryan, can't you handle a cat shifter?"

"You're not going anywhere," I growled, my claws sliding out.

Shifters swarmed the stage, all wanting a piece of the Faulkners. Zeph twisted around with a roar, claws swiping.

"Hey!" I grabbed for his arm and missed. "You don't have to fight anymore."

I might as well have yelled at the ghosts. It was like when I'd been trying to drag him out of the arena the first time around, only worse. Breaking the barrier hadn't been enough to undo whatever extra spell the Faulkners had used on him.

"Right, we're getting out," I yelled in his ear, throwing all my weight onto his arm. He stumbled, and for want of a better option, I threw a knockout spell in his face.

Zeph crumpled backwards, right on top of me. I caught his arms before he hit the ground, and a shifter's punch hit my cheek, sending me staggering. "Ow. Becks, help me—"

I'd lost sight of Becks in the crowd again. Holding Zeph upright, I scanned the chaos for her, dodging a punch every couple of seconds. *What's she playing at?*

The answer came moments later, in the form of a

resounding crash from backstage and the sound of an explosive spell hitting something metal and solid. The crowd surged as a new wave of shifters surged from every stage entrance and exit—cat shifters, rat shifters, ferrets, foxes, wolves. Becks appeared at the head of the group, her fur bloodied, her eyes shining.

"I got them out." She shifted to human, staggering against me. I fell, struggling to support Zeph and Becks at the same time.

"You did great," I said. "But if you keep leaning on me like that, I'm gonna fall."

"I've got you, Cori!" said Ember's voice. "Whoa. Astor, help me out here."

My allies moved in to help, their hands supporting mine. Even though we'd lost sight of the Faulkners, a rush of triumph stirred at the sight of the utter anarchy breaking out. The Faulkners couldn't kill every shifter in the room, and word would spread around the whole of London by tomorrow. Everyone would know what they'd done. They would never be able to show their faces in public again.

The Faulkners wouldn't let it end there, but for now, I let myself bask in the glow of our victory, and the light of a thousand spirits set free.

19

"You did *what?*" said Will, confronting me across the living room.

"I won." I paced in front of the sofa, wide awake and still wired. Greyness lurked in the corners of my vision, remnants of my spirit sight, but no ghosts had tailed me home. Zeph lay unmoving behind me. Astor and Ember had helped me carry him back, but none of us knew if he'd attack us again when he woke up. After the pummelling the troll-shifter had given him, he was lucky to have survived.

"Won?" Will repeated. "The Faulkners got away, and they have a device that can suck out souls. And you have Zeph, but he might wake up and kill us. How in hell is this a victory?"

"We're still alive?" I nodded to my sister, who sat in an armchair sipping from a mug of hot chocolate. Becks had gone for an early night after Kit had healed her, while the dragonling curled up on Kit's arm in the other chair. "And by morning, everyone in the city will know the Faulkners are crooks."

"Guess we don't need to call the Mage Lords, then," said

Ember. "But I'd like to know who the Faulkners got to set up that spirit barrier. They can't have done it themselves."

"Anyone can buy candles on the market," I said. "Or steal them from the necromancers. Hell, the Faulkners probably own a deluxe collection they tricked some poor sod into selling them. Wouldn't put it past them."

"No kidding," Ember said. "I didn't know it was possible to trap so many ghosts in one place."

"It was a key point," I said.

Ember's eyes widened. "What, it was like Hyde Park? When..."

When I died. "Yeah, but not that strong," I said. "Powerful, though. I don't know what would have happened if I hadn't stopped them from using that record player."

"They still have it," Zeph rasped, startling everyone by sitting up.

"You're okay!" I said, moving to his side. "Wait, don't move..."

He sank against the cushions, groaning. "What the hell happened to me?"

"Don't you remember any of it?" I said. "You were like... hypnotised or something."

"I remember, but it's foggy." He dragged a hand over his face as though to reassure himself it was still there. "They healed me first... I remember that. They said they needed me in good shape to fight for them. I wouldn't let them do it without a fuss, so they ended up injecting me with something that knocked me out. I think it... I think it made me susceptible to their orders." He swung his legs over the sofa's side.

"Whoa, take it easy," I said. "That troll-shifter dude pummelled the crap out of you."

"I feel it," he said. "I won, right?"

"Not exactly," I said. "I wrecked the fight and caused a diversion. You were going to kill one another otherwise."

"I would have won." He pushed himself upright, then collapsed back on the sofa.

"Chill," I said, though saying that to a dragon was like asking a fire to stop burning. "Kit healed you, but you'll be sore for a while."

His gaze travelled around the room, stopping on Kit, and the dragonling curled up in his arms. "What—the egg hatched?"

"Yep. Now we have an angry murder dragon in the house, too," I said.

Zeph's face went chalk-white. "No. You have to get rid of it."

"That was the plan."

Zeph pushed himself upright again, leaning to get a closer look at the dragonling. "How on earth did you tame it?"

"Kit claims it heard him talking to it when it was in the egg," Will said. "Believe me, we're getting rid of it one way or another. Is anyone else about to drop dead? No. Good. I'm going to bed."

He walked out of the room. Kit didn't stir, and neither did the dragonling.

Zeph looked at both of them, then Ember, and then Astor. "How in the world did all of you end up living in the same house?"

"The apocalypse happened." I sat down beside him on the sofa, my adrenaline-fuelled state starting to give away to exhaustion. "Zeph, do you remember anything about what happened at the Faulkners' place? I didn't mean for you to get stuck in there."

"I stayed on purpose," he said. "I was sure the Faulkners wouldn't be able to resist making a public display of me, and I was right."

"Uh, yeah, but they *hypnotised* you this time," I said. "You've got to stop doing that. Seriously."

He grinned a little. "I'm not that delicate, Cori. I won't break."

No kidding. He was lucky to be alive after tonight. "Did you see anything else in the Faulkners' house?"

"No… they knocked me out, then when I woke up, I tried to get out. That didn't go well. They were all wearing those dragon-proofed suits, so I got hit pretty badly. They healed me before I got to the arena."

"Why would they do that?" Astor's sharp gaze assessed the other dragon shifter. "Why are you so important to them? You knew they worked with the successors of the Orion League, didn't you?"

"The successors? How would a human know—?" He broke off, his eyes widening as they took in Astor properly for the first time. The former assassin had removed his jacket, revealing the lines of a tattoo that covered the marks he'd worn as an Orion League soldier.

Marks indicating the shifters he'd killed.

"You were one of them." Zeph advanced forwards, his eyes flaming despite his unsteady steps.

"Don't." I stepped in front of him, but he walked around me.

Worse, Astor wasn't backing off. He met Zeph's stare with a challenge.

"Oh, for god's sake!" Ember moved to Astor's side. "Don't start a fight, you two. Yes, Astor was an Orion League soldier. He left them during the invasion, and he helped us destroy them."

Zeph didn't sit down. His eyes didn't lose the faint orange glow, either. "You killed my people. I shouldn't let you leave here alive."

Astor took a step forward. "Want to give it a try?"

I planted myself between them. "You have three seconds to back off or I'll knock both of you out cold. Calm the fuck down. We don't have time to fight each other."

"I have plenty of time," said Astor.

"Astor!" Ember caught his arm. "You should have known this would happen when Zeph found out. It's not worth fighting your allies."

Astor scowled. "I'm more concerned with what our new friend is hiding. I left the League. I don't know how their technology wound up in the home of a pair of wealthy humans who force shifters to fight to their deaths for profit. But I bet *he* does."

I turned my attention to Zeph, not lowering the knockout spell. "Is it true?"

Zeph's eyes had turned ashy grey again. "I would *never* align with the League. They killed everyone I cared about. Burned my whole village to the ground more effectively than a dragon shifter ever could."

"I'm sorry, Zeph," I said, "but—please tell me. How did you know the Faulkners were using the League's techniques?"

"I didn't, but I knew the League was developing more of their anti-dragon shifter technology before the invasion." He spoke quickly, with a quiet current of anger. "They captured me when they destroyed my village and put me in a cage at one of their facilities. Those new dragon-proofed cages, the weapons… they were all in development when I broke out. I hoped they wouldn't survive the invasion, but I was wrong."

The breath punched from my lungs. "You broke out?" I asked, my throat dry. "Were—were the Faulkners there?"

"No," he said. "They were never part of the Orion League. I didn't hear of them until I reached London. That was a couple of years ago. It took me three years to cross the country to get here, after the invasion."

"We'd already destroyed the League by then," Ember said. "How long did they have you as their prisoner?"

"Three months," he said. "Then the faeries destroyed the facility, and I managed to escape in the chaos. I never met Malkin, their leader, but I did see that spirit device when they were developing it. That's one of the things I've been keeping an eye out for."

"What, the record player?" I asked, momentarily distracted from the flood of images his words had stirred up. "Are you serious?"

His eyes were simmering again. "Of course I'm serious."

"Sorry, I just—we were hired to get the record player back from an innocent little old lady who turned out to be a banshee the same day the dragon egg showed up." I released a breath. "I guess that was the Faulkners, too. Probably thought it was funny to call the mercenaries. Bet they were watching us chase the banshee and laughing at us."

Zeph frowned. "The mercenary guild is in the Faulkners' pockets, you think?"

"Darcy would definitely take a bribe if it was big enough," I said. "Great. Guess we've lost our jobs on top of everything else."

"Not necessarily," said Ember. "They might have fooled him, too. Or Jake might have acted alone. Not that he's that intelligent…"

"Never mind the mercenaries," Astor said. "I think the real question is, why was Zeph the only person aside from the Faulkners' people aware of a species of dragon that never existed until recently?"

The air seemed to thicken with tension. Or maybe it was the scent of three riled-up dragon shifters—fire, tinged with the tense warmth of the air before a thunderstorm.

"How do you know they didn't exist until two years ago?"

Zeph's eyes weren't simmering this time, but if anything, his voice sounded even more dangerous than before.

"Astor?" said Ember.

"I didn't," responded Astor. "But it's easy enough to guess, given the evidence. This dragon egg trade is more than a moneymaking scheme for the Faulkners."

"That's all it seems to be, actually," said Zeph. "I suppose you've guessed that the eggs are engineered and so are the dragonlings. No, I have no idea where it happens, before you ask."

Engineered. I'd known, in some way, from the instant we'd found out the other dragon shifters had never heard of wild dragons. It was the only logical conclusion. I looked at the little pink-scaled dragonling curled up sleeping on Kit's arm. He and I had more in common than the dragonling would ever know. He'd been created in a lab similar to the one I'd been kept in, as the League's pet. Perhaps even the same one.

I tasted bile in the back of my throat and clenched my hands to stop them shaking.

"I think the League used dragon shifter DNA to create them, originally," Zeph said, addressing Astor. "The Faulkners' scheme is to sell the eggs and then let them circulate around the city, carefully moderated. Then they somehow end up back in the Faulkners' hands along with a boatload of cash. This one made it all the way to the arena, which wasn't typical. Usually I get to them first."

"And they never caught you at it?" Ember asked. "Until the arena?"

"Not until then," he said. "Where they're actually breeding the dragonlings, though—I've yet to figure it out. It might not be in the city at all."

I found my voice. "What's that blasted record player got to do with the dragon eggs?"

"I don't know," he said. "I never did figure out what *that* was for."

"A likely story," said Astor.

"I've told you everything I know," Zeph said. "Bet *you* haven't."

"My history is none of your business."

Ember kept a firm grip on Astor's arm. "Don't. It's not worth it."

"No, it isn't," I said to Zeph. "The Faulkners know our address. Half the supernaturals in London want their blood, but they'll still be able to bribe some people into taking their side against ours."

"I left a message for the Mage Lords," Ember said. "For all the good it does. I told them what the Faulkners did and that they're on the run. It's up to them whether they want to lend a hand or not." She yawned. "But I'm done for tonight. Please, can you try not to kill one another?"

Astor gave Zeph a distrustful look, then turned to Ember. "All right, but we have an unknown element *and* a newly hatched dragonling in our home along with a bounty on our heads. I'm going to guard the house tonight. I'll warn you if anything gets in."

He made for the door into the shop. I watched Zeph to make sure he didn't pursue the ex-assassin out of the room, but the flames simmering in Zeph's eyes died down and he sank back onto the sofa. "That one's trouble."

"Speak for yourself." I rubbed my eyes, exhaustion dragging at my limbs. "Are you okay sleeping in here? I'd offer you Becks's bed, but she's actually sleeping in it for once. She likes to wander outside at night, but I think the arena shook her up."

Maybe the Faulkners, or people like them, had been responsible for Becks ending up on the streets. That they were running scared could only be a good thing—but I couldn't rid myself of the sense of creeping dread that had stirred when Zeph had mentioned the Orion League's labs.

Ember had set their headquarters on fire. How could they still be tormenting innocent shifters, creating dragonlings, manufacturing ways to hurt us?

Zeph adjusted his position so his legs draped over the arm of the sofa. "All right, I'll sleep here. But that dragonling better not come near me."

Within moments, his breathing had evened out, and his head lolled against the sofa's side. I felt bad leaving him in here after the beating he'd taken in the arena, but there was no help for it.

I turned to the dragonling, who sprawled over Kit's arm with his little head resting against the cushion. We'd have to pry the two apart and release the dragonling into the wild if we were to stand any chance of maintaining our life here in London. But when I watched him curled up, breathing faintly, it was hard to see him as an engineered killing machine.

I woke to the smell of baking. Faint grey light streaming through the window told me it was much too early to get up, but the insistent aroma of chocolate chips said otherwise. Becks wasn't in her bed and the covers were rumpled, so she must have recovered from the events of the night and gone for a wander.

I took a quick shower to wash every trace of the arena off me before dressing in my favourite top and a pair of socks decorated with miniature dragons that Ember had got me for my last birthday. The lack of any sounds from the living room suggested the dragonling had slept through the night, and sure enough, he and Kit were still in the armchair, fast asleep.

Zeph wasn't on the sofa any longer, but I heard the shower through the closed door of the downstairs bathroom.

Will was in the kitchen, the only lit area of the main room, and plates covered the entire table, containing enough cookies to feed an army.

"Will, what are you doing baking at five in the morning?" I asked.

"I'm stressed," he said.

"*You're* stressed?"

"Of course I'm stressed," he said. "My boyfriend has adopted a baby dinosaur, several high-profile people in the supernatural underworld want to kill us, and I can't go more than five minutes without one of you getting beaten up. And everyone expects me to sort out their problems because I'm the eldest and my name's on the bloody mortgage payments. So yes, I'm stress-baking cookies."

Well, when he put it like that... "None of us got killed yet," I said.

"And on top of that, Kit wants to name the angry reptilian bite monster 'Cuddles' and let it sleep in our bed," he added.

"We're not calling him Bitey McBiterson, Will." Kit walked over, picking up a cookie and offering it to the dragonling.

"We're not calling him anything," he said. "Because we're not keeping him."

"But..."

The dragon sank his teeth into Kit's hand instead of the cookie.

"No." Kit tapped him on the nose. "Don't do that."

Will glared at the little dragon, but the wound was already healing. I had to admit Kit's faerie healing power made him the best person to handle the dragonling. The rest of us had yet to make the jump from 'tasty snack' to 'potential parent'.

"Is Astor still guarding the place?" I asked.

"Presumably," Will said. "Becks is out there, too. She said she'll find out if the Mage Lords are planning to issue an arrest warrant for the Faulkner twins or not."

"I bloody hope so," I said. "Not that I wouldn't be happy to rip a few holes in those depraved fucks, but they deserve to rot in a cell at the very least for what they did. Only the Mage Lords would be able to get authorisation to take away all their dragon-proofed crap, too." Not that I liked the idea of it in *their* hands, either. The mages had never gone out of their way to protect us in the past, and their silence on recent events spoke volumes.

Zeph wandered back in. His auburn hair was damp and tousled, and his eyes brightened at the sight of the cookies on the sideboard. He still wore the clothes he had in the arena, but the rest of him looked much cleaner. His T-shirt had seen better days, torn in several places that exposed enough of his tightly muscled torso to make up for the early hour in the morning.

"Don't touch those, you'll burn your fingers..." Will trailed off. "Forgot I'm talking to a dragon. Never mind."

"There are a few perks of being one of us, believe it or not." I picked up a cookie and took a bite. Zeph picked up a second, looking more alert than he had last night. "Zeph, you need some clean clothes."

"The Faulkners stole my hoody," he said, picking up another cookie. "They also stole my wallet, otherwise I'd buy a new outfit."

"Well, none of my clothes are going to fit you," said Will.

He had a point. None of us had any spare clothes suitable for a tall, powerfully-built dragon shifter.

"Don't look at me," I said. "I may have a pair of fluffy

unicorn socks you can borrow, but you'd have to wear them as gloves."

"Ha," said Will.

"There might be some clothes in the shelter's spare room," said Kit. "I'll go—"

"Don't take the dragon into the shelter," Will said. "We can't risk anyone else seeing him."

"Okay." Kit gently lifted the little creature from his arm, but the dragonling wailed when Kit tried to detach him.

"Oh, for god's sake," said Will. "Fine, I'll go to the shelter. Please don't let the cookies burn."

"I'll watch," said Zeph, pulling out a seat at the table and grabbing another cookie.

I did likewise. The smell of baking chocolate chips soothed my nerves, even with the presence of the miniature dragon on Kit's arm. When the dragonling started hissing at the oven, Kit retreated from the kitchen, leaving Zeph and me alone.

"Are you sure you're okay?" I asked Zeph.

"Takes more than a troll-shifter to bring me down," he said. "I have to say, I'm glad for that spell or whatever it was they used on me. It muted most of the pain."

"That's not a disturbing thing to say at all." I bit into another cookie, resting my elbows on the table. "The spell would have pushed you to fight to the death without even being aware of it."

Zeph grinned. "You're worried about me. That's cute."

I thwacked him on the knee, which was inches away from my leg. "Cute? You were hypnotised and tried to fight to the death, and all you had to say was that you would have won. You're worse than my sister, and trust me, that's saying a lot."

"Hmm." He sat back in his seat, still grinning. "I'm flattered."

"Oh, for god's sake." Did he have to keep staring at me like that? It scrambled my thoughts and made it difficult to stay mad at him. Then again, how many times had I had to deal with my sister taking absurd risks? "If you're wondering about the comparison, my sister once shifted to human form in mid-air and face-planted into a bush. She also crash-landed in someone's garden in dragon form and knocked a fence over."

"I've done that," he said. "Several times. It's hard to judge when to switch forms if you're not used to it. The tail is particularly tricky to manage. So many broken windows."

"Ha." I smiled at the mental image, wishing I'd got more of a chance to look at him when he'd shifted. I'd been more concerned with our imminent deaths.

I also kept forgetting he'd grown up with other dragon shifters who'd taught him how to handle the shift. He and I had had totally different upbringings, but like me, he'd lost his entire community, thanks to the Orion League.

I'd lost everything so many times, but I'd always had Ember. I had the feeling it had been a long time since he'd had someone he could trust as much as I did her.

"You should know," I said. "I never had the chance to tell you, but if you want to meet some other dragon shifters, I can introduce you."

"You know others?" Surprise flickered in his eyes. "I thought you and your sister were the only ones."

"The only ones in London," I said. "The others... ah, it's complicated. I'm not supposed to tell anyone, technically speaking, but I'm sure they'd make an exception for another dragon shifter."

He leaned forward, his expression entirely serious now. "Where are they?"

"They're in a small village in the middle of the Scottish Highlands," I said. "The home of the last dragon clan."

He watched open-mouthed as I explained how the mirror

linked us directly to the other dragon shifters. Ember and I might have come to London alone, but our parents had left us a notebook which contained clues that had led us to discover where the other dragons were hiding. Lorne had then hijacked the mirrors to bring his own army to London, but in the process, we'd managed to free the other dragon shifters from his rule.

"A mirror that can transport you across the country?" he asked. "The dragons created it? How?"

"I have no idea," I said. "Same with the Moonbeam. Have you heard of that?"

"It's a legend," he said. "Isn't it?"

"Nope," I said. "It's right here in London, with the Mage Lords. The Moonbeam can create a portal that links to either of the mirrors, as well as hypnotising any shifter that looks at it."

I left out the part where Ember had used it to bring me back from the dead. I'd never been happy we'd had to give it up to the Mage Lords, but bringing people back to life was supposed to be impossible. No wonder I'd come back —different.

"Hypnotising?" he echoed. "How is that possible, if the dragons created it?"

"The Moonbeam can be used to shut down the human side of a shifter until they become pure instinct," I explained. "Kinda like what the Faulkners did to the shifters in the arena, except dragons aren't immune. The League used it on shifters to cause them to lose their reason and attack humans, which gave them an excuse to shoot every shifter they came across."

"That explains how they were able to kill so many of us," Zeph said, his fists clenching. "You said the mages have the Moonbeam now?"

"Yeah, it's locked up in their headquarters," I said. "They

took it back after the League nearly used it to destroy the city. We were allowed to keep the mirror, though."

"So you can visit the other dragons," he said. "How many are left?"

"Fewer by the day," I admitted. "There was a war, before the invasion—I was five years old at the time. By the time the dust settled, the dragon shifters were decimated, reduced to a single village."

"A *war?*" he said. "How? Was this Moonbeam involved?"

"Haven't a clue, but it was kicked off by a dragon shifter who liked power too much." I drew in a breath. "That dragon shifter—Lorne—sold his fellow shifters out to the Orion League in order to keep his position as their leader. Anyone who dissented was killed. I survived because my parents gave their lives to get Ember and me away."

Zeph shook his head. "No. A dragon shifter would never—"

"He did," said Ember, appearing behind me. "The dragons in Scotland don't have a happy history, even pre-invasion. There aren't many of them left."

"This Lorne," said Zeph, looking up at me. "What happened to him?"

"He's locked in the mages' jail," I said. "He's been there for five years. The other dragon shifters suffered a lot when he ruled them. I asked them if they'd ever heard of the dragonlings, and they hadn't. Now I know why."

"Why?" Kit approached the table, his bright green eyes fixed on Zeph.

"He was made in a lab," Zeph said. "Engineered from dragon shifter DNA. Even releasing him into the wild is a risky move. I don't know how he'll react."

"What else is there to do?" said Ember. "We can release him close to the village. Not too close, though—we don't want him attacking the villagers."

"He won't if you let me introduce them first," Kit said.

Zeph looked at the faerie, apparently at a loss for words. I hadn't expected Kit and the dragonling to bond so quickly.

"You have an escape route if the Faulkners come after you," Zeph said, changing the subject. "Through the mirror. Right?"

"It's not that simple," I said. "The mirror stays activated when we're on the other side. That's why we always have someone here, watching it. If we all went through at once, anyone else who found the mirror would be able to follow us and find the dragon shifters."

The door crashed open. Becks skidded into the room in cat form, turning human mid-step.

"They're losing their minds!" she said. "There are shifters everywhere in the streets attacking one another—attacking everyone else they can get near. It's spreading."

Zeph was on his feet in a second. "What?"

"They must have used the same spell they used in the arena." I jumped to my feet, my heart sinking. "Where did it start, do you know?"

"I don't," said Becks, "but they're coming this way."

Crap. If the spell was contagious, then it would hit the shelter before it reached us.

20

"Becks, stay in here," I said. "How did it not affect you?"

"I ran like hell," she wheezed, collapsing against the table. "I don't know where they set it off, but it's spreading."

The dickheads were probably dropping it out of their helicopter. Anywhere they wouldn't be in the firing line. Not that they'd be affected anyway, being human.

The arena had been a test run. I should have destroyed them last night when I'd had the chance. I'd humiliated them and showed that I wasn't afraid, and now they had nothing left to lose.

"Dragons are immune," Zeph said. "That means the three of us stand the best chance of finding them. And we're the only people who can stop it."

"We have to evacuate the shelter," Ember said. "Go and tell Will, Kit."

Kit nodded, his grip slackening on the dragonling. The little dragon took flight in a bound, zipping across the room to the door into the shop—and the open window at the front.

"No!" Kit sprinted after him, but it was too late. The dragonling had tasted freedom, and before any of us reached the window, he was gone in a single beat of leathery wings.

"Kit, don't run after him!" said Becks. "You need to help Will with the others in the shelter. Find the dragon later. He won't be affected by the spell and he can fly—he'll be fine."

Kit turned around, his mouth pulling. "I… okay, yes. I'll help." He ran to the back room and through the door into the shelter.

Dammit. Nobody would notice a wild dragon on the loose with shifters attacking one another, so we'd have to leave him be. Stopping the Faulkners was our priority.

"They must have set the spell up somewhere," I said. "Spells… that's Will's area, but for the effects to spread, it's either contagious or it's somewhere with a lot of reach. Last time it only affected the theatre because the doors were sealed and there was a spirit barrier on the place."

"They can't have sealed the entire city, can they?" said Zeph.

"No," Ember said. "You can't make a circle that big, I don't think. But all magic is amplified on the—"

"Ley Line," I finished, my heart sinking. The Ley Line was the biggest spirit line, and it cut directly through the middle of London.

Right through the spot where I'd died.

Hyde Park was a huge spirit hotspot, and in the last seven years, it'd turned from a tourist attraction to the home of wild fae and anything with strong enough magic to withstand the fluctuating energy of a half-dozen spirit lines. One of those lines passed through the theatre, too, but a key point involving the Ley Line was a hundred times more powerful than any other.

So powerful that the forces of life and death could collide.

I'd never wanted to set foot anywhere near the place again. It was where Lorne and Malkin had tried to sacrifice my sister's life to create a second faerie apocalypse, and in the chaos, I'd been ripped out of my body and cast into Death. If not for Ember and the Moonbeam, I'd still be there, among those lost spirits.

Next time I might not be so lucky.

"I'll fly in," said Ember, the haunted look in her eyes a mirror of my own.

"The Ley Line?" Zeph said, his brow furrowed in puzzlement. "Do you know where it is?"

"Hyde Park," I said, the words sticking in my throat. "If I wanted to amplify a spell to affect everyone in a huge section of London, that's where I'd do it. The line amplifies all magic. If witches use magic there, they often blow themselves up."

The Faulkners must have found a way around it or got out of the line of fire. Dickheads.

Ember's eyes met mine and something clenched inside me. I'd never wished for wings so badly. "Don't tell me to hide underground," I said to her. "There are people dying out there."

"I don't want you to be one of them." Flames flickered in her eyes. "I almost lost you once already."

"Even staying behind is a risk." I heard distant screaming from outside, accompanied by discordant crashing noises and shattering glass. "Sounds like it's catching up to us anyway."

Ember and Zeph looked at one another. Then they ran out into the street. Screeching noises overhead signalled a gargoyle fight. Two gargoyles ripped into one another in mid-air, the echo of their cries carrying over the rooftops, and blood sprinkled down onto the street below in a fine red mist. Even if the effects of the spell hadn't reached here yet, the brawling shifters were knocking at our door. We needed to move quickly if we wanted a home to come back to.

"I'm going to fly," Zeph said. "If you think the spell is at Hyde Park, then I'll go right there. But until it wears off, the streets aren't safe."

"Neither are the skies." I pointed to the gargoyles tearing into one another above the rooftops. "I bet the park's protected, too. That's what they did last time. They used a circle, like the spirit barrier on the arena, to make it as difficult as possible to undo the spell."

"They?" Zeph gave me a questioning look.

"The League," I said, my throat dry. "And Lorne. People will die either way. Unless…"

Unless I found a way to stop it. And I could think of only one thing that allowed total control over a shifter… the Moonbeam.

Ember closed the shop door behind us. "Zeph and I will fly. Cori…"

"I'm going to the Mage Lords' place," I said. "The Moonbeam can neutralise the effects of the spell, I'm sure of it."

Since it only affected shifters, the Moonbeam would have no effect on the Faulkner brothers, but Ember had used it to stop a war in the blink of an eye. The Faulkners' spell couldn't hold a candle to it.

The slight issue was that mages' headquarters lay on the other side of Hyde Park, past the warring shifters. Yet another reason the Faulkners had picked a central spot—it was almost impossible for us to call for help, let alone gather an army.

"I'll drop you off there," Zeph said.

Ember whirled on him. "Zeph—"

"Go," I said. "Please. And for god's sake, be careful."

Ember's eyes blazed as she turned on Zeph. "All right, but if you let anything hurt my sister, I'll make you sorry."

She shifted into dragon form, red scales gleaming, and launched herself into the sky.

I watched her strong wingbeats carry her away, then backed into the shop. "I'm getting some weapons. Then you're going to keep your word, Zeph. No leaving me behind."

"I keep my word," said Zeph. "If you're certain this Moonbeam can help."

"Not like we have a lot of options." I grabbed my boots and laced them quickly, then retrieved some knives from the weapons room. Next, I raided Will's stash of spells—not that I'd be able to use any of them on the Ley Line without risking them backfiring on me. "It worked once before. If nothing else, the Moonbeam will paralyse the shifters for long enough for you and Ember to find the spell and destroy it."

"I hope you're right, but Faulkners might anticipate your plan. And they have anti-dragon weapons."

"Then they're as likely to be able to hit you in the air as anywhere else," I said. "This is our doing. We forced their hands, and hundreds of innocent people will die if we don't stop them."

"I have an inkling this was always their plan." Zeph waited for me by the door. "It'll be more comfortable for you if you climb on my back, but I haven't carried a person before."

"I think I'll manage." I walked with him to a clear spot in the street.

Then he shifted, going from human to dragon in a heartbeat. His scales gleamed blue-white, even brighter than Ember's. Gasps rose from the neighbouring houses as he lowered his tail so that I could climb up it. Without the tail, he was maybe seven feet long, bigger than Ember. A pair of ice-white horns curled either side of his face. His eyes were the same as they were when he was in human form, ashy grey, with the hint of a flame.

"Good god, this is awkward." I shimmied up his tail and wrapped my leg over his back, shuffling forward until I found a suitable position behind his neck. Considering his scales were razor-sharp, I was in for a bumpy ride, but I'd worry about the state of my legs when I landed.

He took off in a bound, wings beating against the strong air current. I leaned forward, gripping his scales to avoid being swept away. Ah, so this was why humans didn't ride on dragons. That, and if he shifted back in mid-flight, we'd both crash-land.

"That way." I pointed, lowering my hand to his eye-level so he could see. A growl rumbled through his body, vibrating beneath my knees. Ow. I wouldn't be able to walk for a week after this.

We dropped below a cloud, and I gasped.

Gargoyles brawled in mid-air, punching each other over the rooftops, while the streets were packed with rats, cats, foxes, wolves, colliding in a clash of violence. Some humans were attempting to use spells to subdue them, judging by the frequent flashes of light, but the Ley Line's effect probably made their spells more volatile, too.

Zeph dipped lower, and I clung on for dear life as the wind buffeted against us. If the Faulkners were flying their helicopter today, they'd have a hell of a job keeping it on course.

Their world domination plan might be thwarted by British weather. Imagine that.

We flew over the streets, and I recognised the area where we'd found the Faulkners' house.

"Can you breathe fire and burn it down?" I said to Zeph.

He growled, meaning no. Even breathing fire *inside* the place hadn't destroyed it, after all.

Evil bastards.

We flew over the bright green mass of Hyde Park. The park was a riot of colour and activity, as though someone had dropped a nest of bees into a busy shopping centre. Faeries, humans and shifters ran amok through the patches of woodland, and if the spell was hidden somewhere inside, it was impossible to tell from the sky.

A dart zipped past, clipping Zeph's claw. Someone was shooting at us. Someone with *really* good aim. They must be on a roof somewhere close.

I shouted an unnecessary warning to Zeph, and he dropped lower over the expanse of green. At once, my vision fogged, transparent shapes appearing me in the gloom.

"No," I gasped. "Not now."

Zeph growled in a questioning way.

"Dead people," I muttered. "Bloody hell. They really did stir up the spirit realm."

Like the brawling shifters weren't enough, everyone in the vicinity would have to deal with a plague of ghosts, too. I blinked to clear the grey from my vision, but everything remained smothered in a smoky filter. I'd never be able to spot the spell unless Zeph flew right above the treetops, and that would put both of us in the firing range of whoever had shot at us.

Zeph kept flying lower, seemingly oblivious to the risk. Faint grey lines rippled out from the park, transparent lines as wide as roads. One was thicker than the others, cutting directly through the trees below.

Spirit lines. I could see the spirit lines. The widest grey line shone brighter than the rest, rippling with power. The Ley Line. I *felt* it, stirring the hair from my head, tugging at my bones, as though it was trying to coax me into Death.

"Zeph, fly away from the park! Something's wrong."

He growled and flew west. As two more darts zipped past,

I ducked low against his scaly neck. "It's too dangerous for you to stay high up."

He growled again. I couldn't see Ember, so she must have flown elsewhere or shifted to human again.

The line grew fainter as we flew out of the park. I'd never been there since the battle five years ago and hadn't known it was possible to *see* the spirit lines. Not from this side of the veil, anyway. The echo of their currents brushed my skin, as though they knew I'd crossed over to the other side once before, and they wanted to claim me again.

My legs were numb from gripping Zeph's neck, but if he landed, he'd end up directly in the middle of the fighting. *How are we supposed to find that spell from up here? I can't see a thing.*

Zeph growled, flying at a sideways angle that made me slide to the right. I held on tighter, my heart pounding. "What's up?"

Two more darts answered the question. Zeph turned to the nearest low-rise rooftop and unleashed a jet of fire that engulfed the archers in an instant.

"Bye bye," I said. "Damn, they have some nerve thinking they can shoot you out of the sky—"

Another dart snagged in my hair, and Zeph tilted to the side, his wings spread wide against the current. My hands held on hard enough to draw blood, but the air current tripled in strength. That was no ordinary breeze. Someone was using elemental magic.

I looked up, seeing a man wearing a cloak on a nearby roof. Not one of the Faulkners—and not a sniper. He was a mage. *What is he doing?*

The air current strengthened, battering Zeph off course. Either one of the mages had betrayed us or he thought *we* were the enemy. Either way, Zeph couldn't communicate in his current form and tell the guy he wasn't a villain.

"Hey!" I yelled. "Cut that out. We work with the mages."

I mean, kind of. I'd never wished I'd taken them up on their job offer more than I did in that moment. That was dragon shifter pride for you. If I'd taken a job with the mages, I might have been able to get the Moonbeam before—

Air blasted me full in the face, sending me flying off Zeph's back. For a moment, I hung suspended in the air, the wind whipping at my clothes. Zeph roared, but I tumbled, too fast for him to reach me.

Images flashed before my eyes.

An army, humans and dragons, tearing into one another. Bullets flying, claws swiping, fae tearing up the earth.

My sister, fighting for our lives.

My friends, held hostage by the Orion League's hunters within a circle of light surrounding the park.

Death, calling me into its embrace.

The Moonbeam, bright enough to hold every shifter in the city in its thrall. My sister, gripping it tightly in her hands, her head raised to the sky, pleading—

My claws reached out, snagging the nearest surface and slowing my fall. Brick crumbled under my touch and I skidded down the side of a low-rise building, my heartbeat roaring in my ears. I slid to a gasping halt on the pavement and my knees gave way. *Holy shit, that was a close one.*

I looked up, struggling to catch my breath. Zeph flew at a tilted angle above my head, his wings fighting the mage's current. Fire burst from his mouth, but the air current caught that, too, sending the flames harmlessly into the clouds. He couldn't even knock the bastard off the roof. The air mage's control was too high.

We'll see about that.

He wouldn't know I'd survived the fall, which gave me an edge. I took off at a run, eyes on my target, until I located the office block he'd been standing on. Faces peered out of the glass windows, watching the battle with wide eyes.

I dug my claws into the wall and began to climb as fast as possible. Zeph's intermittent roaring fuelled my rage, and I reached the rooftop where the Mage Lord stood with his cloak rippling around him. He didn't see me sneak up on him until my arm was around his throat, wrenching him backwards.

The air current briefly stopped, then started again. I'd heard mages had to exercise immense control over their powers or else risk injuring themselves or the people around them. This guy was unleashing everything he had against Zeph, repelling him even in his shifted form. He had some serious power.

"Let go of me, you little worm," snarled the mage.

"Do I even know you?" I yanked him to the floor, but the air current continued to blast into Zeph. He didn't need to be able to see his target to use his power. The guy wasn't a mage I'd met, not that I'd memorised their names and faces. Tall and thin with a forgettable pale face and greasy dark hair, he wriggled like a fish in my grip.

The mage snarled, and the air current died down a little. Zeph regained ground, moving closer.

"Fair warning, if my friend breathes fire and it hits both of us, it won't do a thing to me," I said into his ear. "Dragons are immune to fire. You, however, will be burned to a crisp unless you play nice."

"What do you want?" he said, through clenched teeth.

"Stop trying to kill my friend, for a start. We're not under the control of the spell that's affecting the other shifters, but I'm guessing you know that already." I tightened my grip. "Tell me. Whose side are you on?"

"Not yours," he growled. "You unnatural beasts aren't welcome in my city."

"Any particular reason you don't like me?" I glanced at Zeph, who flew closer. "Because if it's to do with being able to shift into a giant lizard and breathe fire, you're standing on a building and controlling the weather. So maybe think about your definition of *unnatural*. Also, the Orion League used that term to describe all supernaturals. It's not a good look on you."

He broke out of my hold and blasted a current of air at Zeph. The dragon shifter dodged to the right, releasing a snarl.

I grabbed the back of the mage's cloak and tugged him down again. "What the hell is in it for you? Haven't you got enough money or resources? Why help the Faulkners?"

"To ensure safety of our city, of course," he said. "Your people have done nothing but stir up trouble since you came out into the open."

Seriously? "Okay, first of all, we've always been here," I said. "Secondly, the Faulkners force shifters to fight one another for cash. I repeat—not a good look on you."

"They don't aim to kill all the shifters," he said. "Just drive them out of London. This city is no place for wild animals."

"You know... you're right." My claws slid out, piercing his body through the back of his cloak. He gave a startled yell of pain, and the air current died to a low breeze. "You can still save your own neck if you tell me where they set off their spell. The Ley Line, right?"

"How did you—" His eyes went wide. "You won't stop it. You can't. It'll reach the whole country by nightfall."

The whole country. "So I guess it's not all about protecting your city, then. You just want us dead. At least make an effort to *pretend* to be noble, you fucking scumbag."

He twisted away from me, his face ashen. "Let me go, you monster."

"Sure, *I'm* the monster in this scenario." I rolled my eyes at him. "Tell me exactly where they activated their spell and how to turn it off."

"How the devil should I know?" The air stirred, pushing at me, but I didn't give. "You should have stayed dead, Coriander."

I sank my claws in deeper, and he went limp.

21

My breath escaped in a rush, and I let the fallen mage go, claws shifting to bloody hands. The roaring noise of the wind had died down, but the ongoing battle remained. And Zeph was gone.

I walked away from the mage's fallen body, squinting into the fog. *What happened to Zeph?* Had he been struck by a poisoned dart, or worse? I couldn't even see the park from here.

Heart pounding, I lowered myself over the building's side. Climbing down was faster than the reverse and I jumped the last six feet, using my claws to break my fall. It would be useful if I could shift my feet, too, but what I really needed were wings. The fog was even thicker on ground level, and London was too easy to get lost in even without the thick fog blocking the way. A five-minute walk could morph into a five-mile wander through a maze of streets. Not great when you were in a hurry to stop the apocalypse.

Or when there were ghosts everywhere, come to that. The air was thick with the clamour of a thousand spirits stuck on this side of the veil, along with the screams and sounds of the fighting. It was impossible to see if the mages were involved, but if any more of them had betrayed us like the guy on the roof, we were in serious trouble.

I have to get the Moonbeam. Zeph would want me to stop the battle first and rescue him later, but he and Ember were the Faulkners' main targets. They didn't need to keep me alive. I'd lost track of the snipers, but they'd never see me on the ground, not with so much chaos around me. For once, my small, unassuming appearance came in handy. To anyone passing, I was just another powerless human fleeing the violence.

I dove behind a row of bins to avoid two gargoyles slashing at one another, both bearing bloody wounds. Shifting my hands to claws, I used them to shield my head as I sprinted across the street. The only way to stop a rampaging shifter was to use knockout spells, and if I did, they'd be trampled to death by the horde. Besides, my spell stash was running low, and there was no way I was getting home until I shut off the Faulkners' spell.

I ran in a zigzag pattern, veering out of the way of a rampaging troll. The park had emptied, Faerie's denizens revelling in the chaos. Bursts of blue and green light suggested the fae's magic got a boost from the damaged spirit lines, too.

I dodged a frenzied gargoyle, dodging his claws by a hair's breadth. Kicking the gargoyle's feet out from underneath him, I vaulted his body and kept on running. Two faeries duelled in the street, blue and green light clashing in a firework-like display that made the buildings tremble. Ice sprang up where a bolt of blue light struck the road inches from my feet.

"Come on, save your duel for later!" I yelled at them. "Might have escaped your attention, but London's kind of on fire."

My words went unnoticed. Everyone in London with a grudge against another supernatural had gone in for the kill, and a dozen similar duels littered the streets. The faeries weren't under any spell, they were probably just pissed at their park being invaded and giddy with the rush of their magical boost. It wasn't until I reached the road leading into mage territory and slammed headlong into an invisible barrier that I spotted two more cloaked mages.

"Ow!" I rubbed my forehead. The barrier was transparent, and on the other side, the mages stood in defensive stances as though they thought I might attack them.

A gargoyle's claw slashed at me from the side. I dodged and struck him across the beak with my claws, while the mages watched from behind their barrier spell. "I could use a hand here, you know."

"You're not under the spell," said the blond female mage. Lady Clare. I'd met her a couple of times, and I knew she had mind-powers, including reading thoughts. Not really an aggressive ability in a fight. No wonder she was hiding behind a shielding spell.

"No, I'm not." I swiped at the gargoyle's leg as he tried to kick me. "Mind letting me through? I urgently need to speak to the Mage Lords."

"Speak to me from here," she said. "If we drop the barrier, anything might get in."

The gargoyle shrieked when I plunged my claw into his leg. As he fell, I turned back to the mages with an exasperated snarl. "Will you *please* let me through? If you do, I'll tell you how to stop the shifters fighting. I can help you."

The second mage, a young black man who barely looked above apprentice age, peered at me through the barrier. "Should I let her in?"

"Yes, go on," Lady Clare said impatiently.

The barrier flickered and died, and I stepped over the line. The wards flared up again a moment later.

"Seriously?" I snapped, once I was safe. "You're just *watching* the shifters destroy themselves and the faeries duel in the streets."

"We're mind mages," mumbled the apprentice. "We can only affect one person at a time, and we need eye contact to do it right. If we go out there, we'll be torn to pieces."

I'd bet Lady Clare had terrified him into believing that. I turned my glare onto her. "You know what they did?" I asked. "They set up a spell right in the middle of Hyde Park on the key point. It's going haywire, affecting every shifter in the city up and down the Ley Line. I can't get through to stop it."

"Can't you fly in?" she said. "I saw your friend."

"I lost track of him," I said. "One of your people knocked me out of the sky."

"Excuse me?" she said sharply. "One of *my* people?"

"A mage." Caution screamed at me—if I made accusations against her allies, I could say goodbye to the mages' cooperation. But what if they had other traitors in their midst? "Air mage, tall guy wearing a cloak, with wild control levels. He was on the roof over there. Did you see Zeph—the other dragon—getting blown around by a strong air current? That was him."

"I saw the other dragon," said the apprentice.

Lady Clare shook her head. "What? None of my people are on the roofs."

"He was there." I'd also killed him... not that I'd be telling her *that*. If they found his body and noticed the claw wounds, then I might be in trouble if they didn't believe me, but at this rate, London would be buried in bodies by the day's end.

"Don't be absurd," she said. "None of our people would have reason to attack you. Unless you attacked first. Why are you unaffected by the spell on the shifters?"

"Dragon shifters aren't affected." *I should have seen that one coming.* "Don't know why."

"You're a dragon?" the apprentice said, with an expression of interest on his face.

"Joseph, not now," Lady Clare said. "Coriander and her sister Ember have long been an... exception, in the eyes of the Mage Lords. I hope she will reconsider making accusations against us."

"It's not you I'm accusing," I said. "Does the description match anyone you know? Dark hair... maybe thirtyish?"

"Lord Herrod?" the apprentice said. "Isn't he head of security?"

A Mage Lord. The highest rank, and someone with ten times the clout as a mage apprentice, let alone the rest of us. "Did you say head of security?"

"Yes," said Lady Clare, with a disgruntled look at her apprentice. "Why?"

Fear clawed up my throat. "Please tell me someone has checked on the Moonbeam lately."

"That's what you want?" Lady Clare said. "That item is high-security—"

"It might be the only thing that can stop that." I waved a hand at the chaotic battle swamping the street behind the barrier. "Assuming someone didn't already take it."

"What are you implying?" she said.

"I think she's implying someone already stole it," said Joseph, then closed his mouth quickly.

"Not my friends," I said before Lady Clare could start throwing accusations. "But if I was the person behind this and I knew how it worked, I'd want to get hold of it, too."

"You'll do no such thing."

A gargoyle collided with the invisible shield, and a cracking noise ripped along the wards as his bloody claws tore at the barrier. The spell wouldn't last forever. The mages were deluding themselves if they thought they could indefinitely shut out the fighting.

"I'm not plotting against you," I said, exasperation colouring my words. "If I was, I wouldn't have walked right up to you and asked for your help. I'd be up on the roof with Lord Herrod. He betrayed you—just ask someone to check up on him."

Assuming any of the mages were actually participating in the fighting. I sure as hell hadn't seen any. But they had the luxury of picking their battles.

Lady Clare pulled out her phone, fury suffusing her expression, and gave a few terse orders. A moment of silence filled the space, punctuated by shouts from the battle.

Then the blood drained from her face. "Excuse me, what? Who is on security duty, exactly?"

"They took the Moonbeam," I guessed.

She lowered her phone, her eyes narrowing. "You knew, did you? Joseph, take her with you to headquarters."

"I just guessed five minutes ago," I said. "Maybe focus on the real enemy?"

The barrier shook at another blow from the gargoyle, and Joseph backed away. "Er, sorry, Coriander, I'm supposed to take you to headquarters."

Fine. Maybe Lord Smyth will believe me.

Leaving Lady Clare, I walked along with the apprentice through the quiet streets. The discordant sounds of the fighting sounded muted here, as though we walked in a bubble.

Joseph gave me an apologetic look. "Are you really a dragon?"

"Yep." I shifted my claws in demonstration. "You didn't see my sister?"

"No, I only started my apprenticeship three years ago," he said, eyeing my claws with an expression of awe.

That'd make him eighteen or nineteen at most. Younger than me. "Once you take me in there, go somewhere safe, okay? I don't know who took the Moonbeam, but they're unhinged and dangerous."

"Okay." He might believe me, but Lady Clare was a Mage Lord. His word wouldn't outrank hers.

We reached the mages' headquarters, a huge building made of chrome and glass set back behind iron fences. Cloaked mages blocked the road, running around barking orders at one another.

Joseph halted beside the gates. "Lord Smyth?" he called out.

He'd better listen to me. Lord Smyth was the Mage Lords' current leader. He was fair as far as Mage Lords went, but he wouldn't react well to the accusation against his fellow mage. Still, that hardly mattered. *The enemy took the Moonbeam.*

Lord Smyth spotted me. He was a tall black man with a serious face who wore the same style of knee-length black cloak as Lord Herrod and Lady Clare. "Coriander. What are you doing here?"

"Lady Clare sent me here because I guessed that the enemy would want the Moonbeam," I said. "Did you see who it was, and where they took it?"

Lightning crackled in the Mage Lord's eyes. "No, but one of our high-security prisoners escaped. I can add two and two."

"High-security..." I trailed off, raw fear turning my blood to water. "Who?"

I expected the answer before I heard it: "Lorne."

The name punched me in the chest.

The man who'd killed me walked free again.

22

Somehow, I managed to speak. "*He's* the one they were helping. He did this."

The Faulkners were out for themselves, that much was for certain—but the person who had the most to gain from wiping out London's shifters was the dragon shifter who'd tried to do the same once already.

The Moonbeam. Not only had Lorne got out of jail, he had the Moonbeam.

"How the *fuck* did you let him escape?" I said, when the Mage Lord didn't respond.

"He must have had help," said Lord Smyth. The air turned static, making my hair stand on end. Normally I'd be worried about standing close to him with his mage power active—but I was more scared of Lorne than the mages. "All our security cameras melted."

"Melted?" I frowned. "What, he breathed fire?"

"Not him," he said. "We're not certain it was him who stole the Moonbeam, but the two events occurred simultaneously."

Had another dragon shifter broken him out? Impossible.

"Was he the only person who broke out?" I asked.

"He was, but we suspect he has accomplices. Cori, I must ask you to leave," he said. "We have to find this individual before he does irreparable harm."

"I think he already has." Or his allies had, anyway.

The mages had already lost their upper hand. That left me with two choices: get into the park and shut down the spell—or find Lorne by myself.

This time, he might kill me for real.

With the Moonbeam, he had the ability to control any shifter he wanted to, including me. He and the Orion League had worked together for years. He had no issues with betraying his fellow shifters. He had the same ideas as they did about remaking the world with fewer shifters in it. Less competition that way. *Scumbag.*

I turned my back on Lord Smyth, anger sparking. Lorne was counting on my fear. Counting on me being too afraid to fight him, to track him down. But I wouldn't bend. I wouldn't break. And this time, Death would claim him, not me.

I left at a fast walk, wishing more than ever that I could leap into flight. My pace quickened, down streets I was unfamiliar with. How was I even supposed to track Lorne? He might be anywhere. But someone had helped him escape...

A jet of fire burst over my head. I ducked, looking around for the source, and spotted the dragonling sitting on a lamp post.

"How did you get all the way over here?" More to the point, how'd he learned to breathe fire? *Crap. Don't tell me he's going to attack me, too.*

The dragonling flapped his wings and flew down from the lamp post to land beside my leg. I tensed, but he didn't try to bite me.

"What is it?" I couldn't take him with me into the middle

of a battle, but he'd somehow flown all the way here without getting knocked out of the sky. Another puff of fire escaped, melting a hole in the tarmac.

Dragonfire. Real dragonfire.

It can't be. "You didn't," I said. "Please tell me it wasn't you who helped Lorne escape."

The dragonling spat out a wad of paper, singed at the edges and punctured with teeth marks.

Even with the words smudged, I could read the last one... *From You Know Who.*

"Lorne," I whispered. "His people sent the egg. They wanted me to know he planned to get out."

But he'd left the dragonling behind, after using him to help aid his escape. He ducked his head as though ashamed.

"Why? What did they do to you?"

The dragonling shuffled his wings, his head lolling. I might not be able to understand his words, but I'd bet he was as vulnerable to the Moonbeam as any other dragon shifter. Lorne had counted on it.

The dragonling flew a few metres, then sat on the roadside, waiting expectantly for me to catch up. I hesitated, then followed.

A limp body lay further down the road, wearing the uniform of a shifter guard. One of the gargoyles who worked for the Faulkners.

The dragonling perched on his head, prodding him with a claw. *Huh?*

"I can't talk to him. He's dead..." *Oh.*

Dead people couldn't talk... or rather, most living people couldn't hear them. But I could.

The fog was already present, and it didn't take much concentration for me to snap on my spirit sight and spot the dead man's ghost floating a few feet away.

"Hey!" I waved at him. "Can I have a word?"

"They killed me!" he yelped. "The bastards killed me."

"The Faulkners, by any chance?"

He twisted on the spot, his eyes wide. "How'd you know? How can you see me?"

"Everyone can see ghosts today," I said. "If you don't want a shit-ton of people to join you, tell me the truth. Why are you lying dead in a ditch?"

"I stole it for them," he said. "I stole that artefact straight from the mages for them and they *killed* me for it."

"Wait, *you* stole the Moonbeam?" That couldn't be right.

He nodded frantically. "Yes, my bosses told me to use it to summon that little dragon over there. Then I had to take it into the jail and help one of the prisoners get out. I did everything they asked and then they bloody *killed* me."

"Oh." Understanding flared. The Moonbeam enhanced dragon shifters' powers. If activated it in the jail, it would have given Lorne the boost he needed to get out. The Faulkners hadn't wanted their thief to blab about what he'd done. Too bad they hadn't counted on me being able to talk to the dead.

Not that it changed the outcome. Lorne walked free, the Faulkners were still hiding in London somewhere, and—

A tremendous blast of fire bloomed over the rooftops, and a winged shape appeared. A lithe body cloaked in red scales. *Ember. She's okay.*

"Hey!" I waved frantically, but there was no way she'd see me from that high.

More fire exploded overhead, and several human-shaped figures on the rooftops burst into flames. She was taking out the snipers. But the fog was too thick, the fighting constant, and Lorne was free.

Every one of my instincts screamed at me to run, not chase after him. The man wanted me dead. He'd already succeeded once. But if he had the Moonbeam, he could make the shifters do anything. He could make *us* destroy London.

The dragonling took flight, angling higher. Ember spotted him, and our gazes locked. I gave a frantic wave.

A moment later, Ember landed beside me, shifting into human form. "Cori!"

I ran over and hugged her fiercely. "He's out. Lorne is out."

Her body stilled. "No."

"Yes." My voice sounded oddly calm considering the roaring panic in my mind. "He used someone else to steal the Moonbeam for him so it would give him the boost he needed to escape."

"It's burned out," said Ember, the merest hint of uncertainty in her voice. "Last time it got overloaded. He can't use the Moonbeam on every shifter at once anymore."

"Then what did he hope to achieve by stealing it?" Unless it was possible to power it up again. "Never mind. Ember, the spell is in the park. On the Ley Line. Zeph disappeared somewhere near there—one of the mages betrayed us and knocked him out of the sky."

"If we destroy the spell, it won't stop Lorne," she said.

"I know." I saw the same inner battle that waged in my mind reflected in her eyes. "But it'll stop the fighting. We can search for him from the sky."

"If you're sure, Cori." Her gaze went past me to the dragonling. "He can't come with us, though."

I crouched beside the little dragon. "Can you hide somewhere close by? Out of range of the fighting?" That'd probably been his plan, once the Moonbeam had released him from its thrall, but despite his betrayal, his evident misery at being used and his desperate attempts to help made me determined to remove him from the fighting.

I didn't know if he understood my words, but at least he

hadn't tried to chew my fingers off this time. The Moonbeam might contain enough power to control a small dragonling, but if it was true and it had burned out since the battle five years ago, then we might have an edge. Assuming we could *find* Lorne.

Ember shifted into dragon form and I climbed onto her back, settling between her red-scaled shoulders. I held on as tight as I dared as we rose into the clouds, searching for the Moonbeam's glowing light in the fog. Lorne couldn't be in dragon form. He'd fled on foot for a reason—so nobody would be able to track him.

Ghosts rose on either side, spectral forms close enough to touch. Coldness gripped every inch of me, threatening to overwhelm the fire in my veins. Lorne had walked free only in my worst nightmares. The same nightmares where I'd been caged.

It will never happen again.

As Ember had said, if our enemies were back, in any form, we'd have to fight again and again. There was no alternative.

A faint line appeared beneath and around us, transparent but unmistakable. The Ley Line. "Down here!" I said to Ember. "Fly lower. I think we're close."

More lights flared up in the fog, from the park below. In the middle of a crowd of trees, a space had been cleared. Even from here, I could see the outline of a circle. A spell circle, the size of a house.

"There!" I pointed.

A tongue of fire erupted from Ember's mouth, obliterating the spell circle. Fire and light merged in a flood of brightness that illuminated the fog. Ember roared, the sound carrying over the park, and I held on tight as she flew lower.

Please let that have done it.

The whir of a helicopter cut through the general clamour,

and my gut tightened. "Follow that noise!" I shouted. "Let's get the bastards."

Ember let out a rumbling growl, quickening her speed. More darts flew towards us, and when the fog cleared, the helicopter came into view. From within, the Faulkners grinned through the window.

Ember dipped in the air, a feathery dart sticking from between her scales. *No.*

My sister flew on, a stream of fire pouring from her mouth. The flames skimmed the helicopter's side, but her body trembled, and her claws began to turn to human hands.

"NO!"

As Ember fell, I gave a wild leap, grabbing for the helicopter's open hatch. My claws dug into the side, and the helicopter veered off course, skidding to a halt on the roof of one of the low-rise buildings. I clung to the side, gasping.

Ember. They'd knocked her out of the sky.

They'd killed my sister.

A roar trembled in my lungs, whitening my vision. *They're dead meat.*

I leapt off the helicopter onto the rooftop to face my enemies.

The two Faulkners watched me through the open hatch. They had Zeph tied up in the back of the helicopter, and both pointed Orion League-style guns at me.

23

"You're persistent, aren't you?" Bryan Faulkner said. "You still fight us, even after I killed your sister."

"I'll kill you." Claws burst from my skin, the scales creeping higher up my arms—but if I moved, they'd shoot me. Or Zeph. My entire body trembled with adrenaline, and the clicking sound of their guns barely registered.

"It's nothing personal," Logan said. "You must know your kind aren't suited to living in the modern world. We're better off without you here."

My claws burned with the strength of my rage, yet somehow, I held myself back, stopped myself from running deep into the path of his bullet and into true death.

Speaking of death...

I hadn't felt Ember die. She'd told me she'd felt the moment when I'd passed beyond the veil into Death, but when she'd fallen, I hadn't felt anything. She was alive: I was certain.

She'd saved me from Death, and I'd do the same for her.

"If you weren't so focused on trying to kill us, you could have done so much more with those resources of yours," I said to the Faulkner siblings. "Like helping repair the damage the faeries caused to the city. Anything but spreading more hate and destruction. But I guess it's no use trying to talk sense into people like you."

"This is your doing, Coriander," Bryan said. "You pushed us into a corner. If you'd just cooperated—"

"Like *hell*," I said. "You were just waiting for a chance to destroy London's shifters, weren't you? Don't pin this one on me. You'd do it anyway."

Bryan shook his head. "Like I said—it's nothing personal."

"If you bothered to talk to any dragon shifters before you killed them, you'd know we have zero patience for bullshit. And you're full of it."

"Maybe," Logan said. "But I have a gun and your friend. I'm the one who wins this time, Coriander."

"We," added his brother. "The dragonling... you can keep it. The egg served its purpose. We've accumulated an outrageous amount of cash from the fake eggs sold at auction over the last two days, despite the chaos you caused in the arena."

"Congratu-fucking-lations," I said. "Lorne walks free, you take the money and run. I suppose he paid you off, too."

Bryan's mouth twisted. "We're not hoarding cash for the sake of it, Coriander. Money is essential to survive in this world, to protect ourselves against the likes of you. We will be relocating to a remote location far from here, where no monsters such as yourselves will be able to reach us."

A small jet of flame shot past me, followed by a high-pitched screech. Logan cursed as the flame singed his sleeve and fired at the dragonling. The little dragon bounced into the air and the bullet missed wildly.

Crap. What's he doing here? He followed me?

Bryan jumped out of the helicopter, firing the gun. The dragonling dodged and landed on the mobster's head, his claws digging in. The gun fell from his hands, a startled yell escaping.

I ran, grabbing the weapon and crushing it into my clawed hand. Opening my palm, I released the splintered metal pieces with a growl of satisfaction.

Logan snarled and moved to shoot me, but Zeph hit him from behind with his cuffed hands. *Good. He's not hypnotised this time.* Zeph kicked Logan down and climbed over him out of the hatch.

I moved in, giving Logan a kick for good measure. "Zeph, are you okay?"

"I'm fine," he said through gritted teeth. From the blistered state of his hands, the cuffs were covered in the dragon-proofed stuff the Faulkners put on their clothes.

The dragonling sank its teeth into Bryan's arm, and he screamed. Blood streamed into his eyes from the deep furrows in his forehead from the dragon's claws.

Zeph moved away from them, hands still bound. "Dammit. I can't shift like this."

"Hang on." I took his cuffed hands in mine. My palms blistered, but I turned his hands over to see the cuffs. They were sealed with some kind of switch, but my hands hurt too much to get it off. Swearing, I let go for a second, and a bullet bounced off the ground beside me.

"Careful, little worm," snarled Logan.

"You *really* need to figure out when to quit," I said.

The dragonling sank his teeth into Logan's ankle, and he fired again. The bullet missed, and I grabbed his gun hand, wrenching the weapon free. Then I smacked him in the forehead with it and he dropped like a stone. His partner lay crumpled and moaning on the ground, no longer a threat.

"Let's see if this works." I reached for Zeph's hands again. "Hold still."

I shot the bolt on the cuffs, freeing his hands. Then I

shifted my hands to claws, crushing the gun between them. Zeph shook the cuffs off with a grim smile, his hands shifting to opalescent claws.

When Logan saw Zeph was free, he roared, hitting out at the dragonling. "You won't get away. My face will be the last thing you see before you die, worm."

I bared my teeth. "I've stared death in the face before. You're more like Death's kid brother. You're nothing."

A louder roar came from behind me, echoing through my very bones. *Ember.*

She was alive. And in pain.

I backed to the roof's edge.

"Finish them off," I said to Zeph. "I'm going to get my sister."

Using my claws to scale the building was easier than the last time. Fuelled by the sound of my sister's roar of pain, I climbed down until my feet hit the road.

Ember crouched in an alley, her wings pierced with multiple dart wounds. Lorne stood beside her, holding a gun to her head. He hadn't changed much in his five years of captivity. He had a male dragon shifter's tall, muscular build, his copper hair was cut short, and he wore a ragged suit that resembled the gargoyle arena guards' uniform. Maybe that's all he'd been able to change into after escaping jail.

And in his other hand, he held the Moonbeam.

The instant I set eyes on it, the breath left my lungs. The Moonbeam looked remarkably innocuous, a piece of stone that gleamed brighter than anything earthly I'd ever seen. A creation of magic, forged in dragonfire.

If Lorne used its portal ability, he could transport himself into the other dragons' village and reduce it to ashes. Or he could use it to wrap every shifter in London under his spell. I *felt* its magic, humming deeply inside me. The magic that had brought me back to life. And now Lorne wanted to use the very same magic to destroy us.

"Thank you, Coriander," he said. "You've just helped me start a war."

Fear coated the back of my throat. The first time we'd *met*, he'd tried to kill me, and only Ember's intervention had spared my life.

Only Ember's intervention... and the stone he held in his hands.

Ember released a faint growl, and the Moonbeam glowed brighter. Lorne didn't understand. He'd let the Orion League use the Moonbeam to control him and had never made any choices for himself.

Unlike Ember, who'd risked it all to beg the Moonbeam to return me to life.

I drew in a steadying breath, one eye on Ember, and said, "You know, Lorne, that note would have worked better if I actually knew you."

"Excuse me?" he said.

"You Know Who." It wasn't a *Harry Potter* reference—the guy had zero sense of humour or knowledge of popular culture, as far as I was aware. "I have no idea *who* you are. I'm not sure even you do. You helped the Orion League because they let you cling to power, and in the end, they turned you into their puppet. And now here you are, working for their successors like they wouldn't turn on you again in a heartbeat."

"Successors?" He narrowed his eyes. "The real League died out when Malkin betrayed them, as they deserved to. As for me? I will never be caged again."

The Moonbeam gleamed in his hands. A single thought, and he'd be able to use it to turn me into a monster. Make me kill my friends.

"Well done on the jailbreak, then," I said. "Is that what you wanted to hear from me? Because this is kinda like an awkward school reunion here. I spoke to you twice in my life. Unless you count the time you ordered your people to murder me, but even then, I'm not sure it was you who was really pulling the strings."

A muscle ticked in his jaw. "You're face to face with someone who already took your life once before, and that's all you have to say? Have you no regard for your sister's safety?"

Ember spat a plume of fire at him. He held up the Moonbeam as a shield, and the fire went right through it. While his dragon shifter's skin deflected the damage, his gun wasn't so lucky. The ashes of the destroyed gun slipped through his fingers, and his eyes went wide.

"Looks like my sister's doing just fine," I said. "What's the matter, did you forget to hit the 'on' switch?"

His fist clenched on the Moonbeam. It hadn't protected him like it might have done to one of us. The stone might have raised me from the dead, but it wouldn't even protect Lorne from a dragon's fire. Granted, he was still in his human form at the moment… but the fire had touched him. He wasn't invulnerable.

Lorne held up the stone. Its light grew a little brighter, but the curse that slipped from his mouth suggested bitter disappointment. "Kill her, Coriander. Kill your sister."

Nothing happened.

Ember gave another cough, and a jet of fire hit Lorne, igniting his sleeve. He swore, shaking his wrist to dim the flames.

"Did you just try to use the Moonbeam on me?" I laughed for real this time. "Looks like it's not too fond of you after all."

Through gritted teeth, he said, "Then I'll have to use this instead."

He reached into his pocket and pulled out a gleaming metal device.

I blinked. "That looks like a cheap sci-fi movie prop. What does it do, curl your hair?"

Death slammed into me, grey fog smothering my vision. Ghosts approached from all angles as though drawn by an invisible force, and behind it all, Lorne stood tall, outlined in light.

Shit. The metal device in his hand must be what the record player really looked like, under its innocuous disguise. He'd got it from the Faulkners, maybe as part of their deal.

"I'm no necromancer," he said. "Your soul, though... it's different. You came back from the dead, and that comes with a cost."

How the hell does he know that? This man wasn't the same person who'd almost led his own species to extinction, or even the enraged dragon shifter who'd wreaked havoc and destruction on London. His face was calm. Reverent, almost. And he held the power of Death in his hand.

"You and your sister cost me everything, Cori," he said.

"My sister set you free from Malkin's control," I said. "If anything, you should be thanking us."

He turned the device over in his hand. "I got this from a necromancer. It stores spiritual energy, and with the Moonbeam, I'll be able to reset the spirit lines, and reset the supernatural world along with it."

"I thought that was all Malkin's idea."

The League's end goal had been to attack the spirit lines by sacrificing my sister and me, causing the barriers between worlds to split open and trigger a second faerie invasion. I'd been under the impression they'd planned for Lorne himself to die along with everyone else, but maybe he'd had an escape plan. Or maybe he'd taken their plans and twisted them to fit his own ideals.

Whatever his justification for bringing back their batshit *break the spirit lines and kick off another faerie invasion* scheme, I had to stop him.

I launched myself at him with all the shifter speed I possessed, grabbing for the device. He lifted his hand, and an electric shock went through my nerves as my fingers brushed his sleeve. *Damn.*

"You know that dragon-proofed crap can hurt you, too, don't you?" I grabbed his arm, driving Lorne's sleeve towards his own exposed face. The pain was unbearable, but Lorne snarled and twisted, breaking his composure. He smacked me in the forehead with the metal device, forcing me to let go.

I won't submit. I won't die.

The spirit device flashed, and when it did, the drifting ghosts began to disappear.

The device was absorbing their souls. And if I wasn't careful, I'd be joining them.

I slammed into Lorne once more. In the same instant, he shifted, blue scales spreading across his body. He backhanded me with his clawed hand, sending me flying back into Ember. She roared in pain, shooting a jet of flame at Lorne, but he held the device out of reach.

The fog grew clearer. Ghosts brushed against me and I gasped, feeling their touch like a physical presence even as the device sucked them in.

Then Lorne staggered backwards as though shoved by invisible hands.

The ghosts. They'd turned on him. Lorne staggered, but held firm, his half-shifted hand on the spirit device. For every ghost whose soul disappeared into the device, another took its place, shoving at Lorne, driving him backwards even at the cost of their own souls.

I looked at Lorne through the haze of death, like I had when his army of ghosts had dragged me out of my body into Death.

This time, he was the one who looked afraid.

A dizzying heady sensation rippled through me from head to toe. "Just *try* to take my soul."

Among the ghostly lights, the Moonbeam glowed, too. Then white light blasted outwards from the stone, and the spirit device flew from his grip, clattering onto the pavement.

His eyes widened. "What the—?"

Ember breathed fire, and the flames engulfed the spirit device, burning it to cinders.

"YOU!" Lorne took a furious step forward, and the little dragonling crashed into him, tearing and biting. The spirit world snapped off like a switch had been thrown, and I ran at Lorne, grabbing for the Moonbeam.

He shifted, his huge blue scaled form filling the alley. His tail lashed the nearest building, sending debris flying, and his eyes turned on me, glowing with embers.

Then he launched into the air, the Moonbeam clutched in his grip.

"Get *back* here, you bastard!"

There came the sound of a helicopter overhead, following Lorne's departure. Shit. The Faulkners were getting away, too. *Zeph...*

"I won't let you!" I screamed.

Emotions tore through me. Rage, grief, anger, building to a crescendo. My hands turned to claws, and the scales kept climbing up my arms.

"Come on," I growled, and pain splintered my body as the shift took hold, finally, *finally.*

Clawed feet dug into the road beneath me. My wings hit the side of the buildings—my *wings*. I swung my tail, narrowly missing Ember. Oops. Zeph had a point about the tail.

I kicked off the ground, wings beating. My body felt lightweight despite its larger size, and the sound of the wind against my scales sang like a chorus in my ears. I flew higher and landed on the rooftop beside Zeph. His eyes went wide.

Then his own shift took over, and his white-blue scaled form filled the roof beside my own.

I turned to the retreating helicopter. *Good luck trying to out-fly a dragon.*

Fire burst from my lungs, joining with Zeph's, and the Faulkners' screams were extinguished in the inferno of two flames intertwining. In seconds, the hunk of metal was nothing more than ashes, which drifted like rain onto the streets below.

I turned my attention onto the spot where Lorne had vanished, but it was suddenly hard to breathe. Greyness crept in at the corners of my vision.

Zeph caught my arm in his own before I could fall. He was bleeding, too—they'd hurt him when he'd been in human form. In human…

"Dammit!" My human voice was higher than normal, my clumsy feet catching the edge of the roof. "Lorne has the Moonbeam."

"But can he use it?" asked Zeph.

Dizziness swept through me, and I sat down on the roof. "You know, I don't think he can. This isn't the victory he planned for."

My mortal enemy was still out there. That hadn't changed. But the Moonbeam had knocked the spirit device out of Lorne's hands instead of helping him. Not only that, he hadn't been able to control me, and I'd shifted into a dragon for the first time.

Honestly? I felt pretty damn good right now.

I smiled at Zeph. "Let's go back down there and help my sister."

24

"Three hotels on Mayfair—how is *that* fair?" Will looked at Kit in disbelief across the Monopoly board.

"Fair's fair," said Kit, lounging on the sofa. "I have the money."

"Because you took it from the rest of us," Ember said. Her arm was still bandaged, but she was back on her feet after her recovery from the poison. So was I, but it'd taken me two full days to sleep off my first shift. They weren't kidding about the side effects.

And when I'd woken up, Zeph had been gone.

"Cheat," said Becks.

"He wasn't," Astor said. He sat with his back to the sofa, and while his pose was relaxed, I knew he was constantly scanning to make sure nobody was flaunting the rules. That's what happened when you played board games with an ex-assassin. "You're all terrible at cheating."

"Sorry we don't meet your high standards," Will said, rolling his eyes. He sat beside Kit, but at a suitable distance from the little dragonling curled up on his arm. I'd been genuinely surprised to find that he'd found his way home, and even more surprised to find that Kit had talked Will and Becks into keeping him here while I'd been recuperating from my first shift.

Ember and I were supposed to be on bed rest, but the others knew better than to force the issue. Astor had to stop us from attempting one-handed sparring a few times. Dragons didn't cope well with being cooped up. Small wonder that our little game of Monopoly had become so intense. Astor was as ruthless in the game as he was in real life, but it was Kit who'd unscrupulously hoarded all the cash.

Kit set another hotel down on the board. "Your move, Ember."

Ember muttered a curse, picking the dice up. "We should just cut our losses and run."

"That's what the Faulkners tried to do," I said. "And they ended up deep-fried."

"I can't believe you set them on fire and I missed it," said Ember.

"The shift didn't last long." I hadn't tried since. If it took days of bed rest to recover from each shift, no wonder Ember had had a two-year gap between her first and second times turning into a dragon.

Zeph, on the other hand, hadn't even left a note. For all I knew, he had a whole life he'd left behind and intended to head back to it now the Faulkners were dead. Perhaps he planned to continue his search for wherever the dragonlings had been created. We never did find where the League's successors kept their labs, and I knew it was important to Zeph. But it would have been nice if he'd left us a way to contact him.

As for the mages, they'd dropped the accusations against me when they'd found the body of the thief who'd stolen the Moonbeam and helped Lorne escape. Lord Herrod's body had later been retrieved from the roof where he'd attacked us, and while the mages hadn't outright admitted one of their own had conspired against them, they were too smart not to put two and two together with his disappearance during the battle. They knew that Ember and I would never help Lorne after he'd nearly killed us, but the fact remained—he walked free, with the Moonbeam. Which meant we hadn't seen the last of him.

Surrendering was not a dragon shifter trait.

Ember and I had warned the villagers, in case Lorne found a way to reactivate the Moonbeam and returned to reassert himself as their leader. But in the two weeks since the battle, we hadn't heard so much as a whisper about him. It was nice to imagine he'd followed the Faulkners' plan to retire to an island somewhere to live out the rest of his life, but I doubted we'd get that lucky.

"I'm almost out," Ember said, tossing a wad of cash over to Kit. "Your move, Becks."

"I'm nearly out, too," said Becks, waving the handful of notes she had left. "Wish I could trade this for the real deal. Much less of a hazard than solo missions for Darcy."

"I'll be joining you soon," I said. "This bed rest nonsense has gone on for too long."

Besides, I never did get the chance to rip into Jake for his betrayal. According to Becks, he'd stopped showing up at the guild at all and had put out a rumour that he'd been killed in the aftermath of the Faulkners' deaths. Coward.

"One more week," said Ember. "At minimum. You've barely begun to walk again, Cori."

"Three days," I said. "Come on, we need the cash."

The shelter had been lucky and suffered minimal damage, and Will had managed to help the other shifters hide while the violence had been going on. But two weeks with half of us incapacitated and unable to go on missions had taken their toll.

"We do," said Becks. "I'd rather take it from someone who doesn't aid criminals, though."

"We don't know for sure Darcy was involved," I said. "I'd pin the record player stunt on Jake, but he's not that smart."

"Someone else at the guild might have it in for us?" said Ember. "Yeah, no. We'll find new employment."

"Don't look at me." Will surrendered the rest of his cash to Kit. "I can barely sell to paying customers in the shop since the dragonling bit that guy on the ankle last week."

"He was a dick," said Becks. "Right, Kit wins the game. We can all go home. Or go out."

Becks had been even more restless than usual lately. Probably from being stuck indoors with two irritable dragon shifters. I'd wanted to help her out on Darcy's missions, but I hadn't been in any condition to hunt banshees… or even help little old ladies.

Ember growled and pushed the dice over to me. "If I didn't know better, I'd say someone had spelled these dice—"

The doorbell rang, and I tensed. Part of me was expecting word from Lorne. A reminder that he was still out there, and he still wanted us dead. We'd closed the shelter for new families and helped the ones who were already there move elsewhere, just in case. So far nobody had attacked us, but the dragonling was getting increasingly difficult to hide as he grew in size. The entire supernatural community was in shock after the battle, not to mention the humans. I could only assume that's why the Mage Lords hadn't come looking for the dragonling… yet.

I walked into the shop to find that Ember had opened the front door, with Astor close behind her.

"It's your friend, Cori," said Astor.

Sure enough, Zeph rolled a suitcase up to the doorstep.

He wore a dark jacket and jeans and looked altogether less ragged than the last time I'd seen him.

"Hey," said Zeph. "My landlord kicked me out. Are you in need of a new housemate?"

I gawped at him. "A simple note or text would have worked."

"Ah, the Faulkners stole my phone, and I never did get your number." He peered past me into the shop. "I don't mind sleeping on the sofa, and I'll do my own grocery shopping."

"Are you sure?" I said. "You know there are people who want us dead, right?"

"It's not exactly a new experience for me," he said. "My old place… it's not really safe for me to stay there anymore."

"Why, because of Lorne? Did you see him?"

He shook his head. "No. Just the rumours. I mean, too many people saw me shift. Pretty sure that's what led my landlord to kick me out. It didn't exactly get nasty, but it struck me that there are friendlier places I could stay in. If you have room."

"That's up to Will to decide, but I don't see why not," I said. "We're playing Monopoly. Ember was about to flip the board over."

"I was not," she protested.

"Yes, you were." Astor moved aside, giving Zeph an appraising look. Zeph's expression was carefully neutral, but the merest hint of a spark danced in his grey eyes.

"If you're going to fight, do it over the Monopoly board," I said. "Kit hoarded all the money and is claiming innocence."

"Hey, I'm winning fair and square," he said indignantly.

Becks grinned at us. "Hey, Zeph. Good to see you again."

Zeph rested the suitcase against the wall and walked towards the board game setup next to the sofa. "Will, you own the house, right? Do you have room for one more?"

"Oh, for—" He sighed and dropped the fake money he'd been counting. "I'm taking a wild guess that I'm outvoted?"

"I'll earn my keep," Zeph said earnestly. "I just need somewhere to crash for a bit."

"I've heard *that* one before," said Will.

"Yeah, but you're stuck with the rest of us for life now," said Ember. "I like him. I vote we let him stay."

Astor didn't look happy, but he'd go along with Ember's decision. Kit gave Zeph a wave. The dragonling chewed on some of the fake money, while Becks was surreptitiously re-rolling the dice while Astor was distracted by Zeph.

"Are you really certain you want to step into the middle of this?" I asked him. "Last chance to back out."

"I wouldn't miss it," he responded. "Looks like you could use another dragon shifter on your team."

ABOUT THE AUTHOR

Emma is the New York Times and USA Today Bestselling author of the Changeling Chronicles urban fantasy series.

Emma spent her childhood creating imaginary worlds to compensate for a disappointingly average reality, so it was probably inevitable that she ended up writing fantasy novels. When she's not immersed in her own fictional universes, Emma can be found with her head in a book or wandering around the world in search of adventure.

Find out more about Emma's books at
www.emmaladams.com.

www.ingramcontent.com/pod-product-compliance
Lightning Source LLC
LaVergne TN
LVHW041627060526
838200LV00040B/1464